VICTOR SUTHREN

THE BLACK COCKADE

Paul Gallant's
Louisbourg Command

TOR

A TOM DOHERTY ASSOCIATES BOOK

THE BLACK COCKADE

Copyright © 1977 by Victor Suthren

Reprinted by arrangement with St. Martin's Press

First Tor printing: August 1986

A TOR Book

Published by Tom Doherty Associates, Inc.
49 West 24 Street
New York, N.Y. 10010

ISBN: 0-812-58862-2
CAN. ED.: 0-812-58863-0

Printed in the United States

0 9 8 7 6 5 4 3 2 1

There was a distant boom from the New England ships far behind him, sounding over the rattle of the musketry, and then suddenly, with a vicious crunch the ground before him leaped up in a fountain of black, spattering and drenching him.

Gallant staggered on. He could hear faint shouts, and realized dimly they were from the distant ramparts. Shouts of encouragement. He closed his eyes for an instant, trying to will away the agony in his leg. Du Chambom was groaning now, starting to stir, and Gallant gritted his teeth, fighting to keep the unconscious youth from slipping from his shoulders.

Then Gallant stumbled and fell, gasping in pain as his knees crunched down. Du Chambon sprawled in a heap before him, the grey-white shoulder of his coat now matted and deep red.

God help me, thought Gallant wildly. Ahead he could hear the shouts of the men atop the Dauphin, calling him. And behind him, the jeers and whoops of the New Englanders coming on. For a moment Gallant thought of trying to drag Du Chambon into one of the shacks, then as soon struck the thought from his mind. They would die like trapped pigs in there. Move, his mind shrieked silently. Move! Move!

The BLACK COCKADE

For Lindsay

The Track
of Écho

Britain

Lorient

France

Toulon

Spain

Mahon

The
Inlet

Gibraltar

Algiers

Africa

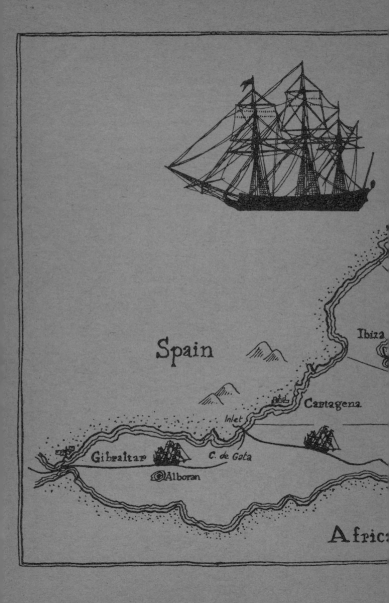

Spain

Ibiza

Cartagena

Inlet

Gibraltar

C. de Gata

Alboran

Africa

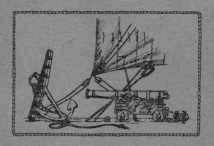

ONE

It was late December, 1744, but the ship was already to the south of the deadly grey seas and howling gales of a North Atlantic winter. Instead she was bowling along before the warm northeast Trades, her canvas aloft taut and full, her bows rising and falling with a hiss and roar as she pushed on over a sea of the deepest blue. High above the masts, even rows of white snowdrift cloud marched westward, the sun that beamed down through them catching a hundred tiny rainbows in the spray. The wind hummed in the taut lines of the rigging, and over those notes and the deep baritone rush of the sea came the steady creak of the masts as they worked against their wedges. Altogether it was a hypnotic symphony that enraptured the man who stood braced against the larboard rail of the quarterdeck, moving his legs automatically to balance against the ship's motion.   Enseigne Paul François Adhémar Gallant, junior officer in the independent companies of naval infantry garrisoning the Fortress of Louisbourg, and now in temporary command of the French corvette *Écho*, licked the salt tang from his lips and looked aloft, eyes searching for signs of strain or wear in the sails. He was tall, almost six feet, and the weight of his uniform hung on a frame more angular than fleshy.

Gallant stood very straight, a feature that marked him as a land officer; no Compagnies Franches officer who had spent a career crouching beneath the deckheads of a man-of-war would have carried himself in so military a fashion. His face was long and deeply tanned, and his brown eyes regarded the world from beneath straight black brows and a wide forehead slightly furrowed by a frown. His jaw line was clean and strong, but about his mouth were lines that suggested an air of gentleness and sensitivity, uncommon in an officer.

Gallant wore the ubiquitous uniform of the troops who not only served as marines in His Most Christian Majesty's warships, but also formed the principal garrisons of the overseas holdings and colonies of France. His grey-white justaucorps was stained and threadbare, the large turned-back blue cuffs frayed and patched along the edges. The brass buttons had none of the parade-ground sheen of the Toulon garrison. The veston and breeches of blue serge were worn and showed signs of frequent repair.

But the lace at Gallant's wrists and throat was clean and immaculately gathered, and he wore the gilt-edged black tricorne at the most courtly angle, with a large black cockade of silk ribbon set on the brim above his left eye. He carried himself and wore his clothing as would a soldier; but in the manner of the military professionals of his age, he was at home upon the sea as upon the land, and was drinking in the joy the dramatic progress of the ship was stirring in him.

The corvette was a live thing, moving majestically on its way through a world of breathtaking beauty. The long backs of the blue and white swells that raced westward with her were sprinkled with diamond-like glints of sunlight. The wind swept clean and cool across the stern, cleansing away all concern or worry from Gallant's mind save a wonder at the beauty of the moment. There was no flaw in the setting of the sails aloft. Each broad rectangle arched out, lifting with power and grace, the energy almost visibly pouring down the lines and spars into the fibre of the hull. There was a rhythm to the lift and fall of the ship that Gallant never tired of; it held him in an embrace of motion and life, as real and comforting as a mother's arms.

With her topsails double-reefed, *Écho* had fought her way back southward across the westerlies to pick up the Trade Winds for the long run westward. The southward track had not been lengthy, but was gruelling nonetheless; a constant shaking out and taking in of the reefs, the pitch and stagger of the ship over greybearded swells, the working of the hull until every seam which could admit water did, and the men below lived in a fetid and damp world of darkness under closed hatches and wedged scuttles. But within forty-eight hours the grey wasteland had faded dramatically into the sunny warmth and steady winds below thirty degrees north latitude, and *Écho* had gratefully swung her bows toward the distant palm-fringed shores of the Antilles two thousand miles beyond the horizon, on the long southern loop to America.

Gallant saw Béssac, the mate, emerge from the forward hatch and stroll aft, wreathes of smoke puffing from his pipe as he scanned proprietorially aloft.

Béssac was an Acadien, a short, powerfully built man whose warmth and humour had soon cemented a friendship with Gallant, whose own family roots were in Louisbourg and Isle Royale. His ship, *Écho*, was registered in the Louisbourg admirauté; her owner, Henri Jolicoeur, had captained her for years on the long triangular trading haul between Cayenne, Louisbourg and l'Orient, in France. For Béssac and his crew, a rough and hardy mixture of Acadiens and Louisbourg men seasoned with the looming black presence of Akiwoya, the corvette's African gunner who had yet to say a word in Gallant's presence, the trading life in the little vessel had brought a precarious but respectable income.

But Jolicoeur had died of a raving fever in l'Orient harbour, leaving the ship in the hands of the local port authorities who soon decided they would send the ship back to her home port for an unravelling of the problems Jolicoeur's death had caused. And, when a penniless Louisbourg officer with sea experience had arrived at dockside seeking passage home, they had been only too happy to put him in temporary Command of *Écho* and charge him with getting her back to the hands of the admirauté in Louisbourg.

The relations between Gallant and Béssac might have been grim in the extreme. But by God's good luck, the mate had greeted Gallant with a patience that soon warmed to acceptance and approval as Gallant's competence became evident. Slowly the crew had come to accept him as well, and in their common love of the sea and the way of a good ship in it, Béssac and Gallant were building a deep friendship with each league *Écho* forged westward.

The marine was about to speak when the maintop lookout hailed the quarterdeck.

"Deck there! A sail, m'sieu'! To the northwest!"

Gallant cupped his hands. "What flag?"

He could see the man shaking a tousled head. "Not visible, enseigne!"

Béssac arrived beside him. "Hm! First sail we've raised this passage, enseigne." He puffed on the pipe. "Likely a merchantman."

Gallant glanced at the broad white Bourbon ensign that streamed over their heads.

"Likely so, Béssac. Nonetheless it might be wise to be a little cautious." He turned to the helmsman. "Steer two points to southward."

"Two points southward, m'sieu'."

Béssac was looking aloft, debating on whether to brace the yards round a touch. At a word from him several seamen made minor adjustments in the course and topsail sheets.

Gallant scanned the northwestern horizon carefully, eyes slitted against the glare. After a moment he made out the other ship, a small white shape on the blue skyline.

The lookout's voice carried down again.

"He's seen us, m'sieu'! He's fallen off his reach to run down on us!"

Béssac saw the expression on Gallant's face. "He may be intending to speak to us, enseigne", he said, squinting at the distant sail. "Or else…"

"Exactly. Your 'or else' is what bothers me." He thought for a moment, his mouth a hard line. "You'd better pass the word that we may have some action coming up. Tell Akiwoya to look to the gun crew. And haul out those cutlass barrels from my cabin."

Béssac's expression was dubious.

"Béssac, a little preparedness is all I'm thinking of. Don't alarm anyone yet. You may be right after all."

The mate nodded. "Oui, enseigne."

Half a turn of the glass later Gallant scrambled up the ratlines to *Écho*'s foretop and squinted at the strange vessel, which was hull up over the horizon and moving strongly toward the corvette, heeling dramatically. As he watched, he saw a flicker of red above the vessel's stern. A British ensign.

Gallant wrapped a leg around a topmast shroud and pursed his lips thoughtfully. The vessel was a topsail schooner, a small and alarmingly fast rig common on the coasts of the English Colonies and much used by traders and the dread "black-birders", the slave vessels. He could see painted gunports on the pitching hull, but no red gleam of muzzles; the ports were for bluff only, but there was nothing of bluff about the glint of sunlight from the vessel's rail, off what were likely more than a half-dozen swivels. And the swivels were an almost dead giveaway for a special kind of ship during wartime: the ship under a letter of marque.

As if to end the argument, a puff of smoke followed by the thump of a gun burst from the schooner's bow, and a geyser of water leaped up a little over half-way to the corvette.

"A Yankee privateer, by God!" said Gallant to the empty air.

He slid down a backstay and regained the quarterdeck, where Béssac waited with an anxious look on his face.

"A privateer, enseigne? That bow chaser shot means he wants us to strike to him!"

Gallant nodded, spitting over the rail. "Right. She's an Englishman. A topsail schooner, likely a Yankee out of the Chesapeake. I've seen those rigs before."

He thought quickly, trying to imagine all the moves he might make with *Écho*, and the chances each one held for survival. The privateer would have no interest in shiphandling round to hold the weather gauge, pumping broadsides in man-o'-war fashion into the corvette. Instead it would crunch in alongside, its swivels belching a hail of shot across *Écho*'s decks, grapnels hooking fast in the corvette's rigging while a ruthless boarding party cut down the remainder of her crew. That was the privateer's way, and if they came in expecting a fight from the corvette, it would be all over in a few bloodsoaked moments.

But if they expected no defence...

"Strike the colours, Béssac!"

Béssac looked at him aghast. "Enseigne?"

Gallant moved to him. "Strike the colours, Béssac. Put her into the wind and let fly the topsail sheets. Make it look good, as if we're a defenceless merchantman fearing for our lives!"

"But..."

"Do it, Béssac! Then issue cutlasses and get the men down behind the rail toward the privateer!"

Comprehension flashed across the mate's face, and in an instant orders were barking from his lips.

He turned after a moment back to Gallant. "Enseigne, you're a crazy man! You know that, eh?"

Gallant grinned crookedly back, recklessness bubbling within him. "Of course, mon ami. But they won't be expecting us to board them, will they? And you never know; luck just might be with us!"

Within a few moments the white flag of France lay crumpled on *Écho*'s quarterdeck as she lay pitching with her bows into the wind, the broad surfaces of her topsails pressed flat back against the topmasts, their sheets loose and writhing.

As the privateer drew nearer, Gallant could see that the ship had an astonishing turn of speed, and was closing the distance rapidly. Its masts were black and raked, Yankee-fashion, and the figurehead flowed back into the lines of a sharp and hollow-cheeked bow far more pronounced than *Écho*'s own. The vessel looked trim and deadly.

The corvette's crew were tight-lipped and tense, every mind intent on the approaching danger. The best topmen and able seamen were clustering at their posts, ready to work feverishly when the command came. Amidships and along the foredeck rail Akiwoya was clustering the bulk of the men crouched out of sight below the rail on the side toward the privateer. In each man's hand a cutlass gleamed, and several had armed themselves with belaying pins as well. Their faces were dark and strained, and here and there Gallant could see lips moving in the words of the *Aperi Domine*. A few men clutched grapnels and lines.

Béssac arrived on the quarterdeck and handed a weapon to Gallant. Very rapidly the schooner closed the gap, and Gallant could see rows of heads as the privateer's men clustered at the rail, ready to swarm aboard.

Gallant kept his cutlass pressed against his leg, and took a quick look around the corvette. With the men crouching behind the weather bulwark, and invisible to the Yankee, *Écho* presented the image of an undermanned French trader waiting helplessly for the hand of fate to fall on her.

Gallant spat. His mouth was dry. The privateer was about three hundred yards away, dead abeam, and moving in quickly. He saw its sails luff briefly as the knife-sharp bows paid off the wind slightly. The Yankee captain was going to swing his bows into the eye of the wind at the precise moment to slam his ship hull-to-hull with *Écho*, a horde of boarders following immediately. Gallant could see the privateer's name on the black bows, a flowing script in white: *William and Anne*.

His knees trembling, the marine strolled studiedly to the wheel, to stand by the shoulder of the white-faced helmsman. His eyes flicked over the crouching men. They were ready, cutlasses hefted expectantly. He could see, when he looked up again, the officers on the quarterdeck of the privateer pointing him out to the men massed at the rail, the mocking laughter carrying to his ears.

A moment more. The privateer was swinging now, canvas thundering aloft, the wedge of sea between the ships suddenly a leaping cauldron. A jeer rose from the massed men waiting to sweep over the corvette's deck.

"Now!"

"Hard to port!" Gallant bellowed.

The wheel spun in a blur, and Gallant felt the deck cant beneath his feet. In the next instant there was a heavy, shuddering impact as *Écho*'s quarter slammed into the waist of the privateer. The men at her rail staggered at the impact, falling, grasping for handholds.

Gallant whirled his cutlass over his head and leaped for the rail. ''Come on!'' he shrieked.

A roar burst from the lips of *Écho*'s men as they sprang to their feet and swarmed up over the rail, vaulting the grinding abyss between the two ships to the privateer's deck. Grapnels flashed in the air to hook on shrouds and rigging, binding the two vessels together.

Flame flashed from pistols and muskets, the reports lost in the bellow and shriek of fighting men's voices. Gallant felt a hot flash in his face as he leaped from the rigging to the Yankee's deck, and a ball hummed by his ear. He thrust out blindly into the sudden cloud of smoke before him and felt the blade thud home. A cry rang in his ears and he wrenched the blade free as a hulking, bare-chested seaman collapsed at his feet with blood spurting from his throat.

All around Gallant was a mad, struggling chaos, the clash and ring of blade on blade mixing with pistol and musket blasts, hoarse shouts, and ghastly screams.

He staggered back as one of the men of *Écho* shouldered into him and fell, kicking, his hands clutching at the half-pike deep in his stomach. Gallant looked up to see a privateer, face contorted with fury, aiming an overhand cut at him with a heavy cutlass. He parried the ringing blow, had his own blow blocked, and then ducked to one side to bring down the man with a backhand cut that bit deep into the man's muscular neck. Gallant heard a voice shouting, hoarse and incoherent, and then realized with a start that it was his own.

For an instant Akiwoya surged into view, locked in combat with a blond giant whose arms were a mass of tattooing. Just as Gallant's eyes ripped away he saw the African level the man with one tremendous punch.

Suddenly an arm fastened like a vice around his neck, and a fierce voice snarled obscenities in his ear. With a reflex action Gallant snapped forward, feeling the man hurtle over his back, the arm tearing loose from his throat. Almost sensing rather than seeing the sprawling body before him, Gallant raised his cutlass and drove it with all his strength into the man's chest, the wretch's scream hideously loud in his ears. Sickened, he staggered back, the writhing body of the privateer wrenching the cutlass from his grasp.

At that instant, without warning, it was all over. The fighting ceased as if on some timed signal. The privateers were backing against the far rail, hands raised in surrender. Smoke drifted across the deck, and the planking was littered with grotesquely sprawled bodies. Here and there a moaning form struggled to rise. The sun glistened on the slick red smears that stained the planking.

Gallant was leaning against the mainmast fiferail, his breath still coming in hot, burning gasps. He looked at his hands. They were trembling and bloody.

Béssac appeared, seemingly unhurt. The long cutlass blade in his hand was scarlet from tip to guard.

"The Yankee captain's over there, m'sieu'. He's dying. Took a body thrust from one of our lads. D'you want to see him?"

Still not sure of his voice, Gallant nodded. He followed the mate to where a heavy-set, balding man in a heavy green coat lay propped against the capstan. From the chest down the man's clothing was soaked in blood, and he was breathing in short, froth-flecked gasps.

"Who are you, capitaine?" he asked.

The man squinted up at him. "Cap'n Abner Wallace... the *William and Anne,* out o'...Boston. She's owned...by..." The man paled with the effort.

"Never mind that, m'sieu'," said Gallant. "Why did you attack us?"

The captain made an effort to smile. "Don't you know... Froggy...there's a war on? Us'ns were...under a letter o' marque..."

"But the war's in Europe, capitaine. We're bound to Louisbourg. There's no war there!"

"When Billy Vaughan convinces...ol'Gov'ner Shirley an'... the Gen'r'l Court, Froggy, ye'll...get yer war, I reckon!"

"What do you mean? Who are these men you're speaking of?"

"Ha...you'll find out! You and...all that Papist coven up

there...when we take Louisbourg...ye'll feel the wrath of Providence and the muscles...of Massachusetts men..."

Gallant stared at the man. "What? What was that?"

He bent forward, trying to catch what the man was whispering. It was too late.

"He's dead, enseigne", said Béssac.

Gallant rose, staring down at the body of the New Englander. Take Louisbourg? What the devil did the man mean?

He looked up to see Béssac and Akiwoya watching him, waiting for orders. He rubbed his brow and squared his shoulders. There was work to be done, and time enough to ponder what the dying man had said.

"There's no use our trying to man this vessel, Béssac. Check below in her stores for anything we can use, but leave them some water and biscuit. Lock the crew below so it'll take some time for them to break out. Toss overboard all their weapons that we can't use and then cut all the sheets and braces."

He moved to the rail.

"By the time they knot and splice it all we'll be over the horizon."

He suddenly noticed the corvette's men were looking at him, grinning, their eyes full of pride and exhilaration over the little victory they had won.

Gallant forced a smile for them, knowing they deserved it. "And while you're at it", he added, "broach a brandy cask for these cut-throats of ours."

The men's cheers ringing in his ears, he went below to his cabin to scrub his hands in sea water and to try and let the shaking and the nausea pass. He made himself repeat the privateer captain's words.

"Take Louisbourg?"

Was there a British expedition moving to besiege the great fortress? That made little sense. The Royal Navy was stretched to the limit in European waters, Gallant knew, with usually no more than a squadron on the North American station; too little to waste on so remote an outpost as Louisbourg. But there might be something else afoot.

The muscles of Massachusetts men...

The English colonies to the south, the old enemies in Boston and elsewhere, were becoming stronger, more ambitious. Their ships roamed everywhere, particularly into Louisbourg's own harbour. Gallant found himself realizing one awesome possibility: were the colonists themselves planning a siege of the fortress town?

Gallant squinted out through the stern windows at the whitecapped swells, realization and conviction slowly building in him as he thought and re-thought those words from dying lips. What he had heard might well have been simply the ravings of the dying. But perhaps it was more than that? Was it, by God, a chance discovery thrown in his lap that might, just might mean the difference between a miserable defeat and successful resistance for the Louisbourg garrison, if a siege was indeed coming?

His heart beat hard against his ribs as he strode out of the cabin, heading for the upper deck.

"Béssac!" he bellowed.

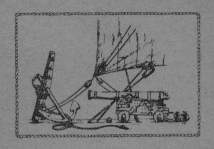

TWO

The Chevalier Louis Dupont Du Chambon, gouverneur-commandante of the Fortress of Louisbourg and of Isle Royale, pressed his fingertips together and stared up at the heavy beams of the Council chamber, a studiedly patient look on his face. Then he looked back at the young officer who stood, hat in hand, at the far end of the table. He cleared his throat.

"M'sieu' Gallant. By all means I have been hearing, from many sources, that what you suggest is possible. Sources of somewhat greater experience than your own, I should add."

He leaned forward over the blue and gold of the fleur de lys table cover. "But I am not in the habit of having my responsibilities dictated to me by a very junior officer! Do you follow?"

Paul Gallant clenched his teeth and looked with a feeling of futility round the impassive faces at the table before meeting again the imperious gaze of the governor. Louis Du Chambon was bearing himself with all the authority of his position, his occupation of it admittedly only temporary. The strong-jawed face, powdered and patched, was framed by a magnificent wig that fell to the shoulders of an exquisitely brocaded coat. From cuffs heavy with lace Du Chambon's ring-laden hands lay smooth and white on the table.

"If you please, Louis", said another voice. "The enseigne may well be repeating nothing that we have not already heard from les sauvages. But he has been trying to obtain an audience before this Council ever since his arrival almost four months ago! And what of the other things we've seen?"

" 'Things', François?"

" 'Things', Louis. You must say that to have seen His Most Christian Majesty's Ship *La Renommée* attacked and driven away from the very mouth of the harbour attests to some..."

Du Chambon shook his head. "There is no proof whatsoever that the vessel was *La Renommée*. None!"

"But Royal Navy warships off our shores!"

Gallant watched with interest the governor's questioner, who sat to one side of the table. François Bigot, the Intendant, a neat, small hawk of a man whose vital and powerful post as administrator allowed him to speak with the governor almost at a level of equality, was directing a well-manicured finger at Du Chambon.

"No proof, Excellency? What of the sauvage Benoit sent out with others from Port Toulouse to investigate what the English were doing at Canceau across the Strait, and who barely escaped with his life? Didn't he babble about transports, and more importantly, men-of-war? And what of the master of that little brig out of Saint Jean de Luz? He swears he was broadsided by an English sixty-four! A sixty-four, on a blockade right out there!"

He stabbed the finger toward the window, through which over the rooftops of the town the grey Atlantic could be seen, cloaked with its attendant wall of fog which had not dispersed in five weeks.

"And what of those goélettes we seized, packed with game and provisions."

"Enough, François, enough!" Du Chambon raised protesting hands. "You have made your point. But what is it you wish me to do, hein? The *Société* has sailed for France, carrying letters from myself to the Minister, detailing our position. I am doing everything possible to be aware of Bostonnais activity!"

His eyes flicked meaningfully to the impassive sergeant who stood cradling his halberd at the doorway of the chamber, and lowered his voice.

"And, messieurs, just what do you think a lot of rumour and babble about an impending attack would do to my mutinous garrison? The treasonous dogs would be as likely to slit our throats and sack the town, and then where would we be!"

Gallant watched Du Chambon's face flush with anger, and he had to admit he understood the governor's worry on that particular point. Four months earlier, in the depth of winter, the soldiery of the garrison had suddenly mutinied, led by the disgruntled Swiss mercenaries of the Karrer regiment. It had been a relatively short-lived and thankfully bloodless revolt; the whole garrison of the Karrer and the colony troops of the Compagnies Franches de la Marine had paraded themselves inside the looming King's Bastion while a bayonet-wielding squad had cruised the town streets, drums thundering. Only the long-service men, the sergeants and capitaines d'armes, had refused to join the mutiny, and it had only been after a few officers had faced the bayonets, rashly promising redress of many of the soldiers' grievances, that the companies had fallen out and returned to their duties.

Not that their complaints were unjustified. The men lived in verminous squalor in the dank and rotting barrack rooms in the King's Bastion, their lives a mean routine of wretched food, poor pay, insufficient clothing, a disease-ridden boredom. Almost the only solace they could obtain came from gambling or the syphilitic embrace of the women in the soldiers' brothel.

For Gallant and a few other officers whose horror of these conditions led them to try and correct these injustices, the effort soon faded against the bitter truth that the misuse and exploitation of the soldiers was often carried out for the profit of the most important men of the town. Even François Bigot himself had glibly reported mixing bad flour with new to make biscuits for issue to the soldiers, and had helped balance his rather shadowy accounts by simply cutting the daily bread ration in half.

But the men still had a spark of pride and self-respect. Or would have, with proper leadership. And if an attack on Louisbourg was being contemplated by the energetic and imaginative men in the turbulent colonies of England to the south, Du Chambon would need the musket, and loyalty, of every ill-treated soldat in the fortress.

The governor was speaking: "…and so to give us men we can depend on I have sent out a call for the fishermen of Baleine and Lorambec to augment the town militia here."

"Excellency", said Gallant, into the silence that followed. "I know your concern about the garrison. But from what I see in my own company I know they are men who can be appealed to. They want to prove they are loyal, and in spite of everything they want to think of themselves as soldiers. Even if you disagree that the New Englanders intend to assault us, would it not be wise, Excellency, to appeal to their honour? To call on them to stand with you for their own sakes, and that of France?"

Du Chambon pondered for a moment, looking over the faces of his advisory council who were for the most part looking at Gallant with mixed expressions. Other than the governor and Bigot, the faces were all strange to Gallant. There were two merchants, recent arrivals from France, who traded to the Caribbean and Québec; a resplendent officer who was evidently the latest military administrator, the lieutenant du roy; the sombrely draped figure of the procurer général, Du Chambon's legal advisor; and a scribbling clerk, who sat at a small table to one side.

Du Chambon broke into a not unpleasant smile.

"You're impertinent, Gallant. But I sense that the majority of these gentlemen seem to agree with you." He stood up abruptly, a signal that the meeting was at an end. "I shall therefore issue, as you put it, an 'appeal' to them as Frenchmen. Perhaps", and here he looked briefly at the procureur, "a promise of pardon is possible as well."

He stopped as he moved toward the door, looking at each of the men in turn.

"But I wish to hear no more loose tongues babbling about an attack, for the present. Proof is what I need, messieurs! Proof!"

A few moments later Gallant stepped out the door from the governor's wing of the long barracks, after having waited respectfully for the other members of the council to precede him. As his feet touched the uneven cobblestones, the sentry by the door stiffened to attention. The man's uniform was almost in rags, but showed long and laborious efforts at patching. And the musket was gleaming and spotless.

They think of themselves as soldiers, said Gallant to himself, sadly.

Setting his hat firmly on his head, Gallant returned the salute and struck off from the cobblestones across the grass of the parade, hands automatically moving to their quarterdeck position behind his back. The fog bank was flowing and eddying back and forth across the fortress, and above his head the ramparts were vanishing into its wet whiteness.

Gallant shivered. If Du Chambon was convinced that all Louisbourg had to worry about were the pestilential Boston privateers, there was no point trying to convince him that a major English attack was on its way. There was no hope that he could be prodded into the kind of preparation a siege threat called for. No. If the attack did come, it would fall on a Louisbourg woefully unprepared. The list of inadequacies was endless: too few guns, too few well-trained gun crews, no progress on the dismantled landside walls of the Royal Battery down along the harbour...

He pulled his coat closer about him against the chill of the fog. Rounding the corner of the Governor's animal stockade he crossed the open square and trudged up along the ramp leading to the platform where two twenty-four pound guns pointed their snouts into the fog toward the marshes that bordered the seacoast west of the fortress. A threadbare Compagnies Franches sentry was pacing behind the guns, and just as the man touched his musket in salute to Gallant, the platform was bathed in a sudden shaft of brilliant morning sunshine. Looking up, Gallant saw that a patch of blue was overhead, the fog's white tendrils unexpectedly breaking and eddying as it often did to tease with glimpses of sunlight.

From this height he could see that the fog still cloaked the western half of the town and the seacoast beyond, but had curled back from the harbour mouth and the eastern half, so that Gallant's view was uninterrupted down over the low town roofs to the twinkling harbour and the grey mass of the Royal Battery some distance along its shores, directly opposite the harbour mouth.

Louisbourg harbour was a long, kidney-shaped inlet of the Atlantic that lay parallel to the seacoast rather than running in from it. Its narrow mouth was closed on the north side by a high and wooded arm of land that bore on its rocky tip a tall stone lighthouse. The southern side of the harbour was formed by a broad, flat triangle of land which reached out toward a series of small islands in the harbour mouth, the channel between them and the lighthouse point being measured in mere yards.

It was on this broad, flat southern arm of land, a low and marshy expanse dominated by the higher ground inland, that the grey stone and timber of Louisbourg rose, its twin-spired skyline half-hidden behind the mighty fortifications that cut across the base of the triangle from harbour side to sea. From where Gallant stood on the high ramparts of the King's Bastion he could look out over the long chimneyed roof of the barracks into the town itself, out toward the channel islands where, on one island, a menacing battery blocked easy passage of the channel; from the sturdy round tower of the lighthouse his eyes could trace the fishing sheds and shacks of the fishermen, flanked by the sprawling fish racks, clustered round the sides of the harbour right up to the very walls of the fortress. There, close by the harbour, the fortifications began with the Dauphin demi-bastion, its massive semi-circular battery of ten twenty-four pound guns dominating the inner harbour. From the Dauphin a long and climbing curtain wall rose to the King's Bastion, where Gallant stood; then on to the Queen's Bastion, another great angle of masonry thrust out into the evergreen and ooze of the encircling marsh; and ending at the sea again with the Princess demi-bastion. Other walls and other bastions facing seaward linked round the town to join it and its harbour quay in a seemingly impregnable improbability: the stern might of a Vauban fortress set on a dark and savage New World coast.

But to Gallant, there was no sense of incongruity. He drank in the play of sun on the dark, tiled roofs over which the chimney smoke swirled and spread, on the grey, rough-hewn stone and plum-coloured woodwork of the King's buildings; he delighted in the contrast of the gleaming masonry with the rolling, shadowed mass of evergreen hills that stretched away to landward.

For all its beauty and clear light he had found the Mediterranean world somehow too gentle, too accepting. This new world about him was a harsh, powerful one, demanding and callous in its cold, its starkness. It stirred something within Gallant, burnishing to diamond brightness his sense of taut, aware existence. He revelled in the swirling fogs, the brilliant chill of the sea-washed air, the incredible power of the storms that swept in from a thousand miles of ocean to shriek and thunder at the coast and the buildings that clung doggedly to it, barnacles of human endurance. Gallant's heart and spirit were northern in a way neither he nor anyone not born there could fully understand; but he knew that this truth of his character had been made more clear to him by the past year's events, and it was with remarkable serenity and sense of place that he looked out over the land which, more than any other, was his.

Three leagues to the northward, along the lush bands of the Miré river, his father had first driven a mattock into a stump-dotted clearing in 1720. That clearing had grown through love and backbreaking labour into a prosperous farm, now tended by Gallant's younger brother Philippe.

Every chance Gallant had to leave his garrison duties, he would shoulder a small pack and trudge over the marshy track outside the town walls, snaking through the gloomy bush to the settlements along the distant river. The joy and the warmth of the family welcome never faded. It was home there for Gallant, in all the full richness of the word's meaning, and in the moments when his thoughts turned to his own death, he found he could not imagine his burial being anywhere except in the embrace of the soil his family's toil had made their own, and his.

The deep chime of the barrack clock tower bell startled Gallant, and he squinted at the broad face of the clock. A quarter-hour before eleven. In fifteen minutes he would be able to watch the duty guard company fall in below him on the square, tumbling out of the barracks to the hollow thump of the summoning drum.

Gallant looked back toward the harbour. Amidst the mass of hulls riding in the anchorage he quickly picked out the sleek lines of the *Écho*. He smiled, imagining Béssac and Akiwoya bustling about the ship, making a thousand last-minute preparations for sea.

That, at least, had been a story with a happy ending. Soon after the corvette's arrival in mid-winter, Gallant had been brusquely ordered back to active duty, leaving his two friends to deal almost unaided with the Admiralty Court's disposal of the corvette. But the key members of the Court had decided to appoint Béssac Master and Akiwoya Mate, and to order the vessel to sail it to a French home port of registry, Saint-Malo. There a higher admirauté would rule on whether the two men could claim the vessel as their own. There was the brokerage to deal with, but this would likely be the case, Gallant had been assured. Now the two men and the loyal Acadien crew were but a few hours away from departure.

Gallant would be sorry to see them go. Every free moment had meant a scramble down to the quayside to ride a lighter out to the ship, even to spend only a few warm minutes with his friends.

"Fog's clearing to westward, enseigne."

Gallant looked up. The sky was in fact opening up, more than just a little blue showing. Perhaps he had time to wander down to the barbier-chirurgien to have his queue reset before the Guard feel in...

"Sweet Christ save us!" The sentry's voice cracked, and he dropped his musket, fumbling for it as he stared pop-eyed westward.

Gallant squinted out where the man was pointing, toward the wide, shimmering gunmetal surface of Gabarus Bay, which majestically came into view as the fog rolled away seaward. A good two miles west of Louisbourg, the bay itself was more than six miles deep and almost as much across, and from the ramparts Gallant could see almost its entire area.

"Peste!" he said, and spat. He knew he had been right!

The bay was covered with ships. Schooners, brigs, snows, pinks, cutters, luggers, full-rigged vessels. Ships of every size and variety. Ships in enormous numbers, the dark hulks of men-o'-war looming here and there among them.

"Holy Mother, enseigne!" stuttered the sentry, a pox-faced youth. "Who are they?"

"The English, soldat. New Englanders, to be exact. We're about to have ourselves besieged in earnest, I think!"

Beside him the youth moaned, turning pale. Gallant shielded his eyes against the sun. There was something else moving out there, among the ships. He squinted, then gave a long, low whistle.

Boats! Landing boats, by the hundreds, moving for shore!

Gallant spun on the sentry and seized him by the shoulders.

"Now listen, man! Carefully and well! You are to go as swiftly as you can out through the arch of the Place d'Armes guardhouse. There you'll find the officer of the guard, understand? Tell him that ships — Christ, a fleet — is visible in Gabarus Bay, and that I am going to the Town Major with the rest of the news! Do you follow?"

The youth nodded, eyes gaping with fright.

"Pray God you do! Now go!"

As the youth clattered off down the ramp, Gallant looked for an instant at the incongruously beautiful scene. The fortress town, sunwashed and tranquil under a spring sky. And beyond, to the westward, the shimmer of clustering white sails on a multitude of ships coming to anchor on sparkling waters.

He jammed his hat firmly on his head. That peace is no more, he thought glumly. In the next instant he was pounding down the other ramp toward the door in the governor's wing of the barrack block that marked the cabinet of the Town Major.

Twenty minutes later the fortified town of Louisbourg was anything but tranquil. The square in front of the King's Bastion was filled with the ordered ranks of the garrison soldiery, rushing at the double out the barrack doors and shuffling into line under the sharp, impatient eyes of their sergeants. From everywhere in the town drums rolled, thundering the alarm among the low, squat buildings, voices raised in shouts and orders over the roll. The deep pealing of the clock bell was joined by the lighter notes of the hospital bell. The streets below were suddenly choked with knots of running, shouting people, their voices a cacophony of oaths, cries and the panicky wail of women. Even the harbour had leaped to life, small skiffs and lighters being oared with considerable frenzy back and forth, as if sweaty labour might somehow keep at bay the horrors, both real and imagined, of the threat which had materialized to the west of the town.

And it was an anything but tranquil Louis Du Chambon who stood before the altar in the chapel and looked round at the hurriedly convened assembly of his regular and militia officers.

"Landing now, you claim, enseigne Gallant?"

"Yes, m'sieu', I swear it! Their boats were pulling for Point Blanche and the beaches beyond! You can see them from the ramparts!"

"Excellency, we must act, and act at once!" boomed a deep voice from one side. It belonged to Poupet de la Boularderie, a leathery and white-haired old veteran officer of the Régiment de Richelieu, who had arrived that morning by boat from his Bras d'Or lands.

"Boularderie is right, Excellency! We must make a move against them now, or we are lost!" A chorus of shouts went up among the men in agreement.

Du Chambon waved a hand airily about him. "Our walls still stand, messieurs. Let us not, shall we say, over-react. When we have had time to assess carefully..."

An angry murmer came from the men. Gallant was about to speak when, to his relief, de la Boularderie shouldered his big frame to the front of the crowd.

"Excellency", he growled, "with all due respect to you, if we wait any further the only thing we shall have time to assess will be the surrender terms dictated by les anglais!"

A hoarse shout of agreement greeted these words. Stung, Du

Chambon reddened under his powder.

"What, then, do you propose?" he said savagely.

"Look, Excellency. There are woods covering the points where the English are landing. Under cover of those woods a force could advance within half a pistol shot of the beaches undetected!"

"And?"

"These Englishmen out there are a New England militia, not British regulars, by the look of them! By the time those misérables stagger ashore in the confusion and upset of such landings they'll be frozen to the bone, to boot!"

"Perhaps, but..."

De la Boularderie swept off his hat in a dramatic gesture. "Excellency, give me half the garrison! I'll march them to the beaches now and drive the Yankees into the sea!"

"And I, Excellency!" Morpain, the Port Captain, had stepped forward as well. "I'll take as many militia of the town as are willing, and go as well!"

Du Chambon frowned and shook his head. "Non", he said at length. "I can spare no man beyond these walls."

Loud voices rose in dismay until at last Du Chambon raised his hands in protest.

"What, are you all fools? Very well, very well! Morpain, if you can find any townsmen moronic enough to go with you, you may go! M'sieu' de la Boularderie, I cannot entrust my soldiery to your command, but you may go with a half-company of the Troupes, if you are willing. My own son, Mesillac Du Chambon, will go! Gallant here may command. But mind, Gallant, a half-company only!"

Leaving the astonished assembly staring, Du Chambon strode through their midst out the chapel door.

Poupet de la Boularderie looked round him, his face a grim mask. "Very well, messieurs. Let us be off!"

Gallant's company volunteered to a man, and Gallant was forced to select only the steadiest twenty-four. Young Du Chambon was feeling such shame over his father's hesitancy that Gallant left him to see to the cartridge issue while he visited the quartermaster himself. He returned with a nine-round waistbelt cartridge box, a haversack of spare rounds, and a musket.

Mesillac had armed himself at the first alarm, and so it was only a few minutes later that Gallant led his men out the central archway of the Bastion.

The march down through the town toward the Dauphin gate was an appalling experience. Gallant strode ahead of his company, literally pushing shouting, panic-striken people to one side to make room for his men to pass. Everywhere he looked the scene was the same: wailing and panicky women with sniffling children clutching at their skirts, wild-eyed sailors and townsmen running about in a useless and sickening lather of fear. The word of the attacking fleet had spread like lightning, and the panicked crowds shoved past Gallant and young Du Chambon, ignoring their calls for calm. The two officers realized the futility of trying to halt the panic, and moved their men on. Finally the Dauphin gate swung shut behind them, and they clumped out over the small bridge into the open air. The silence hummed in their ears.

Gallant shook his head, listening now to the crunch of the men's shoes on the roadway. There would be no holding Louisbourg with that kind of panic afoot.

Behind them a ragged little party of townsmen puffed to catch up, and with scarcely a look at them Gallant and Du Chambon swung the detachment on into the marshy ground toward the distant New England landings. The spongy hummocks and wet ooze between made the going hard, and the men were soon toiling on in silence, the only sounds the squelch of their shoes, the hum of insects, and their own heavy breathing. Behind, the townsmen sweated and cursed, and when Gallant looked back over the scene he found it hard to imagine they were not on some routine and familiar exercise.

Finally the trees before them cleared enough to give a glimpse of the landing area, now only a mile or two distant. De la Boularderie puffed up from the tail of the company and joined Gallant as he squinted at the scene ahead.

Gallant had to admit it was impressive enough. The vast fleet of ships, the small, beetle shapes of boats plying in, and now, on the flat and stony beach, the multicoloured pattern of many men drawn up in military formation.

At his side, de la Boularderie gasped.

"There must be almost a thousand men ashore there, enseigne! Peste! There's nothing we could do against them with this paltry lot of ours!"

"What do you suggest?" said Gallant.

"Go back." The old man stood back and spat forcefully. "Go back now, while we have a chance to make it."

"What?" Gallant turned to see Morpain sloshing up from his ragtag company. His face was livid with rage. "Go back? Like cowards? By the Christ, never!"

Now ahead Gallant could see some rapid movement in the massed formations. Waves of men were spreading out, moving toward them; others were moving with lightning speed inland, already outflanking them. A few of the closest were dropping to their knees and squeezing off impossible long shots at the approaching Frenchmen, the puffs of white smoke small and perfect in the distance. A flash showed on the side of one of the New England ships off to their left, and seconds later the air was filled with a ripping sound. A hissing jet of mud and water suddenly leaped up a few yards in front of Gallant. Then more flashes flickered, the rumble of the gunnery carrying now on the wind. Now the air was filled with howling and ripping sounds, and heavy shot was punching into the marsh around them, throwing up stinking geysers of mud and weed.

There was a sudden rush of air behind him and a strangled shriek, and he felt something warm splash against his neck. He glanced over his shoulder, whipping his head back again before he lost control of his stomach. A ball had ploughed through the rear rank of his party, leaving nine of the twelve men bloody, twitching pulp in the mire. He spat, willing back the retch, listening to the sloshing feet.

"Fools! Cowards! Come back!" he heard Morpain yell.

Gallant spun around. The townsmen had broken, and were running and struggling back across the marsh toward the distant walls. Railing at them was Morpain, his voice hoarse with rage.

"Come back!" shouted Gallant futilely. Then his neck stiffened, as off to the north he saw a line of New Englanders moving in after Morpain's fleeing townsmen. The Bostonnais had already got right around behind them!

Gallant glanced ahead. At least two companies were moving rapidly in a loose open order toward them, the sun glinting off barrels and bayonets. They had to get to cover!

"Break ranks, soldats, and run in a crouch!" he barked. "That ditch over there, behind the hummocks! Take cover there! Come on!"

Muskets held high, the men splashed, falling and stumbling, over to a depression that lay half-hidden by a series of low mounds. They ignored the mud and water that sloshed around their legs, sinking down into it, breath coming in great gasps. Gallant hung back, pushing on the straggling ones, finally helping de la Boularderie stagger in to sprawl full length in the water at the bottom of the ditch.

Gallant scrubbed at the dirt caking the lock of his light musket. "Prime and Load! Make Ready! Fire at your own targets! And keep firing!"

The men bit their cartridges and emptied the cartridges into the muzzles. Ramrods clinked in barrels and hammers clicked back.

A sudden fusillade sounded far behind them, and Gallant turned to see a party of whooping New Englanders fall on Morpain and the hapless townsmen. He swore helplessly, watching the tomahawk blades of the Yankees flash in the sun. Screams carried faintly on the wind.

"Poor bastards", muttered Messillac Du Chambon, and turned away to hide the tears that streamed down his cheeks.

In the next second a hail of fire broke over the little party where they crouched, balls splatting into the mud on every side. From almost every angle rifle and musket fire poured in on them, so accurate that several soldiers barely managed to get off a round before a ball punched into them, and they sprawled with a moan in the mire.

There was a ragged cheer well over to his right, in a low ditch where Gallant had seen de la Boularderie move with three men to find better cover. Gallant swung round in time to see a roaring knot of New Englanders, their faces ruddy with effort and likely rum, swarm over the position. Before several whining balls sent Gallant scrambling for new cover he saw the old man's hands raise in surrender, a beefy New Englander snatching the musket from his hands with a crow of triumph.

Gallant looked wildly round for Du Chambon. The young man had lost his musket and was slumped down in a bloody pool, cradling the unconscious form of a sergeant. With a start Gallant realized that no French were firing.

He rose and sloshed in a crouch over to Du Chambon's side. As he moved a ball snatched his hat from his head and sent it spinning into the mud. He squatted down beside Du Chambon and shook him roughly.

"Mesillac! Is he dead? Answer me!"

Du Chambon nodded, not flinching as a ball thudded into the hummock beside his ear.

Gallant looked up, despair flooding him. Then he stared. The New Englanders' firing was dying away. They were standing up, watching, knowing it was almost all over.

A mad thought seized him.

"Come on, Mesillac! Stand up!" Throwing aside his musket Gallant slung one of Du Chambon's arms around his neck and pulled up, staggering and splashing for balance. "Stand up, hein? You want to die in this place?"

Du Chambon rose as if in a daze, revealing the bloody hole below his shoulder. He slumped against Gallant. With his eyes closed, waiting for the killing hail of shot, Gallant lifted one foot out of the sucking mire and took a step back in the direction of the fortress. Then another.

The New Englanders watched as if astonished for a brief moment of silence. For a few precious seconds the two men were stumbling unmolested off through the marsh toward the distant walls.

Then, with a chorus of yells, a storm of fire rippled along the New England line, and Du Chambon crumpled under the impact of another ball.

Something clipped Gallant's leg viciously and he fell to one knee, then fought to get up, to rise again. He would not give in!

He clenched his teeth against the pain, a sob breaking uncontrollably through his lips. With enormous, gasping effort, he pulled Du Chambon's limp-rag body from the mire and got him across his shoulders before rising on trembling legs. He began to walk again, feeling for every step, the fire and awful pain in his leg seeming to flow up through his entire body. He fought for balance, fingers wrapped like hooks into the cloth of Du Chambon's coat.

There was a distant boom from the New England ships far behind him, sounding over the rattle of the musketry, and then suddenly, with a vicious crunch the ground before him leaped up in a fountain of black, spattering and drenching him.

Gallant staggered on. He could hear faint shouts, and realized dimly they were from the distant ramparts. Shouts of encouragement. He closed his eyes for an instant, trying to will away the agony in his leg. Du Chambom was groaning now, starting to stir, and Gallant gritted his teeth, fighting to keep the unconscious youth from slipping from his shoulders.

They were nearing the Dauphin gate now, passing the few scattered shacks that lay outside. Their doors gaped ajar. The fishermen's families had already fled into the town, and now he was stumbling along a rutted, spongy track that was littered with odds and ends, personal belongings, pots, little sacks of valuables: the rubbish of fear.

Then Gallant stumbled and fell, gasping in pain as his knees crunched down. Du Chambon sprawled in a heap before him, the grey-white shoulder of his coat now matted and deep red.

God help me, thought Gallant wildly. Ahead he could hear the shouts of the men atop the Dauphin, calling him. And behind him, the jeers and whoops of the New Englanders coming on. For a moment Gallant thought of trying to drag Du Chambon into one of the shacks, then as soon struck the thought from his mind. They would die like trapped pigs in there.

A ball slapped into the mud before his face, spattering filth into his eyes. With a curse he fought to his feet and dragged Du Chambon up across his shoulders, sobs of pain escaping through his gretted teeth. Move, his mind shrieked silently. Move! Move!

From ahead in the Dauphin the yells were louder, more urgent. He lurched forward one step, two, then more. A blast off to the right rang in his ears, and he turned in time to see a gout of smoke wash over the grey lip of the King's Bastion. Thank God! They were firing the twenty-fours at the pursuing New Englanders, and now there was the sputter of muskets, too. Maybe under that cover he could make it.

Then before he expected it his feet thudded hollowly over the bridge, and the great gates of the Dauphin were swinging open, shouts and orders ringing in his ears. Hands were reaching for him now, hands that slapped him in joy, lifted Du Chambon's weight from him, grasped his own hands and arms, holding him as the tumult suddenly rang too loudly in his ears. A great roaring darkness came out of nowhere and overtook him, and he pitched forward into arms outstretched to catch him.

The screaming was like a knife cutting into the fog that seemed closed over Gallant's brain. It was the screaming of a man, regular and piercing, full of horror and despair and agony. Almost before his eyes snapped open Gallant could feel a cold sweat break out all over him. He was in darkness, a darkness lit by lanterns that cast a sick, yellow light over the rows of men who lay moaning along the walls.

On a rough table, their breeches stained darkly, their shirts soaked in sweat, four men were holding down a fifth whose nakedness was more appalling to Gallant's stare because of the streaks of blood and phlegm that laced across his body. The man was screaming with his eyes rolled downward, straining so terribly against the strength of his captors that every cord in his neck stood out like a bowstring. His eyes were fixed in terror and agony on the surgeon in a bloody apron who hunched over his lower body, his back to Gallant, shoulders working with terrible intense effort.

Gallant's head spun and his own pain coursed up his leg into his vitals like spreading flame. The scene overwhelmed him, and he hung his head over the edge of his cot and gagged, straining until there was nothing left but painful empty heaving.

The wretch on the table shrieked in a last extremity of suffering and slumped back. The surgeon, arms gore to the elbow, stood up and threw down a heavy iron probe. He spat and wiped his hands on the apron, like a butcher ending a bad job.

"Merde! He's gone. Thought that splinter'd gone too deep. Right, then, out with him. Who's next?"

"The ensiegne's awake, m'sieu' ", said one of the assistants.

Gallant stared at the fiendish spectre of the surgeon's form as it moved toward him and crouched over his leg.

"Awake, hein? How's the leg, enseigne?"

Gallant's throat was aflame. He tried to speak but could not make a sound.

"Ha! No fever! Good! Won't have to cut if off! Rouleau! Bring the brandy for M'sieu'." The surgeon held out an impatient hand to another of the assistants. The third and fourth were carrying the body from the table toward the door.

The surgeon seized a dark, squat bottle from the assistant and jerked the cork out with his teeth. A lantern gleamed off a silver fang, and he winked in the gloom at Gallant.

"Hold your breath, enseigne. This'll smart somewhat."

Gallant's breeches had been ripped away from his wound exposing it to the air. The surgeon emptied the bottle directly on to Gallant's leg.

With a roar Gallant sat up, the reflex snap of his leg to the liquid flame piercing his flesh and sending the bottle smashing against the brick.

"Jésus Christ!" Gallant threw a wild fist at the surgeon, who leaned back, roaring with laughter.

There was a flash of daylight at the door, and two men in Compagnies Franches uniform and an artillery officer pushed in. They stood for a moment searching the gloom.

"Over here, capitaine!" boomed the surgeon, jabbing a thumb at Gallant. "He's all right. No worms'll chew him!"

"Gallant! For God's sake!" said the officer, striding over to Gallant's cot. As he knelt down, Gallant recognized the strong open features of Chassin de Thierry, young commander of the Royal Battery. Thierry had befriended Gallant immediately after his return, and the marine was flooded with relief to see him.

"Chassin! Thank Christ! For the sake of the Virgin, Chassin, get me out of here!" Gallant fought to sit up and swung his legs over the edge of the cot, reeling with light-headedness.

"Steady, Paul. We'll get you out. You two! Lend a hand to the enseigne here!"

The two soldiers slung Gallant's arms over their shoulders and helped him to his feet. With Thierry leading they stepped out of the gloom into bright sunlight.

Gallant swore again, as much as from the pain in his leg as with surprise. They had emerged on the right flank of the King's Bastion, and were standing in the courtyard, amidst a hive of activity. Everywhere men were moving rapidly to and fro, carrying stores of all kinds, weapons, tools, or clutching muskets. Carts and wagons were being loaded or emptied of bales or barrels, their oxen or horses stamping nervously at the desperate speed of the workmen and the urgency of their shouts. At least two groups of women, children and the elderly were being herded under cover.

Gallant opened his mouth to speak when a low whooshing sound filled the air, and Thierry hurled him flat on his face with one powerful arm. As Gallant thudded down, his ears rang with a tremendous concussion. Fragments of wood and tile rained down around them, and he looked up to see a jagged hole in the dark slate roof of the barracks almost above his head belch out a thick column of smoke and wood ash that swirled down over the courtyard in choking clouds. From within Gallant heard shouts and screams.

Thierry was on his feet again, the soldiers lifting Gallant to his feet between them.

"Well, it's begun", said Thierry, through pursed lips. "They've started to use my guns against us!"

"Your own guns! Holy Mother of God, what is going on?" said Gallant in exasperation.

Thierry and the two soldiers moved Gallant rapidly down the central archway and out through the gate ignoring the attempts of the jittery sentry to salute.

"Tell you in a moment, Paul. First things first; you need a dressing on that wound. The idiots! To have had you carried into that charnel pit!"

In a moment they had crossed out over the broad bridge to the townside place d'armes and turned left, half-dragging Gallant up on to the porch of the guardhouse there. As Gallant was put down on the bench, Thierry bellowed, and a small, black-coated man darted out of the officer's room doorway and was instantly examining Gallant's leg.

"Yes. Yes. No evil humours. Bind that in an instant!" The black coat skipped back into the doorway and reappeared with a strip of clean linen. In two minutes Gallant's thigh was firmly and reassuringly strapped up and the little man, clutching a heavy leather satchel, had scuttled into the archway.

Gallant stared at his leg, which felt remarkably better. "Who was that..." he began.

"Good, hein? Came in with one of the Compagnie des Indes ships a month ago. If he says you'll do, believe him!" Thierry slapped his friend on the shoulder. "Glad you're still kicking!"

Gallant shook his head. "If I'd had to stay in there one more hour..." He did not finish the sentence, as another shell bomb burst with an ear-splitting report just above the clock tower spire, sending splinters thudding into the porch over their heads.

Thierry shook his head. "Damn me, I knew this would happen if they didn't mine that place!"

"Chassin, you still haven't told me what is really going on! Last thing I remember was coming in through the Dauphin with Mesillac digging into my shoulder blades, and then I passed out. What...?"

"That's right. And Mesillac will live, thanks to you. You went out like a snuffed candle. That was Tuesday."

"Tuesday? What's today, then?"

"Friday."

"Friday?" Gallant was aghast.

Thierry grasped his arm. "You were delirious. Raving. Half-awake or asleep. You'd been in the hospital until the damned brethren said they could do no more for you. I was going to have taken you to a room at Grandchamp's, but Bigot had you moved. Took me hours to find you."

Gallant was perplexed. "Why did Bigot...?"

Thierry spat in the dust and hefted his hanger in its scabbard. "Nothing that little lizard does surprises me!"

"But what were you saying just now, about your guns? The Battery?"

Thierry spat again. "Taken."

"Taken?"

"By the New Englanders. Those are our own guns blasting at us. The Yankees got one drilled out and firing at noon today!"

Gallant just stared.

Thierry shook his head. "Look, Paul. We've only a minute or two. His Excellency is screaming for you to be brought into his cabinet dead or alive and I've got to get back to my crews in the Dauphin." He snorted. "For all the good they can do! And you've got to get cleaned up. You should see yourself. But this is what's been happening."

In the dirt in front of the guardhouse porch Thierry used the tip of his hanger to draw a crude map of the kidney-shaped Louisbourg harbour, drawing in the town walls, the Grand Battery halfway around the harbour on its inland side, Lighthouse Point across the channel from the town, and the Island Battery in the harbour mouth. He talked rapidly, poking at the map, ignoring the squads of men who doubled past and the whooshing descent of the shell bombs, which were striking regularly now into the landward side of the casernes and the town buildings.

"All right. You went lock-stepping out and nearly committed suicide on Tuesday afternoon. A few others got away from that besides yourself and Mesillac. Morpain's people had a few get back. Him too, but he took a ball or tomahawk blow. His negre brought him in. De la Boularderie was taken."

"I know. I saw that happen."

"Hope they treat the old whoreson well. When everyone straggled in I think we lost about sixteen, maybe seventeen."

Gallant shook his head. "Sacristi, Chassin, we could've done more if we'd had enough men!"

"Yes, yes. I know." Thierry cleared his throat and spat. "So after you all dragged your tails in, the Bostonnais, behaving like the thugs they are, showed up and gave us some insults and jeers. They plundered most of the houses there and got over by my people in the Grand Battery. We gave them a musket volley and they backed off. For the moment."

"But then?" said Gallant. "Did the gouverneur order a sally?"

Thierry snorted. "His Excellency didn't order a purge for his lapdog, Paul. Nothing! By the next morning the New Englanders had landed at least two thousand of the heathenish bastards, had started a camp along that brook there, west of the Pointe Blanche, and had marched right around my battery to the nor'east, right up the head of the harbour!" He bit a lip. "I watched them burn out every poor bastard habitant up there. I knew then I couldn't hold the battery against them. Not with the rest of us sitting on our tails and watching them do it! Christ in heaven! I could hear the screams of the women right till dawn!"

"But why give up the Royal Battery, Chassin?"

"No 'why' to it, Paul. It's done. Wednesday night."

Gallant stared at him. "You're joking."

"Wish I was, mon ami. Look, the landward defences were flattened! Shovelled out nice and level for that consummate idiot M'sieu' Verrier to tinker with! Christ save us from engineers! I couldn't have held off a corporal's guard, let alone two thousand of those tomahawk-wielding illegitimates!"

"So you..."

"So I reported to His Excellency that we should blow the whole thing to Hell, spike the guns, and at least try and defend this place!" He waved the hanger in the air. "And he and the Council bought the idea. Except for one. Verrier!"

"Why?"

"Verrier threw a tantrum. Told me I wasn't going to blow to pieces one of the finest pieces of stonework in the Americas over some backwater war that'd be over in six months! I protested. Even His Excellency was with me on that one. But..."

Both men flinched as a solid shot punched a spray of tiles from the roof and then thumped into the dry ditch not thirty feet from where they crouched.

"You see the result. I was ordered to spike the guns, carry in the stores, but leave the bloody ramparts! Christ in Heaven, any fool would've known they'd simply bush the guns and turn the damn place against us!"

Thierry wiped his hand across his mouth. "Anyway, I was out of there by midnight. The bastard Bostonnais were squatting in there the next day. And it only took till today for this to start!''

Gallant stood up carefully, flexing the hurt leg. He was woozy with weakness and hunger, and his leg pulsed with pain. "All right. They've got the battery. What else?"

"His Excellency sent off four boatloads of the Compagnies to try and take back the place, but the anglais just laughed at 'em. And we've sunk all the ships in the harbour."

"What?" Gallant's heart sank.

Thierry smiled crookedly. "All except your corvette, Paul. Although God knows why not. We also sent out a party to burn everything outside the walls. Got a chance then to get back a bit of our own. Some of the Swiss went along as escort and trounced a mob of the Bostonnais who tried to break up the work. Nice bayonet work." He sniffed. "They're not as tough as all their strutting makes out."

"So that's it?"

"All I can tell now, Paul. The swine look to be trying to set up some batteries closer in. We keep sending parties out to try and get in any of the habitants who are trapped out there.

"And you?"

"Hah! I've got years of work to do in a few hours. Every time we fire a round the gun platforms disintegrate a bit more. That's why you haven't been hearing too much from our own guns. We're too busy trying to prop them up!"

Thierry pushed his tricorne over his eyes. "Bien. I've got to get back to my guns. As soon as you're able, hurry over to the Town Major's office and tell him you're reporting as M. Du Chambon ordered. Do it soon, or they'll have me on a gibbet!"

With a wink Thierry strode away.

"Thanks for the rescue, Chassin'', said Gallant.

Thierry stopped and showed the crooked smile again. "Look, enseigne. It was my neck I was thinking about!"

Wincing at the fire in his leg, Gallant limped along the place d'armes and struck out down the Rue d'Orléans, toward his rooms which were across the rutted tracks from the hospital. The fog had swirled back in over the town, and the chill mists curling around the low buildings set a scene of gloom and foreboding that echoed with the crunching detonations of the bombardment. Gallant's stomach knotted as everywhere he looked the shapes of frightened women and cursing men appeared and vanished in the fog, that same terrible look of aimless fear in their eyes. At one point he pressed himself against a wall to let a jabbering gang of wild-eyed fishermen shove past, a pathetic dread twisting their faces.

Gallant shook his head. He cursed Bigot, the Conseil Supérieur, cursed Du Chambon himself for his milk-gutted indecision, and Verrier for his narrow idiocy. If only the fools had listened to the warning he tried to give!

Still swearing under his breath he shouldered at last through the doorway and into the kitchen of the little widow who tended his rooms. With one look at Gallant's dishevelled and bloody appearance the good creature threw her apron over her head and crouched, wailing, under her table. It took slow and infuriating coaxing before Gallant managed to put her to giving him some bread and fish broth, and later, a jug of hot water to shave and wash.

Weak though he still felt, Gallant quietly thanked God for the little doctor. As his razor scraped his chin, the pain in his leg was noticeably lessened, and it was no longer necessary to grit his teeth when he put his full weight on the leg.

The widow had vanished under her table again as several New England shot had plunged into buildings nearby. Gallant gave up trying to reassure her and hurriedly pulled on a clean uniform. As he settled the tricorne on his head and adjusted the silk of the black cockade he ducked out into the fog and moved back toward the King's bastion, whose dark bulk was mantled now not only with the fog but the smoke of several fires.

Gallant was standing at the foot of the same broad conference table where the drama now unfolding had begun, so few days yet so seemingly long ago. But this time the austere figure at the far end of the room was attended only by a clerk, who was scuttling out, his arms clutching a sheaf of written orders.

Du Chambon looked pale and haggard. "A bloody and sad business, Gallant." He sighed. "We watched you...your skirmish of the other day from the ramparts. And now all this. Mon Dieu, but war is a hateful thing! But your effort was commendable, even if…"

Gallant smiled, grimly without humour. "A defeat, Excellency. The New Englanders were ashore in the hundreds. They cut us to pieces!"

"A rout such as that, was it?"

Gallant smiled, grimly and without humour. "A defeat, Ex-most of them stumbling townsmen at that, could do little."

Du Chambon's slender hands raised in apology. "Yes, yes enseigne, I realize." He sighed again. "Forgive me. At least I might thank the man who saved the life of my son."

Gallant coloured, caught unprepared. "Any man would have done the same, Excellency. Messillac is a brave man and fine officer."

"I shall nevertheless be in your debt always."

"Thank you, Excellency."

Du Chambon's eyes were a cold grey. For a brief instant they had glowed with warmth at Gallant's reply. But only for an instant.

After a moment he went on. "I have now a travel order for you, enseigne. A vital one." The set mask of the administrator was firmly in place once more.

"Excellency?"

"When you have had an hour…no more…to gather what you need and settle accounts with your company captain, you will take ship, Gallant. For France."

"France!" Gallant was shocked. "But Excellency!"

"Do not interrupt." Du Chambon's hands were visibly trembling. He lifted a sealed envelope from the table and handed it to Gallant. "You will carry this word of what is transpiring here out through that blockade. And you will give your life, if it comes to that, to see that it is delivered."

The grey eyes looked into Gallant's own with a heavy anguish in them. "I have dreaded what is happening now for a very long time, Gallant. You are going to carry my request for help, for a relieving expedition, for anything from that court which plays while France and God's fortunes are ill-used, ignored..."

For a moment Du Chambon could not go on, and Gallant stared at the envelope in his hands.

When Du Chambon spoke again his voice was hoarse with emotion. "But there is more to this than a simple plea for assistance now. If Louisbourg falls, Gallant, it is the beginning of the end for France in America! Lose this island, and we lose control of the Saint-Laurent. Lose that, and it all goes: the Ohio, the Mississippi. All of it. All gone. France will lose a continent and power and riches beyond the imagining of the gentlemen at Versailles. If she keeps this continent there is no limit to her greatness. This is what the King must understand."

Gallant nodded, wordlessly.

"The vessel you arrived in, the corvette *Écho*", Du Chambon continued. "You'll ship in her, by my authority. Her master is notified that you are coming aboard, and that he is to sail at nightfall. You are to take command of the ship the moment you board her, Gallant. And you must not fail to pass through the blockade."

Gallant leaned forward over the great table. "Excellency, are you certain that my place is not here, with my men? You need every musket. Every officer."

Du Chambon rose and took Gallant's hand in a grip of surprising strength. "You will be ten times the value if you succeed on this mission, enseigne. Louisbourg must live, must survive, if France is to have any future in the New World. By getting my letter through, you will have rendered your country an incalculable service."

He nodded in dismissal. "Now get to your ship, enseigne. By nightfall I want you clear and at sea! We can only hold out so long!"

Gallant looked into the grey eyes for a long moment. "I shall be, m'sieu' ", he said finally. With a swirl of his coat skirts he left the cabinet.

And true to his word, the midnight moon that rose over the dark face of the Atlantic that night washed its coppery light over a new object as it rose: the hurrying form of a small ship, working eastward into the open vastness of the sea, leaving behind it the firelit mass of Louisbourg on its dark shore, a shore off which hovered a line of cruising vessels that had not seen the little ship slip like a minnow from the coast and vanish in quicksilver silence into the dark sea night.

THREE

"Damn it all to Hell!"

Commodore Sir Roger Gannon Fitzsimmons of His Britannic Majesty's Navy snapped shut the small telescope and dropped it on a desk cluttered with charts. A snort of disgust issued from the beaklike nose that projected from between black and piercing eyes.

"Treed, by God! But how am I going to get at him?"

His powerful jaw, its line not yet obscured by the growing jowls his age and a certain weakness for port were bringing him, jutted foward and down. He thrust his hands under the voluminous skirts of his coat and began to stamp up and down his cabin. Through long practice his pace passed along the flanks of the two twenty-four pound guns that cramped the opposite sides of his cabin, but swung him about on the return route before his knees thumped into the planking of the ship's side. The deck was covered with heavy canvas that had been painted in a black and white checkerboard, and Fitzsimmons' feet unconsciously stepped neatly from one colour to the other and back again: white, black, white, black.

39

He ducked low enough to pass under the gun tools, the rammers, sponges, worms and other long-handled pieces slung on their racks under the deckhead without looking at them, at ease in the cramped little space by benefit of long experience, like a miner in a coal shaft.

Beneath Sir Roger's wig his mind flicked once more over the immediate possibilities open to him, now that the corvette had been trapped by his squadron in this Spanish inlet. They were all too few.

"Coggs! Blazes, man, where are you!"

In response to this bellow the shaggy head of his steward appeared at Fitzsimmons' doorway. "Zur?"

"Fetch me out a tot of Madiera. I'm parched, but I want something to drink I don't have to strain through my teeth. My throat feels like a trollop's…"

Coggs, who was a devout Presbyterian, winced at his Commodore's obscenity. He padded over to a bulkhead rack and freed a bottle and small wine glass.

Fitzsimmons' ships had tracked and intercepted *Écho* in the eastern Atlantic, near the great north-western bulge on the African continent at Cape Spartel. Unexpectedly, the quarry had displayed such sailing wizardry that it had taken an exasperating pursuit of several days to bring it to bay.

He sucked a tooth pensively.

Fitzsimmons was known as a man who responded to frustration with undisguised fury. Now, with the French corvette lying scarcely more than gun range away, her inaccessability was building in the Commodore one of the thunderous storms that periodically terrorized his squadron and shook his own command from keelson to main truck.

Coggs appeared at his elbow, setting down the glass on Fitzsimmons' desk before scuttling wordlessly, crablike, out of the cabin.

Fitzsimmons' day-to-day facial expression was that of a man who normally expected to find a weevil in the Bread of Life; after downing in one gulp the glass he looked for a moment as if every such suspicion had been simultaneously fulfilled.

God, he thought. Sheer turpentine, and water to boot. That chandler'll be selling us urine next!

He paused in the pacing of his cage and eyed the topmasts of the corvette through the slanting windows of his cabin. Just visible above the low spit that formed the outer barrier of the inlet, the masts seemed to draw toward one another, then away. *Écho* was swinging on her hawser to the gentle ebb tide. That meant the inlet was wide enough, once through the mouth, to make mooring off bow and stern unnecessary. It was still a tricky spot to have got into.

Neatly done, fitting himself in there, Fitzsimmons thought. The Frenchman must have had a touch on the wheel delicate enough to be a woman's.

The Commodore glanced at the pine steeple clock which ticked self-importantly from its perch above his cot, then peered back at the Frenchman. Almost three bells in the afternoon watch. A jaunty green burgee waved languidly in the zephyrs from the corvette's fore truck, and the sight of it set Fitzsimmons' teeth to grinding. He would, he swore to himself with an ingenious obscenity, put an end to this absurd chase even if it meant blasting the corvette into kindling.

Fitzsimmons' anger was understandable. *Écho* simply outsailed the plodding, worm-riven hulls of his British squadron. Single-decked, meant to carry less than twenty guns, the corvette showed the clarity and logic of French ship design. Function showed in every graceful compound line of the blue and tan hull and the remarkably tall rig, marked by the characteristically French topmasts of equal size.

But to the Commodore's eyes she was too light, too underbowed, too French for his roastbeef taste in ships. Yet he admitted to himself grudgingly that the delicate Frenchman had sailed the wind out of his frigates, to say nothing of the humiliation of his own fouled and leaking *Redoubtable*. *Écho* held her own in winds foul and fair; she was able to work to windward like a witch, her yards braced so tightly around that they lay almost fore and aft, her low, hurrying hull buried in a welter of foam and the periodic garland of glittering, high-tossed spray. Animated by a lightfooted vitality, *Écho* was as remote from the oaken stolidity of His Britannic Majesty's Ship *Redoubtable* as a jeweller's tool from a smith's hammer.

It disturbed Fitzsimmons somewhat that this very quality in

the corvette increased his determination to destroy or take her; normally he was a man whose heart was gladdened by beauty, and both his seaman's eye and heart agreed that the French vessel was beautiful. But she had caused him to pay too high a price in his pride at a time when England's pride on the seas was in rather short supply.

Even had the austere gentlemen of the Board of Admiralty not evidently concluded that sufficient grounds existed to order the interception of *Écho*, Fitzsimmons' grim relish in his task would have been undiminished. Further, it provided an opportunity to strike back at the scheming French. The problem which puzzled the Commodore's quick mind was that of the means he should adopt to achieve his aim.

Fitzsimmons turned back to the table and frowned at the topmost chart. Scribbled over its neat lines and numerals were small inky additions showing the positions of the French corvette and his own anchored squadron. As well as *Redoubtable*, 64, Fitzsimmons had the sixth-rate *Hector*, 24, and *Vigilant*, 24, the prize gun brig *Amalie*, and an ungainly little bomb ketch, inappropriately named *Slyph*, under his immediate command. A third vessel, the fifth-rate *Heracles*, 30, was repairing storm damage and replenishing at Gibraltar, under order to rejoin the squadron at the earliest opportunity.

The Commodore sighed and shook his head. It was mid-1745. England was at war, with not only Spain but France as well, although His Most Christian Majesty Louis XV still continued to make the absurd pretension that France acted merely as an "auxiliary" of Spain. It was , in fact, all-out war with the French, for the third time in fifty years.

English naval achievements, ever the sop of the London mob and the salvation of politicians, seemed in short supply at present. Fitzsimmons' squadron and other Royal Navy units were strained to the breaking point in a long, tedious blockade and harassment of coastal shipping along the French and Spanish shores, principally in an effort to prevent the movement of troops and military stores from these coasts to Italy. Weeks of hovering off Valencia, Livorno or Marseille, contending with the unpredictable treachery of Mediterranean winter winds, line squalls, ill-marked charts, and dwindling stores, ever conscious of the possibility that the French Navy would slip out of Toulon before a northerly gale that would force the British back from the coasts, and entrap lone vessels or force unequal encounters with patrolling British units before the Royal Navy could concentrate in strength: this had been Fitzsimmons' lot for over a year and a half, a grinding routine broken only by brief replenishments at Port Mahon or Gibraltar.

And the memory of Admiral Mathews' humiliation following his failure to smash the Toulon fleet when it had been in his grasp was still fresh; The French fleet of Court la Bruyère had eluded Mathews' attacks and the wretched English Admiral had been sacked as a result, compounding the gloom that hung over His Britannic Majesty's ships in the Mediterranean.

Yet in the face of a desperate need for every available vessel, the Admiralty's orders had led to the sending of Fitzsimmons and his valuable squadron to intercept and destroy a little Frenchman whose broadside would do little damage to a Thames barge. Perhaps insanity was in vogue in Whitehall, mused the Commodore.

Fitzsimmons' mind turned to the interview, barely a week past, which had begun this extraordinary chase. Fitzsimmons' squadron had limped into the roads at Gibraltar, licking its wounds from a twenty-hour gale that had driven them from a point fifteen leagues south-south-east of Formentera to near disaster in predawn darkness on the hidden shoals of Alboran. *Sylph* had remained afloat at the last through the extreme measure of cutting her stays and letting the mainmast go by the board; every other vessel had suffered damage to rigging and weatherdeck fittings, and the pumps in Fitzsimmons' own *Redoubtable* had barely managed to keep ahead of the rush into her already weakened hull. The northeast winds had abated, and through great luck as much as anything else the squadron had managed to limp into the lee of the massive Rock more or less in company.

Redoubtable had barely swung to her hawser before a skiff had shot away from the oaken cliffs of *Namur*, 90, flagship of Vice-Admiral William Rowley, commanding in the Mediterranean, which was anchored a short distance away. It had deposited before Fitzsimmons a prancing ninny of a lieutenant, who had looked about the debris-strewn quarterdeck with a horrified expression of disgust before presenting a sealed note to the haggard Commodore.

Fitzsimmons smiled at the recollection. The glowering look he had fixed on the lieutenant as he took the note from the latter's slim and delicate paw had caused the creature to recoil as if struck, and to scurry back over the ship's side in a welter of mismanaged hat salutes, entangled hanger scabbard, and flouncing feathers. The lieutenant had missed his footing on the battens and had literally tumbled heels up into the arms of his boat coxswain, whose pained expression of martyrdom had sent the watching Redoubtables into hoots and guffaws.

The note had been a brief summons to repair on board *Namur* immediately and report to Rowley. Exhausted, Fitzsimmons had washed and shaved and struggled into his formal dress before leaving the direction of the squadron's repairs to his Flag Captain.

Twenty minutes later Fitzsimmons ducked through the doorway into *Namur*'s great cabin past an immobile marine sentry. The cabin was sparsely furnished: a small dining table, several chairs, a rack on one bulkhead which held several leatherbound books, a bundled collection of rolled charts propped in a corner.

To one side a low doorway opened into the stuffy, cramped cotspace Rowley slept in.

The most striking feature of the cabin was the tall, slanting stern windows which swept in a graceful curve across the stern of the ship, forming the fourth side of the cabin. Off through the windows the panorama of Gibraltar harbour lay shimmering in the bright, crystalline light, the massive hump of the Rock towering behind.

Before these windows, and in front of which Fitzsimmons now stood, was a broad walnut table behind which sat the round, perspiring figure of the Admiral.

Rowley was a fat, choleric-seeming man who looked intensely uncomfortable in the snug linen stock which had a firm grip about his throat. His hands were small and red, looking oddly placed in the great rolling cuffs of his blue frock coat. He had removed his heavily powdered wig, and rivulets of sweat were running over the shaven dome of his head, making it glisten.

With a laced handkerchief he mopped his brow and motioned to a chair in front of his desk.

"Sit down, Commodore. Your return is a surprise to us all. Haven't put Redoubtable over some reef, I trust." The Admiral's eyes were hard little points in a soft, pink face. "Pinch of snuff?"

Fitzsimmons declined the proferred silver box.

"Thank you, no, sir."

"Ah. Ever the man of principle. Well..." The box vanished into a waistcoat pocket. "Can't say as I recommend the stuff. Damned bad for the insides somehow, what?"

"So I've heard, sir", said Fitzsimmons, in a noncommital tone.

"Yes." The Admiral squirmed in his chair. "I've...um...had my glass on your squadron since you put in, Fitzsimmons. You appear to have taken rather a beating. Pity."

"Bad luck, sir."

Rowley nodded, slowly. The small, porcine eyes were fixed on Fitzsimmons with an intent glitter.

"How serious is your damage, would you say? When might you put to sea again?"

The Commodore hesitated a moment. What was the little man up to? Rowley was an experienced sea officer; it must be obvious to him that Fitzsimmons was not in a position to make judgements yet on the state of his ships.

"It's difficult to say at this time, sir. We've just come to anchor, and I've not had the opportunity to consult my captains. Our time will be extended as well by the need to reprovision: much of our shot, powder, carpenters' stores and other things were jettisoned."

"Come, come. Were you that nervous, Fitzsimmons?"

"In our efforts to reach here, sir, I felt it a justified action." Fitzsimmons chose his words carefully, his sense for danger now alert. He had the feeling that the Admiral had been watching the squadron with a sharp and attentive eye from the moment their approach to the roads was signalled, and was now looking for some nod, some inconsistency from Fitzsimmons. The Commodore was sure of one thing at least: something was afoot, and it meant him no good.

"Indeed. Well, I suppose that judging by the look of her your little bomb ketch is fortunate to be here at all."

Fitzsimmons interrupted, his anger now beginning to rise. "I have no way of knowing the precise state of the ketch, sir; her people were obliged to cut away the main mast, and only escaped destruction on Alboran through the greatest luck. The wind abated. They were able to jury rig a staysail on the mizzen which allowed them to keep in company after a fashion. I should have towed them had this not been possible.

Fitzsimmons' mind still had vivdly implanted in it the sight of the tiny *Sylph*, stern lantern a winking, circling pinpoint of light in the roaring blackness of the gale, seeming to vanish entirely under enormous breaking seas, only to struggle up again, her upperworks and scuppers streaming veils of seafoam.

"Thank God we were not scattered, not withstanding the distance we were driven, sir. As to *Redoubtable*, she has always been somewhat weak in the hull; the worm has been at her too long, and I fear this added strain may have caused her to begin taking water excessively."

The lace handkerchief passed once more over the glistening pate. "Mmmm. Yes. I see."

Rowley leant forward over the desk, in what Fitzsimmons presumed was meant to be a confidential attitude.

"But now tell me, Commodore. You must be able to tell me. How soon can you complete your repairs and other business and get to sea, eh?"

Fitzsimmons bit his lip, holding back the answer that had sprung unbidden to his lips. How the devil can I tell you that, you vast toad, he thought. I haven't so much as rolled an eyeball at any of the damned scows yet!

But it was evident an answer of some kind had to come.

He sighed. "Provided the mast house can provide *Sylph* with an appropriate piece, I might surmise that once she is alongside the shear hulk she might effect repairs within perhaps a week, all else being sound. All of my vessels have suffered rigging damage, sir; I doubt whether there's an unspliced or unknotted brace or sheet anywhere in the squadron.'' Fitzsimmons ran his hand across his brow, the fatigue beginning to take its toll.

"I have no report yet on any major structural damage to the other vessels", he went on, "but *Redoubtable* is making water heavily. I feel she must be careened.''

"Might that be avoided?''

"Not correctly, sir. If the ship is to be made fit for sea to any reasonable degree.''

The little eyes snapped open. "I am quite aware of what is involved in getting a vessel to sea after storm damage, Mr. Fitzsimmons.''

"Then, sir, you will understand...''

"But I am faced with a critical situation which demands that I put every vessel to sea which is in any condition to seakeep. And I want you and your squadron there at the most immediate opportunity. Do you follow me, Commodore? The most immediate opportunity.''

"I do follow you, sir", said Fitzsimmons. "But I cannot take a squadron to sea which I do not consider seaworthy, regardless of how pressing the 'critical situation', if it simply results in the needless loss of men and vessels.''

"You risk impertinency, Fitzsimmons. I direct this question to you again. When will you be prepared to put to sea?''

On this last question Rowley had risen half out of his chair, his fat little fists pressing into the documents scattered before him, his voice rising in intensity.

Fitzsimmons willed himself into a cool and controlled reply. "With fortune and no serious damage, five days, sir. Perhaps four." The figure was absurd, but it appeared he had to throw out some appeasement.

"Make it three.''

"Very...well, sir. Three.''

"Three days. Good, good.'' Rowley slumped back into his armchair and plied the sodden handkerchief once more.

Fitzsimmons was fighting down the urge to walk out of the cabin without a word; but for the most part he felt simply sick at heart, and despair rose like a bubble through the fatigue until his temples throbbed like drumheads. He knew that on the basis of the visible damage in *Redoubtable* herself, the squadron would be at sea again in three days only as a result of driving his already strained crews without sleep through the coming nights. Even as the Commodore had swung down over the side to his waiting boat's crew, *Redoubtable*'s sailmaker, Crofts, had been sitting hunched on the foredeck, surrounded by his mates, stitching the great rents in the topgallants and headsails. They faced six hours' work on one sail alone.

The starboard watch, under the keen eye and inexhaustible blasphemy of the Third, Crammer, had already begun to strike the splintered foretop and main topgallant yards. By now, with luck, they would have begun to prepare the new Baltic fir spars Fitzsimmons had bought as a last resort at Deptford, albeit for a preposterous high price.

But three days.

The Admiral's voice had become easier and almost amicable in tone. "I'm sure I can count on you to slip in time, Fitzsimmons. As to your victualling and provisioning, have no fears." He made what was meant to be a broad, generous gesture of the hand. "The Storekeeper has been instructed to provide you with the best he has available, and is awaiting the visits of your pursers. The Clerk of the Cheque will smooth over any financial...shall we say...inconveniences, as a personal gesture from me."

Rowley was beaming. "I have as well arranged for the freshwater lighters to be alongside you in the morning watch, tomorrow."

"Tomorrow..." Fitzsimmons choked back the outburst. "That is this is most thoughtful of you, sir", he said after a moment.

"Now. As to your orders."

Rowley slid his armchair back from the table and pulled a large manila envelope, bearing a red seal, from a drawer in the table. This he handed across to Fitzsimmons.

"You are to retain these unopened for the present. They are to be examined only upon the event you satisfy the initial phase of your responsibilities." Rowley settled back into his chair.

Fitzsimmons slid the heavy envelope into his coat. "I see, sir."

"Do you, in fact", said Rowley, with the trace of an edge to his voice. The little eyes were once more hard and brittle-looking in the florid face.

Fitzsimmons clenched his teeth and willed himself to be silent. He was astounded at the unpredictable incivility of the man, and sensed a danger in allowing himself to be provoked.

Rowley went on, reverting to the former smooth tones. "The *Iphigenia* sloop put in from Portsmouth last evening with a most secret despatch to me", he sniffed. "It contained a very interesting message indeed, a message I gather we've received in time due only to the excellent passage Preston made in coming out. In short, Fitzsimmons, I am ordered to detach a portion of the ships under my command to carry out a most trifing task."

The snuff box reappeared, and Rowley snorted back two enormous gobbets, coughed, spat hugely into a brass pot to one side of the table, and continued.

"Normally I would not consider for a moment the sending of my ships off to the ends of the earth on some ill-conceived notion of Their Lordships while we are fighting a desperate struggle here, a struggle which depends on me."

Fitzsimmons was astounded to see what appeared to be a childlike pout pass over the Admiral's features.

Rowley appeared to catch himself, shot a look at Fitzsimmons, then set his face back into the businesslike mask once again.

"It is my intention of carrying out my responsibility to the Crown to the letter, while allowing no-one grounds to criticize me. I do not intend, sir, to go the way of Admiral Mathews after his nasty little business off Toulon! Therefore, Commodore, you will use your squadron to carry out these idiotic orders in the shortest possible time and return to your duties with me. I had not planned on all this. But I shall use you to clean this little mess up!"

Rowley then gave Fitzsimmons a detailed description of the vessel, the date of her escape from Louisburg, and the suspected harbour for which it was bound.

Almost without warning Rowley had put an abrupt end to the

interview, and Fitzsimmons had clambered back down *Namur's* side to his boat, the twittering of the side party's pipes ringing in his ears.

As the boat's crew pulled evenly and strongly back for *Redoubtable*, Fitzsimmons had sat in the sternsheets lost in thought. He had been appalled at the prospect of racing to fit his shaken squadron for sea only to have it employed in such a seemingly trifling way. For a moment he had been tempted to agree with the opinion of the Admiralty voiced by Rowley. But his natural sense led him to determine to keep his mind open on the matter; Their Lordships, he reminded himself, were not often fools.

After herculean effort and the constant presence of Rowley's toady bearing irksome little messages from the Admiral, Fitzsimmons had managed to report his squadron as ready to slip and proceed after four days. One vessel, *Heracles*, required hull planking work and would follow as soon as possible.

Rowley had been in such a lather to see Fitzsimmons off that he returned a signal within the half-hour of Fitzsimmons' note, ordering him to sea immediately. Shortly before noon of that day the wind had slowly hauled around fair for the Strait, and in stately succession the Commodore's squadron had slipped, stood on a reach out into open water, and soon wore around to the westward.

Much to Fitzsimmons' surprise, *Vigilant* had made the interception five days later, while the squadron lazed northward across the steady Trades, spread in line abreast across the sea, with only topgallants visible to the next ship in line. The little vessel had been seen tacking hard up to the eastward, some twenty leagues to the west of Cape Spartel. With the wind holding steady from the northeast under fair skies, Fitzsimmons had expected to point up sufficiently to get the weather gauge of the Frenchman, and then run swiftly down for the capture; the surprise had been most disagreeable when the corvette's speed and uncanny windward ability turned what should have been a simple affair into an exasperating chase. Now, however, the end of the business seemed near.

The Commodore's eyes flicked to the locked drawer of his

tiny writing desk. In there lay the orders, the seal now broken, which detailed Fitzsimmons' clear and simple orders: the French corvette was carrying an appeal for aid from the besieged Louisbourg, and he was ordered to see that the message did not get through, by destroying the corvette and all aboard her if necessary. It was a simple, and brutal little job. Or so it had first seemed.

Fitzsimmons eyed the carefully penned outline of the corvette's hull on the chart. Small scrap of lumber though she was, Écho had been handled and positioned in such a way as to make it almost impossible for Fitzsimmons to act against her. He was forced to lurk about offshore under very unfavourable circumstances in the hope that the little vessel would attempt an escape, and so run the murderous gauntlet of the British broadsides.

The inlet lay at the mouth of an intermittent little rivulet which cut down through grey limestone bluffs to the sea, forming a long, oval basin no more than a hundred yards wide running in at an angle to the shoreline. To the landward side of the inlet the uneven face of the bluffs rose sheer from the water, pocketed here and there with narrow ledges to which clung dusty, unbleached scrub. To the seaward side, the inlet took its elongated form from a low sandspit which was in reality a system of low dunes joining outcrops of rock. The spit ended with a narrow, beached point, across from which the bluffs rose vertically. The inlet mouth thus formed was no more than thirty to forty feet in width, in depth at low water scarcely more than the probable draft of Écho.

Once in the inlet, the anchorage area widened enough to let the corvette swing in little more than her own length if anchored on two cables by the bows, to shorten the riding radius. A narrow channel, marked by deeper aquamarine colour than the medium green to either side, snaked out from the inlet mouth, bounded on both sides by shoals and outcrops continually awash in the gentle Mediterranean swells. With these shallows extending some distance to either side along the coast, the only path of approach to the corvette's lair was along the narrow channel to the inlet mouth.

The Commodore scratched his chin. To add to the problem, the French had rendered the approach almost impossible by setting up a bronze six-pounder in the rocks at the end of the spit. The gun was sheltered from the flat trajectories of Fitzsimmons' long guns, and the seaward extent of the shoals prevented *Sylph* from warping herself in to mortar range without bringing herself in turn within range of the six-pounder.

The French had proven they could handle the little gun; the foolhardiness of a day approach under anything but a thick fog was obvious. The one attempt which had been made to send in a party of seamen and marines at night by cutter had ended in a humiliating and bloody disaster. The French gun crew had spotted the faint phospherescence under the cutter's bows as it glided toward the inlet mouth, and had loosed a hail of round shot which shattered the boat's mast and killed or wounded more than half the hapless, cursing men before they managed to put out several sweeps and pull clear to seaward. The last round had driven right through the packed boat from stern to stem just above the waterline, making a bloody horror of the dead and wounded tumbled on the floorboards, and forcing the remainder to bail desperately with hats, cartridge boxes, and shoes. A boat from *Hector* had gone alongside the listing cutter and taken off the survivors scant seconds before the craft had suddenly capsized, spilling the dead into the inky waters. The next morning, as darkness faded, several of the swollen corpses had drifted through the anchored ships, watched by men who lined the rails and swore under their breaths. Fitzsimmons thought it likely that this was going to prove a costly exercise in terms of men as well as time.

The Commodore opened the door of his cabin, wincing as the burly marine sentry clumped to attention in the passageway.

"Pass the word for Mr. Pollett, sentry."

"Mr. Pollett. Aye, aye, zur." The marine hefted up his musket and rolled off down the passageway. He was a big man, and his tasselled grenadier-style cap narrowly missed the swinging lantern at the foot of the companionway.

Fitzsimmons listened for a moment to the thud of the man's boots as the latter reached the upper deck. Then he turned and stared out through the great stern windows at the breeze-ruffled surface of the sea, his lips pursed contemplatively.

A polite cough in the doorway stopped his train of thought.

"Ah, John. Please come in and sit, would you?" Fitzsimmons gestured toward a chair beside the chart-stewn desk, while folding his own frame into a large Spanish armchair.

John Pollett, captain of His Britannic Majesty's Ship *Redoubtable*, doffed his tricorne and eased himself down on the indicated chair. "Thank you, sir. You wished to see me?"

"Yes...um...sorry to take you away from your duties with your people, John. I trust there are no problems?" Fitzsimmons spoke with a casual tone, for he constantly sought, as did most responsible commanders, to avoid even the implication that he was meddling in his flag captain's running of his ship.

Pollett smiled and shook his head slightly.

"Quite routine, sir."

"Good. Have you managed to get the remaining repairs in hand?"

Pollett nodded. "The people have been hard at it. I've given the offwatchmen a 'Make and Mend" for the present. Meade is to exercise the larboard battery gun crews in the First Dog, with your permission, sir. The lack of gun action has taken the edge off."

Pollett spoke quietly, with measured words. He was a plain man of tall and gaunt appearance, who wore his sombre dress as if it had been flung at him rather than put on. The long progress to commissioning and finally post rank had given him the shovel hands and mahogany complexion of the veteran seaman, and service in most of the world's oceans had weathered his forthright Tyneside features into hard and deeply cleft planes. About his eyes, which were of that startlingly pale blue often seen in men of the ancient Danelaw, were lines that nonetheless evidenced amusement.

"Very good. Please feel free to employ one of my lovely cotmates here as well", said Fitzsimmons, nodding at the larboard twenty-four lurking behind Pollett.

"You're most kind, sir", replied Pollett, deadpan.

The two passed several minutes in further talk on the intricacies of gun drills, and to a third observor who had not caught the twinkling eyes on both sides it would have appeared that the Commodore and Pollett were cloaking a distant relationship with an overlay of polite, possibly pleasant but certainly formal terms of expression.

The truth was quite otherwise. Pollett and Fitzsimmons had a hearty liking for one another, mixed with mutual respect. Both were rarities, men of humbler origins who had succeeded in the navy of George II through good fortune and a mastery of their profession. They also had found, to their mutual inner satisfaction, that they shared the heretical view that a ship of war ran best under a stern discipline which nonetheless embraced a humanitarian concern for the welfare of its crewmen. The uniqueness of this conviction in an age which saw an unparallelled use of the lash in His Majesty's men-of-war had given them the basis for a fine, if unspoken regard for one another.

Pollett had come to admire the Commodore's imagination and common sense; Fitzsimmons entertained an unreserved faith in Pollett's ability to sail and fight *Redoubtable*, and indeed had put his pennant aboard her for that reason. He would not have been averse to flying it in a mere frigate. Both men were aware of how sensitive to friction their working relationship was; both were equally determined to use the oil of courteous formality Naval custom provided in order to prevent this friction.

Fitzsimmons laid a long finger beside his nose. "How are your marines?"

Pollett shook his head in disgust.

"Tolerably well, sir, under the circumstances. I've lost three lads today I didn't want to. Captain Edgehill says he's losing his best musketman. Sansom does his best with 'em, but that damned round shot..."

"Mmm. The Frogs knew what they were about."

"Yes, damn them." Pollett bit a lip. "Bastards."

Pollett was visibly incensed at the damage his carefully trained ship's complement had suffered, and colour rose beneath the deep tan as he spoke.

The problem was compounded by the hard fact that there was very little Sansom or any other surgeon could do for the wounded men, other than cauterize with hot pitch, swath in linen bandages, or ply the knife after treating the victim to a mouthful of neat rum and a leather wad to bite through in agony. The Captain was realistically expecting that those men with any major wound would die.''

"Damn pity, John", said Fitzsimmons after a moment. "That's why we've got to get the fellow out of his mudbank. Force the issue one way or another.''

Pollett nodded, slowly.

Fitzsimmons went on. "There seems to be no way to get within gun or mortar range of him. I'll fry in hellfire before I'd send in another driblet of people for him to chew up and spit back at us. And I think we tempt Fate somewhat by sitting at anchor here for any length of time; these are not what we might call safe waters.''

The Commodore scratched at a flea bite under his waistcoat. "I feel as well that it is time you all know what I do, albeit little, about this odd venture we are engaged in.''

A spark glinted in Pollett's eyes. "Conference of captains, sir?''

Fitzsimmons nodded, rising from his chair.

"Just so. Here in my cabin at two bells in the First. I'd appreciate it if you would see that the appropriate signal is made, John. We must thrash out some quick and practical scheme, and I shall want everyone's tuppence of opinion on the matter.''

A few minutes after Pollett left the cabin Fitzsimmons heard Meade, *Redoubtable*'s Second Officer, bellowing at a midshipman who was supervising the flag hoist. There was a slap of bare feet near the main larboard taffrail, and Fitzsimmons heard the small halyard blocks squeal as the signal, Fitzsimmons' own concoction of coloured flags, rose into the air. Almost as the blocks ceased their noise a swivel gun on the foredeck thumped, a small cloud of blue smoke curling over the rail to drift aft over the water past Fitzsimmons' cabin windows.

By evening, Pollett's gun exercise had been carried out, and the efforts of the sweating crew who had manhandled the two thousand pound bulk of the gun in Fitzsimmons' day cabin had left little trace other than a damp area or two on the painted canvas. As Fitzsimmons had requested earlier, the guns had been left in the run-back position, breeching set up, the great tackles hooked to the iron deadeyes to either side of the gunport. The vent covers and tampions were set off to one side, handspikes leant in readiness against the dull red oaken carriages, and the long rammers and sponges on the racks overhead had their retaining strops cast off. Notched match tubs, full of water but without the smouldering matches themselves, and buckets of sand to be scattered for absorption and traction on the deck, were clustered in neat rows behind the guns. At least six rounds of solid shot had been brought up to the racks for each gun, and below in the magazines the gunner's mates had loaded the paper-bound cartridges into dark leathern buckets, ready for the hands of the scampering boys who would carry the charges to each gun.

By Fitzsimmons' order, each ship in the squadron was in the same state of semi-readiness. Fitzsimmons' unease at being anchored inshore in the homegrounds of the French and Spanish navies had not led him to prepare for flight or action as fully as a less preoccupied commander might have done. *Écho*'s saucy contempt for the power of his squadron had come to hold the mind of the Commodore in a remarkably strong grip.

Fitzsimmons' day cabin had been prepared for the conference of captains as much as was possible amidst the clutter caused by the guns. A few more feet of room had been provided by the taking down of the partition that masked the Commodore's cot from the remainder of the cabin. A trestle table had been set up athwartships, and extra lanterns hung from the low deckhead.

Outside the stern windows the sea remained calm, tinged now with a deep velvet blue as night approached. A chill was in the air, and the watchmen pacing the deck or sitting aloft in the tops shivered and drew their coats more closely around them.

Within minutes of the faint double chime of *Redoubtable*'s bell the first boats were bumping against the oak walls of the flagship bearing the various commanders, and those gentlemen scrambling with varying degrees of agility up the battens and over the rail to the deck, where a side party, the marines, and Pollett awaited them. They were greeted, in the case of the frigate captains, with a ponderous musket-slapping Present from the white-gaitered marines, and a graceful spontoon salute from Edgehill; Lieutenant Robinson of *Sylph* received only the twittering cry of a boatswain's pipe as he slung a gangly leg over the rail.

In turn, each officer raised his hat briefly to Pollet, and aft to where the huge ensign curled loosely from the sternstaff. Pollett returned the salutes and led the men below.

Within ten minutes all four ships' commanders were ranged along the sides of the table in Fitzsimmons' cabin, awaiting the Commodore's opening words with a variety of facial expressions.

Fitzsimmons eased himself into the Spanish chair and quickly scanned the faces of the men through whom he carried out the instructions of the Admiralty and, somewhat more distantly, those who governed England. Of his captains, only Thomas of the gun brig *Amalie* was absent, suffering a recurrence of malarial fever.

As ever, Fitzsimmons' eye was alert for the pale, strained expression, the averted eye. His interest in his captains went a good deal beyond the simple demands of obedience and competence.

On his immediate left sat Ledger, of *Hector*. Ledger had a square, bullish head settled firmly on a barrel body, and looked about him with a steadfastness of expression that mirrored together his strengths and failings. Tenacious and singleminded, Ledger compensated for the somewhat unimaginative approach he took to his profession with a dogged fearlessness and intense energy. Fitzsimmons thought him somewhat too conventional a man for frigate command: dash and verve were more the things for those ships. Yet at the same time he valued the certainty that in whatever perilous circumstances might arise, Ledger and *Hector* were utterly reliable.

At Fitzsimmons' right hand sat Molyneaux, captain of the other Frigate, *Vigilant*. Adrian Richard de Vere Molyneaux was an aristocrat; tall and slim, gifted with an easy, catlike grace, his darkly handsome features set in a somewhat cruel cast. He wore a beautifully cut full wig at all times, unfailingly outshining the somewhat threadbare other gentlemen with the exquisiteness of his small clothes. Molyneaux had entered the Navy quite late;

more, it was said, as a result of an ultimatum from his father than any desire to serve the interests of the Crown.

A well-known habitué of the Pump Room, reputedly a beau and notoriously a bedmate of a prodigious number of the delectable young women London garnered in the Season, Molyneaux carried himself as if socializing at the Cocoa Tree or the St. James' or "displaying" in Vauxhall rather than commanding a ship of war of the Royal Navy. His reputation as a rake had already been the topic of much amused talk in the wardrooms of Fitzsimmons' squadron. The latest tale credited Molyneaux with disrobing one well-known beauty in a coach at full gallop through Charing Cross; the girl was reputed to have had a remarkably delicious pair of breasts, and Molyneaux had wagered with another rake one hundred pounds that the former would verify that fact within a week of the wager. The reaction of the young beauty in question was said to have been, in fact, an ill-concealed eagerness.

To the blockade-weary and weatherbeaten officers of the squadron, the agreeable image of fondling a beautiful and willing girl in a thundering carriage off to nowhere was powerful spirits for gossip around the dining table, and the tale had grown and enlarged until Molyneaux had the aura of a Lothario.

Molyneaux had greeted the growing pressure for a distinctive officer's uniform with complete disdain, and even now sat in the resplendent elegance of deep orange velvet, lined and cuffed with shot green silk, a cravat of the most delicate Low Countries lace at his throat.

Yet for all his manner of a fop, Molyneaux had never given Fitzsimmons cause to fault his seamanship; by far the most able vessel of the squadron, *Vigilant*'s response to Molyneaux's direction was evincing an undeniable capability for the responsibility. For all that he had entered late into the Navy, Molyneaux was already demonstrating that he had the capability to rise as far within its ranks as he chose.

Notwithstanding all of this, Fitzsimmons continued to be irked by Molyneaux's affectations of limp-wristed ennui, knowing full well that the muscles under all that silk and lace were steel-hard. He also could not abide Molyneaux's habits of scenting himself with an overpowering lavender water, and toying with a light ivory and lace fan. More seriously, Fitzsimmons had picked up, via the undeclared network of a lower deck whisperings, that Molyneaux was quick to use the lash on his men, and reportedly displayed visible enjoyment at the sufferings of the poor wretch writhing on the gratings.

For his own part, Molyneaux rested comfortably on the secure rock of his own superior social foundations, and dismissed the disapproval he sensed from time to time in his rough-hewn Commodore. He relied for his advancement on the sure effect his family's influence would have upon the Lord Commissioners and other appropriate gentlemen in Whitehall, if luck in war brought him nothing. He granted himself a tolerance of the lesser men he served with and their endless struggles for advancement and recognition, provided their efforts did not cross his own. He believed for the most part that there was no fault in using human beings as he saw fit to satisfy his needs or hungers, whether the moaning girl pressed beneath his hard body in her boudoir or the wretched seaman feeling the bite of his coxswain's lash. It would not have crossed Molyneaux's mind to trouble himself over the thought that such an attitude had brought him few friends in life, and none at all during his brief but promising career at sea.

Pollett, at the far end of the table, was flanked by young Robinson, the tall and angular junior lieutenant to whom Fitzsimmons had given *Sylph*. Robinson was exceedingly shy and spent much of his time attempting to keep his Adam's apple from bulging out over the top of his neckcloth. For all his youth he had conducted himself well during the desperate hours of the storm, a steadiness that had been previewed when, during a confused night raid on the small port of Sète, he had taken the *Amalie* with a boat's crew, losing but one man. He had merited Fitzsimmons' trust since by handling the clumsy and difficult bomb ketch with as sure a hand as might be expected from one so junior.

Fitzsimmons cleared his throat.

"If you please, gentlemen. I think you all know why we are here in conference: the little Frenchman over there. We have been playing hare and hounds with him for some time, and I feel obliged to tell you, as far as I am able, why it is Their Lordships feel the corvette merits our attention and this absurd chase.''

The assembled officers glanced meaningfully at one another, and Robinson tugged at his neckcloth. Perhaps at last the reasons behind the extraordinary events of the last days were to be clarified.

''The case is this...yes, yes, please come in, Captain Edgehill.''

The marine slipped in quietly beside Robinson.

Fitzsimmons began again. ''The Admiralty has informed us, gentlemen, that the French fortress of Louisbourg on Cape Breton Island has been assaulted by an army of His Majesty's subjects in America supported by the Royal Navy. Although word is not in yet, it appears that the siege will be successful.''

''Good'', said Edgehill quietly.

Fitzsimmons gestured out toward *Écho*.

''By all appearances one French vessel only was able to slip out of the blockade we put on the harbour there. That one. Our spies report it carries with it an appeal for help to the court of France, and I presume our task is simply to make certain that appeal does not go through, and thereby prevent the French from interfering with the seige. That is, if the Yankees drag it on that long, which they are quite capable of doing!''

He look at the serious, attentive faces.

''Hence, our activities of the last while, gentlemen.''

After a moment Fitzsimmons went on. ''He's put himself in a very clever position. We can't get at him directly. Naturally this means the fellow can't get out as well. I have no desire to repeat unnecessarily the business with the cutter. But the extreme hazard of our situation here and the necessity of putting this matter to rest at the earliest opportunity leads me to ask, no, require that a solution surfaces among us here this evening.''

''But what in God's name could it...'' began Robinson at the far end of the table, and immediately flushed as the frigatemen turned to look at him, an eyebrow raised here and there. ''I mean...that is...''

''Quite all right, Mr. Robinson. Granted, it is a silly sort of thing to be engaged in, considering the desperate straits we have been in with this wretched coastal blockade.''

The Commodore's jaw set. ''Hence, gentlemen, I now ask for your suggestions as to how to bring this matter to a head.''

Robinson, at the far end of the table, was the first to break the uncomfortable silence. ''If you please, sir.''

''By all means, Mr. Robinson'', said Fitzsimmons.

''I've been aloft for some time studying the French anchorage through a glass, sir. And as we know, the bluffs appear to rise vertically from both the anchorage and the seaward faces along the shoreline for some distance to either side.''

''Correct.''

''But it's not, sir. The vertical face, I mean.'' The young man's expression was bright and eager. ''I think I've found way up it.''

The other captains sat up in their chairs.

''To which side?'' said Pollett.

''On the eastern side, sir. Perhaps a quarter-league along the bluff face, just past a point where the bluffs angle inland a bit. It's quite concealed from the French anchorage; they'd not spot a boat putting in there, I'm sure of it.''

''Does it appear that some kind of footway might be found up it?'' said Fitzsimmons.

Robinson nodded. ''Yes. It appears to be a dried-up waterfall course or split in the rock face. Lots of projecting shelves and ledges.''

Ledger coughed. ''Damned lot of good it would do to get a party up there. What would they do? Roll boulders down at the Frogs? You'd need to wrestle a gun up there.''

Fitzsimmons put his fingers to his lips, pensively. ''Mr. Ledger has a point, Mr. Robinson. What do you think? Could a gun be handled up that slope?''

''No, sir. I don't think so. Not even a three-pounder, I think.''

''Well, there you are'', said Ledger, turning back to Fitzsimmons.

Robinson went on. ''But we could do it with a coehorn.''

Fitzsimmons' ears tingled. ''A what?''

"A coehorn mortar, sir. They fire about a three-inch shell. Weigh about seven and a half stone, counting the carriage. We've got one in the gunner's stores in *Sylph*."

Captain Edgehill leaned forward to look along at Robinson. "How would you get a bit of ordnance like that up such a sheer slope, Lieutenant?"

"Fairly basic, sir", replied Robinson. "If that bluff has any sort of stable surface at the top, we can lash up a sheerlegs and run a purchase down to a boat below. Set a party of hands to the falls up on the cliff top, and a few on some kind of lateral steadying stays, and we'd have her up."

"But where do we hoist the thing from? There's no beach."

"As I said, sir. You wouldn't need it. You'd hoist it directly out of the boat."

"Is the fissure well round out of sight of the Frenchmen, including those out on the end of the spit? Such that lanterns could be used and not seen by them?" said Fitzsimmons.

"Oh, yes, sir", replied the young man. "Not unless they caught some glow in the sky or some such. They'd not be able to see you until you could spit on their foredeck from the bluff. If you wanted to, sir."

Fitzsimmons controlled a smile. "I see. So presumably we could carry this off at night."

"I think so, sir. It might be a little difficult making the climb up in the dark."

Fitzsimmons looked at Pollett, who was trying with difficulty to cover a broad grin behind one hand.

"What do you think the chances would be of putting together the necessary spars, tack, line and so on on short notice, Mr. Pollett?"

"Could do it before the watch changes, sir."

Fitzsimmons glanced out through the stern windows, and then back at the officers' faces. They were still now, watching him, waiting for the statement, the order.

"Very well. We shall carry out the landing of the mortar, along with its crew and a small marine guard, tonight. The intention is to be that of opening fire on the corvette from a position above it on the bluffs before sunrise", said Fitzsimmons.

Robinson sat up with a start. "Tonight, sir?"

"No time to waste, Mr. Robinson. As soon as we adjourn here you will repair on board *Sylph* and prepare the coehorn for transport, including powder, shot...I suppose in this case shells...and gun tools. Detail off your most experienced gunners, although I imagine you have little more than one crew to choose from."

Robinson nodded mutely, looking quite pale.

The Commodore turned to Pollett. "*Redoubtable* is best able, I imagine, to provide the necessary rigger's and carpenter's stores, Mr. Pollett. I'll trust you to see that the necessary materials and the purchases required to haul all this up the bluffs are made up."

Pollett nodded. "Aye, aye, sir."

"As to the boat", said Fitzsimmons, turning to Ledger, "can you provide a cutter under oars and a crew of your most reliable hands, to transport and haul up the mortar? One of *Redoubtable*'s boats will carry in Mr. Edgehill and his marines."

"That I can, sir", replied Ledger. "I had my doubts, but you'll get the very best from the Hectors."

"Good. I'll expect the boats loaded and alongside *Redoubtable* no later than fifteen minutes after the turn of the glass. Mr. Pollett, you will be in overall command. Once ashore, Captain Edgehill will command, with responsibility for the gunner being yours, Mr. Robinson. Any further questions, gentlemen?"

The table was silent. Pollett was by now grinning openly.

"Very well." Fitzsimmons rose. "That's all for the moment gentlemen."

He looked for one last long moment at the faces around the table. "This is a serious problem, gentlemen. Bear in mind that if that fellow gets his message through there may be hell to pay in the Americas. And I needn't remind you what more headaches in Whitehall would mean to your careers." He smiled without mirth.

Fitzsimmons moved to the door of the cabin and then paused.

"Therefore you must get him. Without fail!"

Within minutes the captains had dispersed to their ships, their boats bearing them away with their heads full of thought on the night's plan.

Outside the Commodore's cabin, night was nearly upon the anchored squadron, turning the deep aqua of the sea into a midnight hue. Within the shadows of the land the sharp outline of the corvette's spars were no longer distinguishable, and the English vessels moved slowly to their hawsers on the low, glassy swells. The sky remained a deep indigo except for a band of faintly glowing red along the western horizon, behind the bluffs. From *Redoubtable* and the other ships, the faint glow of hooded anchor lights joined with the mellower light spilling from the great stern cabins to cast undulating bands of warmth on the dark water. From each ship carried the distant, over-water sounds of voices and the muffled clump of movement, mingling with the gentle creak of rigging and the slap of the wavelets on the hull's undercurves. Above the slowly circling mastheads the blazing brilliance of the starlight wheeled in unwinking splendour through the arch of the sky.

Shoreward, in the inky shadows where *Écho* lay, nothing could be seen other than the tiny pinpoint of light from the lantern the corvette hoisted in her fore shrouds each night, almost as a disdainful gesture. All appeared motionless. But a discreet activity was underway there, had there been light enough to see it.

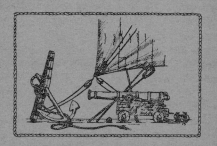

FOUR

As darkness fell over the inlet, the shadows of the surrounding bluffs had left less and less of *Écho*'s rigging bathed in the golden light, until finally only the tips of the fore and main masts caught the dying rays.

From where he stood, leaning comfortably against the mizzen fiferail with a blackened stub of clay pipe clenched firmly in his teeth, Théopile-Auguste Béssac had watched the sun's last touches with a momentary warm inner contentment that masked the anxiety of the last days. Many ships and voyages had brought him to this present pass in life with little save a battered sea chest, calloused hands, and an innate scepticism toward most of his fellow men. But Béssac loved ships, and he was in love with this one with a true lover's fervour.

As mate, his eyes were rarely off the rigging, continually calculating the set of lifts and braces, the tensions of halyards, the workings of clewlines and buntlines. In an age when the theoretical knowledge of complex mathematics was restricted to relatively few people, the mate comprehended the forces at work in the network of rope and spar overhead with the thoroughness of watchmaker.

No formula had devised the line and form of *Écho*'s hull and rigging; it was the product of two hundred and fifty years of ocean-faring experience. From a similar well of experience Béssac drew his instinct for knowing down to an inch what his ship would do under the forces of wind or water.

As he puffed the rich, pungent tobacco his hand rested in a loose-fingered clasp on a staysail halyard, in the manner of a musician's hand poised over the instrument. More by sense than by thought, Béssac knew what the line did, and what its trace was among the welter of crossing and converging lines overhead. He knew the strengths and weaknesses of it, and its exact part in the complex spiderweb that towered above the corvette's duck-like hull.

Béssac was not a leader of men, in the real sense. He had no feel for the direction of people in grand schemes, and abhorred the thought of bearing the ultimate responsibility in any situation. But left alone with men who would obey him without question, he could unleash the endlessly interconnected purchases and leverages of the corvette's rig and send the graceful little ship driving in a froth of seafoam across the heaving ocean swells. The crewmen he viewed as instruments toward that end, although there was no lack of human sympathy in him. His concern was to tune and adjust the hundred lines and cables with gruff commands to the straining seamen until the interwoven mechanism of wood, rope, and canvas fairly came alive with the driving rush of its passage through the sea.

Unknowingly, Béssac was one of those few who escape mere proficiency in their work to achieve mastery and eventually something akin to artistry. But of all this the blocky little mate was unaware, and did what he did because it simply seemed appropriate.

Béssac's pipe crackled and began to grow cold. He rummaged in the pockets of his stained seacoat for a plug, and began hewing off another tarry segment with his sheath knife. The pint of warm red wine he had downed with the evening's fish stew had settled warmly in his veins, and he decided to extend the luxury of the smoke.

As he wedged the tobacco firmly into the blackened bowl and

began searching his pockets for his flint striker, he watched the progress up the shrouds of several seamen whom he had set to replacing worn and rotten ratlines on the larboard side of the mainmast.

A flash of colour caught his eye in the gloom, and he turned to see Paul Gallant appear up the midships hatch and step out on deck.

"A fine evening, m'sieu' ", offered Béssac, amiably.

"What? Oh, indeed. Very much so, Béssac", replied Gallant, who had stood for a moment with hands clasped behind his back, sensing the cool dusk air. "A fine evening indeed. Do you think we'll be without a breeze this night as well?" He walked slowly over to Béssac.

The mate glanced up at the darkening arch of the sky. A few wisps of cloud were lit by the setting sun, floating like pink feathers against the inky blue.

"Hmm. I wager you're right, enseigne. There's little wind to be had behind those, for a day or so, at the least. But then..." The mate did not finish.

"I had not thought the Mediterranean was such a calm sea, Béssac. Where are the howling winds under cloudless skies you were telling me about in mid-Atlantic, eh?"

Gallant leant his hands on the rail and peered down where the light slap of water touched the corvette's side. "One could not sail a canoe in this place."

"Bien", said Béssac, with a thoughtful draw on his pipe, "the winds are there, and in their own good time, they come." He looked aloft at the seamen suspended on the shrouds. "Aloft there! Keep a firm hand on those fids! You want to kill someone?"

"What are the signs for wind? said the marine.

The mate laughed. "Indeed, m'sieu', there are often none at' all. A flat calm can turn to a gale before a good topman can run from one end of a yard to another. That is the way of this sea: you either have more wind than you need, or you have none at all."

"I gather you've sailed these waters often, then."

Gallant watched the glow from Béssac's pipe light the mate's features as he scratched a spark into the tuft of tinder in his small tinderbox, blew the spark into a glowing ember, and then lit the tobacco, exhaling a cloud of pungent smoke into the air.

"Enough. Actually, I suppose you could say a great deal, in fact. When I was a young man." Another pull on the glowing pipe followed. "When one is young one remembers with such clarity. I've sailed many seas since those days and yet I recall the nature of this one more clearly than any other." The mate paused. "As you must remember our own home waters, Monsieur Gallant."

"Yes." The shadow of a smile touched Gallant's features, now growing indistinct in the darkness and the weak light of the anchor lantern.

"I remember another place where the winds can be like this", he said. "The straits between Isle Royale and Isle Saint-Jean. On a hot summer day, the sea there can be as calm as this, and you can stand on the rocks and hear the sea-beasts surfacing and blowing offshore. And the birds! So many ... so many."

The marine looked out over the inlet. "It can be beautiful, for all the wilderness."

Gallant absently bunched one fist and tapped it into his other open palm. "How long has it been, Béssac?"

"M'sieu'?"

"How long? Since we left Louisbourg?"

Béssac thought for a moment. "At the change of the glass tonight, exactly twenty-nine days, enseigne."

"Twenty-nine days!" The marine shook his head. "Can they still be holding out against the Bostonnais?" Gallant's lips became a tight line.

"We must get out of here, Béssac, somehow! I keep torturing myself that if only I could put this letter into the hands of the King or the Minister that help might get there in time."

Béssac shrugged. "Who can say with such sieges, m'sieu'? I'm not a soldier. It's in God's hands, regardless."

Gallant looked seaward, his eyes searching out the dark shapes of the English hulls.

"And this waiting is really quite astounding, isn't it? The English are very surprising. From what I've been told of them I would have expected more than one small boat attack on us!"

He glanced upward at the bluffs, now looming darkly over the inlet. "Up there, for example. What would prevent an agile party of men from carrying a gun up there and dropping shot on us at will?"

"The coastline hereabouts is not that obliging, enseigne", said Béssac, gesturing with his pipe. "There are easier places to land; northward, toward Garrucha, or even three or four leagues southward, to Cabo de Gata. Good places for boats."

"But not here?"

"Not here. We've sheltered ourselves well. There isn't a goat's toehold that I can recall for half a league or more to either or us, and any further than that would be useless to the English. These bluffs fade only gradually down the coast into lowlands, and until that there isn't a thing a rosbif's hobnails would grip on. For all that fine flotilla riding out there, the English are in a predicament if they intend to wait for us."

He pointed along the coast with his pipe. "After all, they have but to be seen by a Spaniard out of Cartagena, or even some fisherman's lugger, and they will be in for a great deal of trouble."

Gallant nodded. "But these winds are unpredictable. Spaniards or not, they might have two more days of calm to move on us, eh?"

The mate grunted.

"Maybe yes. Maybe no." The pipe jutted out at a sharp angle. "It would be even more unpleasant for them if they were to be happened upon in this calm by the galleys."

The marine looked at him sharply.

"The galleys? They pass along these coasts?"

"Bien oui", affirmed Béssac, with an accompanying puff of heavy smoke from the pipe. "But not as much as they once did, enseigne. The patrol galleys, at least, were always abroad on these coasts."

"But how soon...how often..."

The mate raised his hands, laughing at Gallant's sudden eagerness. "Oh, I don't remember the patrol routine. We did it as a matter of regularity, as I recall."

" 'We'? But then...you served in them?"

Gallant was looking at the dark figure of the mate. The galleys!

The galleys no longer played their former role as the well-publicized backbone of French naval authority in the Mediterranean. Nonetheless the legend had persisted, a legend that had grown around the vessels since their conversion by the King's Minister Colbert from the purely naval vessel into the supreme punishment for any number of crimes. A legend that had frightened the wits out of every child old enough to drive exasperated parents into using it to coerce them. To Gallant, as to many others, the galleys seemed a mysterious and menacing aspect of the maritime power of France more shrouded in hearsay and rumour than formed from solid fact.

Gallant's mind recalled a·volcanic sermon he had listened to in the tightly packed chapel at Louisbourg, one of the more memorable efforts of Père Caradec that had electrified the wide-eyed children crouched on the floor. In almost satanic terms, Caradec had formed in the malleable young minds so horrifying a picture of the ordeal suffered by men in the galleys that Gallant's flesh creeped involuntarily, even as the memory flashed through his head.

The galleys had seemed a universe apart from the exciting visits of the stately French men-of-war that periodically put into the harbour at Louisbourg. In comparison to the stinking cod schooners and the drab little coastal traders that usually cluttered the harbour, these seemed immense, graceful arks of adventure and discovery, particularly so to a small boy gazing out at them as he scrambled about the quayside. Their crews would spill out of the lighters that plied in from the anchorage to the jetties: arrogant and resplendent officers in red and blue, looking archly about them at the low, weatherworn buildings and wrinkling their noses at the stench of drying cod; jolly, brown-faced seamen with dangling stocking caps and glittering eyes, who rolled along with a bandy-legged gait, their blackened hands swinging across their bodies, and vanished into the crowded quayside bars that rang long into the night with the clink and roar of such places. On rare occasions one of these would gather together a goggle-eyed group of children who had been playing on the quay amidst the barrels and bales, piles of putrefying rubbish, and the manure of roaming pigs; shifting a tobacco plug about a gap-toothed mouth, the old man would fill the children's heads...and dreams, for some nights thereafter... with tales of islands of fire, monsters that crushed ships, strange birds and creatures, and thrilling, bloody seafights with the English or the buccaneers.

And here and there among these enthralling revelations would come a mention of the galleys, couched in fearsome and strange curses; curses accompanied by much self-crossing and looks of dread or loathing.

"Surely to God, Béssac, you did not man an oar in one?"

Béssac chuckled. "My God, no. It was a long time ago, you understand. I had signed off a Netherlander, a Haarlem flute after a hellish voyage to the Spice Islands. Java. Half the crew died there at Batavia, and the rest of us almost died trying to get home. There was only the intervention of the Sweet Virgin herself which would have put me to sea again. Or so I thought."

Béssac sucked noisely on his pipe.

"But, I had no gentlemanly skills, so to speak. And no money. So I followed a chain of convicts being marched from Nantes to Marseille and took ship in a line galley as a rambarde."

"A which?"

"A petty officer. Handling the few guns and those great, impossible lateens."

He spat vigorously over the rail. "I did my business and ignored what was not my affair."

"What would you do, most times?" said Gallant.

"When a fair wind came up they'd let the oarsmen rest and we'd set the lateens. We made them fill, all right, although I'd not like to have to handle them again. Big, too big, for me."

Béssac sent another cloud of smoke rising up through *Écho's* rigging.

"Those poor devils on the sweeps, on the other hand, could drive the ship at a good two or three knots all day, given some rest." The mate fell silent.

Gallant grimaced slightly as he imagined the living hell life must have seemed to the wretched oarsmen.

"And the galleys cruised these waters quite often?"

"Yes, indeed", said Béssac. "Those oars ruled these seas, enseigne, regardless of how much we cherish our tall rigs and deep keels. You may be sure we would not have been beyond the reach of the galleys, were it they who anchored out there. This calm would have meant nothing to them, of course."

He gestured toward the distant lights of the English squadron, now glimmering across the sea surface.

Gallant's eyes had grown thoughtful. After a long pause, in which he had paced slowly up and down the deck, he turned to the mate again.

"In such a galley, do the sweeps move the ship handily, even though she might be of fair size?"

"Of a certainty. The largest could carry our little corvette here as cargo and still turn in her own length. And after all, even a corvette like this is moved on sweeps from time to time, although not very often...or very far."

Gallant looked again at the water, then out toward the inlet mouth, beyond which in the distance the shadowy hulls of the English vessels rode.

"I see", he said. "Yes."

Béssac turned his attention to the working party, who were finishing up their work and springing gingerly down the shaking ratlines to the deck. From the corner of his eye he noticed that the marine was standing motionless at the rail.

Some fifteen minutes later, Béssac was turning his attention to the assembly of the few stores to be taken out to the lonely gunners on the spit. He looked up to see Gallant approaching him.

"We must escape from here before the English devise some means of getting at us; they'll not simply row in boat after boat", said Gallant.

"So you said before. But how, enseigne? You tell me how to get out of here. Do we make all sail and exit grandly through their midst?"

Béssac waved a hand in an expansive gesture.

Gallant smiled. "That isn't likely, given the winds here, as you know full well. No, I indeed suggest that we escape out of here to sea, but somewhat differently.''

The pair moved to the rail overlooking the corvette's waist-deck, and then hiked back up toward the stern.

"And how might that be?" said Béssac.

Gallant regarded him.

"I suggest we try to row out."

Béssac was silent for a second, then let out a guffaw.

"Row?"

"Indeed so, Béssac."

Béssac cocked an eye at him. "By Saint Peter, I believe you're serious!"

"I wouldn't have suggested it otherwise, Béssac, as you said yourself, ships the size of *Écho* are regularly moved about by sweeps. The sweep ports are there in our sides and the sweeps..."

"And the sweeps were put ashore long before this voyage."

"What?"

"Surely you've noticed. We do not have any aboard. I rarely had need of them. And getting into this sort of trap was the last thing I might have expected. Row. My God!"

Gallant puffed in exasperation. "Béssac, the English know we cannot set a headsail in here without their knowledge. This calm may go on for a full day or more yet. If we tried to tow out with the boats, the thrashing would have shot whistling about our ears before we felt the first swells under the keel!"

"So?"

"So if we improvise some sweeps, we might creep through them before their watchmen could raise the alarm in time. There is no moon. We might be well to seaward by dawn, and able to catch a breeze. It might work!"

Béssac stopped, resting a hand on a small bronze swivel gun.

"Do you realize the deadweight of this ship, enseigne? You talk of thrashing while trying to tow out. Our sweeps would whip the water white in here before we budged an inch, and the English would be waiting for us with their linstocks smoking!"

Gallant moved closer. "There is a way. The English know we have men constantly on the gun at the spit, and that we change them at the same time every night. At the usual time for the change, we pay out the cable on the starboard anchor and lower it into a boat. Perhaps the jolly boat. Have it pulled out to the spit while the cable is paid out. The gun crew could bed it down somehow in the shallows near the spit. With enough effort on the capstan after raising the larboard anchor, we can kedge for the inlet mouth. If we slip the pawls and hold the tension by main strength, we might do it without a sound!''

"Go on.''

"Once through the inlet mouth we cut the starboard cable, our sweeps, and pull for a gap in the English line.''

Béssac looked sceptical. "And...you think we'd not be seen doing all that?''

"Perhaps not'', Gallant shrugged. "Perhaps we would. But what other chance do we have? Wait for the English to come in and get us?''

"Well...er...''Béssac scratched his chin. "Have you given any thought as to what to use for sweeps, then? We have nothing as far as I can see. How would you set them up? Use the gun-ports? Or the old sweep ports themselves? And what of the star-board anchor, not to mention the gun on the spit, which you seem to suggest we abandon? A ship is as good as dead without her anchors!''

Gallant pointed forward at the double-gallows spar rack set above the gratings in *Écho*'s waist. "You've got what look like topgallant yards there. I counted eight a few minutes ago, all of a size. They'd do for the sweeps. And as for the gun and the an-chor, Béssac'', he said, with another shrug, "better to pay with them than with our lives. We will manage somehow, once we are free.''

Béssac's eyebrows raised at the marine's cool appraisal. He waved a hand toward the inlet mouth.

"You realize, I hope, the narrowness of the inlet mouth, eh? It was one reason for my choice of this place as shelter. With your sweeps projecting outboard our beam may be almost doubled.''

"Yes, agreed. But the spit is not very high. If we lower the butt ends of the sweeps on that side as far as we can, and steer as closely to the spit as the shallows will allow, we might clear it and slip through!''

The marine faced Béssac directly.

"Well? What do you say, eh?''

Béssac removed his weatherworn tricorne and took from inside it an enormous red handkerchief. He blew his nose with gusto.

"I'll be frank with you, enseigne", he said. "I think you're out of your mind."

Then he beamed a crooked, wrinkled smile at the anxious look that had come over the marine's face.

"But I'll be damned as a Protestant if something in me doesn't say try it!''

Gallant broke into a grin almost in spite of himself, as Béssac clamped his tricorne down firmly on the crown of his head and spat manfully over the rail.

The mate stirred out the boatswain's mates from where they dozed under the longboat and sent them in turn scurrying below to rout out the sleeping watchmen. Within minutes the slap of running feet on planking and a general hubbub traced the mates' progress as their blasphemous tongues and more than gentle cuffs drove the men out of the privacy of dreams up the companionways leading to the upper deck.

"Do you think we should tell the men what it is we have in mind?'' said Gallant, as they watched *Écho*'s seamen begin to crowd out on to the weatherdeck.

"Hmmm. Yes. A good point, enseigne.'' Béssac called to the mates, who were appearing up the forecastle hatchway in the wake of a knot of scrambling men.

"Muster the men aft! Here, below us!''

Before long the sixty-odd men were gathered in the waist of the vessel, their numbers joined by the watchmen from aloft, whom Béssac had signalled down from their perches in the tops.

The men stood in expectant poses, the pale light of the anchor lantern touching them, watching the two officers who stood at the quarterdeck rail above them.

Not unlike most seamen of their age, they were prepared to work their vessel, fight for it with gun and blade if necessary, and face an endless series of risks simply as the reality of their lives.

And if the tall marine standing at the mate's side was going to add more pepper to that reality, so much the better. A few men licked their lips and pushed their tuques low over their eyes.

Béssac waved a hand toward Gallant.

"We have a plan which may, if Providence wills, obtain an escape for us from the English."

The men looked at one another meaningfully.

"But it will require that you all work with the utmost speed and effort over the next hours."

Here Béssac turned to the barrel-chested ship's carpenter, standing in his leather apron to one side with the senior men.

"We will be needing a major effort from you and your mates, for the things we will need. Can I depend on it?"

Guimond nodded with a short jerk of his head. "I'd build you a skiff to sail through Hell if you want, messieurs!"

Béssac grinned broadly at the man, and a ripple of chuckles went through the crewmen. Gallant perceived with growing appreciation the deftness of Béssac's control over his crew, and the apparently strong devotion that was reciprocated from them.

"Bon, Guimond", said Gallant. "I shall keep that particular offer in mind!"

More laughter.

A firm edge came into Gallant's voice. "We have many things to do, and cannot afford to waste a moment. M'sieu' Béssac, you will take the watch below and position eight...no, six of the spare yards, which I believe are mostly t'gallants, on the gun deck. Shift enough of our cargo to give access to the gunports. You'll need one of Guimond's mates to take the wedges out of the gunports."

Gallant then turned to the second mate, a tall, hawk-faced man who rarely spoke except to drive on an unwilling hand with an acid tongue or, less often, the swing of a three-foot rope end that always swung in his hand.

"Perilly?"

The man knuckled a forelock.

Gallant pointed to the gently swinging anchor lantern in the foremast shrouds. "If we manage to leave here, I wish the English to understand we have not, at least as far as that lantern is concerned. You may use the longboat and one of M. Béssac's spars, and another lantern. Do you follow me?"

"I think I do, enseigne!" A rare sharklike grin split the lean face.

"Good. Take whom you need from the off-watchmen."

"You others", and here he referred to the landsmen, carpenter's mates, and the cook's helpers, "will fall in forward. We'll lay out the niplines to pay out the starboard hawser, and lower the anchor from the cathead into the jollyboat. Béssac, before going below you'll see that the boat is brought round under the bows. Detail off two good hands as the boat crew."

Gallant paused and looked over the men's faces, a good many of which were wearing looks of puzzlement.

"Bien, mes enfants. You are wondering what this is all about", said the marine. A twinkle leapt in his eye. "Well, my brave ones, do your work and then we'll tell you! Dismiss the hands, Béssac!"

Gallant turned away even as a curt order from Béssac sent the crewmen, now excited and wondering, tumbling forward and aft to begin their assigned tasks.

"Silence there!"

Perilly's snarl cut like a knife through the drumming of running feet and the hushed chatter of the men. Within a few moments the mates had led their respective teams to their places, while Gallant, followed by the hawser party, moved quickly forward along the waist and up the short forecastle ladders to the canting foredeck.

Béssac soon had returned from below with his men to begin taking the lashings off the spare spars, which lay on the timber gallows above the gratings amidships. Below the gallows was the jollyboat, and Béssac set a few men to rigging a purchase from the starboard mainyard, to lower it over the side. Once over, it would be hauled forward to the bows and positioned below the starboard cathead, from which the great iron hook of *Écho's* other anchor hung.

The corvette's longboat, normally lashed down alongside the

jollyboat, had been lowered over the side earlier to transport the gun to the spit; Perilly's men were already tying it on at the mizzen chains, swarming out on the cro'jack yard to rig a tackle over the boat as well as several insecure-looking boatswain's chairs.

Gallant remarked to himself again on the openness of the foredeck. Écho's armament now consisted only of the waist battery of four guns, one of which was at the spithead. The two bow chasers the corvette once carried were long gone, and in the fairly uncluttered area abaft the timber bitts at the foot of the bowsprit Gallant set his men to the laborious hauling of the hawser out of the cable tier, the men grunting in uneven response to a barely whispered chant.

As the great, slime-coated rope appeared, the marine set several of the men to flaking it out in broad figure-eight loops. Two men were put to taking the turns off the cat tackle which clutched the heavy anchor to the projecting arm of the cathead.

Shortly, a thump alongside under the cheek of Écho's bows announced the arrival of the jollyboat. One man hooked on to the gaping mouth of the hawse while the other waved up at Gallant.

"Ready, enseigne."

Mentally crossing his fingers, the marine turned to the men stationed on the cat tackle falls.

"All right. Cast off the last turn. Lower away together. Handsomely, now...handsomely..."

He looked over the side. " 'Ware in the boat, there. Take it square amidships, or it'll capsize you."

The three-fold purchase of the tackle still meant the task of lowering the huge wood and iron anchor was a straining effort for the men. Without the enormous power of the capstan, the bulk of the hook became ponderously heavy. Their feet planting and slithering on the deck, muscles bunching into knots, the men eased out the line with slow and careful effort, their breath coming in gasps. The anchor sank under the squealing blocks toward the waiting boat, its black flukes turning slowly.

Below in the boat the seamen eased their craft under the slowly descending anchor. Soon it hung no more than a foot above the boat's thwarts.

Gallant held up a hand to the straining seamen on the tackle.

"Enough! Lower away...lower...easy, now...! Hold the strain!"

The anchor's crown was resting on the floorboards of the boat, which had sunk deeply into the still, dark water. Through the gloom Gallant could see that the boatmen had managed to rotate the descending hook so that the great spade flukes reached out over either side. The long shank tilted forward, and the yellow wooden beam of the stock now held a foot or so above the boat's gunwales.

"Lower away easy...easy...'Vast hauling!"

The anchor bit into the wood of the small boat, leaving its freeboard scarcely more than a hand's breadth high.

"Think she'll do it, enseigne?" said one of the men in the boat.

"That's up to you, isn't it? I wouldn't dance a jig in there just now."

The man answered with a rueful grin.

"Very well", said Gallant. "Cast off the tackle."

With infinite care to their balance and footing, the boatmen cut away the mousing from the bill of the tackle block.

After a word from Gallant the boatmen were soon straining at their oars, slowly pulling the boat and its enormous burden toward the distant spit.

Above on the foredeck the marine watched attentively as the men paying out the hawser handed the great cable, grunting with their efforts as they eased enough slack out through the hawse to prevent the line from suddenly coming under tension and spilling the boat's contents into the sea.

A scuff of shoes sounded on the foredeck ladder, and Gallant turned to see Béssac emerge, panting, from below.

"The spars are below on the gun deck, enseigne." He gestured toward the ladder.

Gallant followed the mate below to the dim gun deck, where the spars had been laid out, three to a side. Béssac's people had already cleared away the mess tables, tumbril racks, and heavily lashed crates and bales from the midships area of the deck, between six gunports which were approximately in the ship's centre.

Gallant smiled at the mate. "You seem to have thought of this even before I mentioned it to you, Béssac. Even with all your doubts.''

The mate cracked a smile, his face a rosy mask in the glow of the smudgy lantern which hung above the nearest gunport.

''It was not too difficult to see what you had in mind, monsieur. The talk of the galleys, the spars, the lack of wind. I started thinking about something like it myself the moment we talked of my days in the oarships.''

Gallant nodded. ''So you understand more than I, I suspect, what the problem is?''

Béssac returned the nod.

Gallant went over again the idea of rigging sweeps and rowing for the open sea. The men of Béssac's party, who were standing in a quiet group around the spars on the deck, shot astonished glances at one another.

''But tell me, Béssac. Supposing we put, shall we say, eight men on a sweep; how do they actually haul on them?''

Béssac pointed to the ship's side.

''The gunports will have to be where we ship 'em, enseigne. They'll not fit in the old sweep ports. The gunports are only about two feet across; that will be small enough to give us a solid thole if we pack something around the yards. The old felt curtains from the forward magazine, say. The clearance is not that great, anyway. It was touch and go feeding the spars in from outboard as it was.''

''Will they be hard to handle?''

''Hopefully not, m'sieu' '', said the mate. ''The greater part of their weight will be outboard, so I'll have a line fixed from the inboard end of each sweep to the gun tackle deadeyes.'' He pointed to the two iron eyebolts that projected from beside each gunport.

''To haul on the sweeps, I'll lash a series of lines to each spar, loosely enough so that each man can bind his arms to it as he sees best. They'll stand like this...facing forward. That way they'll push the sweeps. Put their bodies into it.''

Béssac bent over and spat out through the near gunport. ''It'll work, all right, enseigne.''

Gallant nodded. ''I see. Very well, then. Set matters up, but don't put the sweeps outboard as yet. Then bring your men on deck again." The marine paused at the foot of the ladder. "I think then will be the time to tell our people what we have in store for them."

When Gallant regained the upper deck, he was surprised to find that Perilly and his men had already finished their part of the preparations.

Alongside *Écho* the longboat rode, a single oversize mast rising from its floorboards. Near the top of the makeshift mast, which was snugly stayed fore and aft as well as to either side, hung a large anchor lantern similar to the one burning in the corvette's foreshrouds. Gallant noted that Perilly had seen to the placing of the lantern so that it was almost precisely the height above the water as the actual anchor light.

Gallant grunted. "Exactly what was needed. Do you think you can light that lantern with ease, in the bargain?"

Perilly snapped his fingers at a slim youth below in the boat, tossing him a small tinder box. Within seconds the youth had shinnied to the top of the pole, and after a few strikes of the flint was holding a burning ember near the open lantern.

Gallant nodded again with satisfaction. "Bon."

He turned to Béssac, who had come up after grouping his men in the after part of the corvette's waist. "I gather you're done as well, Béssac?"

"Putting the last lines on now, enseigne."

Gallant directed Béssac to assemble the rest of *Écho*'s men with his own.

Almost as he did so, a thump alongside indicated the arrival of the jollyboat bearing the men from the spit battery, who were already full of intense energy from whatever the boat's oarsmen had told them of what was afoot. The first who clambered over the rail was the huge African Akiwoya, who knuckled his brow to Gallant as soon as he spotted him at the quarterdeck rail.

"The anchor is implanted, monsieur! As firm a place as we could drop it into." The man grinned. "We had to overturn the boat to do it. A good bath for all of us!"

"Well done", said Gallant. "What did you do to make our precious gun useless to the English?" He winced inwardly at the thought of losing the valuable six-pounder.

"Nothing to fear, m'sieu'!" A broad grin split the African's face, his teeth gleaming whitely in the darkness. "They're not going to unspike it in this lifetime!"

Gallant motioned for the man and the rest of the crew to join the other assembled crewmen. Then he turned to face them all. In a rush he felt a good deal more uncertain about the wisdom of his scheme. It also somewhat startled him that should the plan fail he felt a greater worry over losing the respect of the rough, sea-hardened merchantmen than facing the British broadsides. The men were watching him silently through the gloom about them.

"We told you that we may have a means of escaping from the English. It is only fair that you learn now what we have in mind. Our only real hope for leaving here would be an offshore gale that would drive the English out to sea and allow us to slip free. But you can see what little wind we have. And the English will try again soon, in greater force, to come in for us."

He licked his lips. "So we must leave. Tonight."

A murmuring passed through the men. The huge African from the spithead gun crew stepped forward, knuckling his brow to Gallant.

"Your pardon, m'sieu' ", he said. "But we would have no heart to abandon *Écho* to the English. She is everything to us. She is our home. And we will fight for her!"

Voices from the other men rose in agreement.

Gallant held up protesting hands. "Wait, please! Do not misunderstand, matelot Akiwoya. We intend that *Écho* should not be left here!"

Gallant leaned forward over the rail, gripping it tightly.

"We are going to take her to sea!"

Akiwoya's broad grin joined those of his crewmates, and now laughter passed through the men. Apparently the gentilhomme was suffering a touch of ship fever.

"May we ask, if you permit, how, enseigne?" said Akiwoya.

Gallant's scalp tingled, and he felt his face burning. These were no sullen Louisbourg soldiery, obedient like slow cattle to his orders. These men he had to convince and win over to an audacious determination to carry out the scheme. Only then would it work; only then would they ignore the insanity of rowing out to sea under the noses of the English. Ignore it, and do it!

He glanced at the men of Béssac's party, who already knew the details of the scheme. Their faces were impassive.

"We will row her out. We'll make her a galley and row her out."

For an excruciating moment the men stood as if frozen, staring at Gallant with expressionless eyes.

Then slowly, out of the cavernous depths of Akiwoya's thick chest came laughter. A low rumbling that grew and built on itself, deep and resonant, until at last the gunner stood hands on hips, head thrown back, roaring.

And now, with him, the men. One, two, then several, then all. Cackling and chuckling, clapping each other on the shoulders, wiping tears from streaming eyes.

The ghastly feeling that they were hooting at him in mockery put Gallant's cheeks aflame. He had begun to turn away when Akiwoya waved up at him, shouting above the laughter. Shouting, and soon joined by the other men, nodding their heads vigorously and pressing forward behind the gunner. The African's voice became comprehensible over the noise.

"By the Virgin, enseigne, you're a rare one!" roared out Akiwoya. "Row out! Into all that out there! Sweet Jesus, yes! We'll row her all the way to Barbary!" Beside the gunner the men were shouting the same things.

They were with him!

Gallant found himself grinning like an idiot. The sense of relief was enormous. He shot a glance at Béssac, whose eyes were twinkling back at him through the gloom.

The men quieted as Gallant raised a hand for silence.

"M'sieu' Béssac will divide you among the sweeps and the other tasks we need to do. We should light the lantern at the longboat's masthead when we douse our own. We'll up anchor, and to get steerage way we'll stand to the capstan and haul ourselves out to the spithead, where the starboard anchor is set in the shallows. We cut the cable as we pass the spit. Then, once clear, we set ourselves to the sweeps and pull as best we can for the open sea.''

The men's faces were sombre now, attentive, as the realization of what this all meant sank home.

"With luck, it may be possible in the darkness to slip through the anchored line of English and be well to seaward by dawn. There, we may pick up an offshore breeze.''

"You can see what lies ahead, mes braves. It will require everything we can put into it. We'll make the attempt when the glass turns twice in the middle watch. See to it that each man knows his station. Perilly?''

"M'sieu'?''

"See to it that every man who did not eat is sent to the galley. And see to it that my brandy cask is broached and set up outside my cabin. Before we leave there'll be a tasse all around!''

This promise of extra brandy set the men to cheering again, and the upturned faces were eager and animated. Teeth flashed in the darkness, and more than one man spat and rubbed his palms in anticipation.

The men looked at Gallant with the beginnings of a greater respect in their eyes. This Acadien did not lack for courage. And a courageous man they, like their fellows of other nations and other times, would follow into the very mouth of Hell itself.

Within a few minutes Béssac and Perilly had divided the men into teams for each task. The huge gunner, Akiwoya, hurried below to prepare his store of cartridges for the small guns remaining in *Écho*, and to fill his heavy priming horn. Men were soon clearing the decks of the ship's gear and cargo as far as was possible, lashing down firmly what could not be moved, and generally attempting in a make-do fashion the clearing for action which was a smoothly oiled routine in a vessel of war.

The effort was slowed by the sending to the cookfires of those men who had missed the evening meal, or claimed to have missed it. Béssac's sweating teams laboured to set the heavy sweeps in the gunports, packing the spars with almost any material that came to hand to keep them relatively firm in place.

Slowly the work had its effect, until had there been sufficient light an observor on the bluffs would have remarked that the corvette had grown six short, sticklike legs, somewhat like a millpond water beetle. Toward the end of the first watch *Écho* had become as ready as ever she might be for her attempt to slip from the clutches of the Royal Navy.

Gallant turned to Béssac as they stood on the quarterdeck.

"Would you care for some wine?" he said.

FIVE

"Are they still astern of us?" said Edgehill.

"Can't say, sir. I've lost them for the moment."

Lieutenant Anthony Robinson peered into the night behind him, trying to make out the faint twinkle of phosphorescence from the blades of Pollett's oars somewhere astern.

Redoubtable's boat, with the sergeant and ten privates of the marines, was following the boat carrying Edgehill and Robinson, guided by the glow of a hooded hurricane lamp Robinson's coxswain had lashed to the boat's ensign staff. Robinson had last seen the dark shape of the other boat as it crossed a rivulet of light from one of *Redoubtable*'s stern windows, but it was lost in the darkness now.

He looked up at the night sky. Bloody millions of stars up there, he thought, and still not enough to see by.

Robinson looked ahead to where he sensed rather than saw the dark mass of the shoreline. He stood, feet braced in the sternsheets of the boat, holding the tiller behind him at the small of his back. Beside him, on the larboard side of the stern thwart, sat Captain Edgehill.

On the midships' thwarts *Sylph*'s mortar crew, including the grizzled mastergunner O'Brien, sat huddled around the little coehorn mortar. The carrying poles for the little piece of ordnance lay fore and aft along the middle of the thwarts. Ahead in the boat, the oarsmen from *Hector* hauled their looms slowly to O'Brien's low count.

"Damn."

Robinson strained to see some break in the dark mass ahead. The cleft should be coming visible about now.

"Wot's that yew said, zur?" said O'Brien.

"Nothing. I can't see the damned cleft. Way enough."

The oarsmen ceased pulling and lifted their blades out of the water, pulling them quietly inboard until they rested across both gunwales.

In a moment *Redoubtable*'s boat materialized out of the darkness, its occupants' faces gleaming palely. A hoarse whisper carried across.

"What's the matter, Captain Edgehill?"

"Small problem", answered the marine. "Trying to locate the cleft."

"I can't seem to pick it out, sir", said Robinson. "We might be dead on it, we might not."

Pollett grunted. "Well, there's no sense in sitting out here rafting. Push in and if need be we'll skirt the shore until we do find it."

Robinson wiped his brow, which was damp with sweat in spite of the cool night air.

"Out oars. Give way together."

The blades dipped soundlessly into the dark water again and the boats resumed their progress. They had now been under way some twenty minutes since leaving from *Redoubtable*'s seaward side.

Robinson's eyes strained into the dark for several minutes. O'Brien looked inquiringly at the two officers as to their ears there came now the lap and wash of the swells along the rocky shoreline.

Then he saw it. The cleft, barely visible as a thin wedge of lighter sky into the inky mass of the bluffs.

"There we are. Starboard a point is where we're going. Pull in easily, now."

Within a few minutes the boat was barely two or three yards off an almost sheer face of rock. The bowman and O'Brien fended the boat off as it swung beam on to shore, the knobbly rocks touched by the thin light of the stern lamp. At a word from Robinson the oarsmen tossed their oars, holding them vertically before them.

Redoubtable's boat came alongside rapidly, to the accompaniment of scuffles and bumping as oars were dragged inboard and laid dripping on the thwarts amidst the men. The marines were not used to moving the long sweeps with ease, and the Redoubtables in the boat snickered at their clumsiness.

"Quiet, damn you!" Pollett's hoarse whisper came out of the gloom. "Mister Robinson! Where in Hell are we? I see nothing but the whoreson cliff face!"

"This is it all right, sir. I'm sending a man up to scout it now."

The lieutenant tapped O'Brien's shoulder. "Get a man each on the bow and stern lines. If we can't grapple on anything ashore moor us on two grapnels. There must be some small ledges ashore to get on. And keep fending off. Tinker?"

"Here, sir." A whisper came from forward in the boat, and a slightly built seaman clambered aft over the thwarts.

"Right. Up you go, right to the top. Here's the lantern. Give us a flash when you make it up. Flash twice if you can't get all the way, and come back down. Do you remember the other signals?"

"Aye, sir."

"All right. And for God's sake watch your footing."

"Sir. I'll make it, never fear."

The man paused for a second, as if gauging the distance, and then sprang ashore, a coil of light manila line slung over his shoulders. After clinging for a moment to a precarious foothold, he began to work his way up to the dark gap of the cleft.

"Oi, up yew go, Dick, an' nab a rum doxy!" said a voice out of Robinson's boat.

"And the next man to utter a sound will have a hundred

lashes!'' Pollett's low, menacing tone cut dead the tittering in the boat crews.

For some fifteen minutes the two boats bobbed in silence at the foot of the bluffs. Aside from the men tending the lines and fending off, the remainder huddled on the thwarts, glancing occasionally at their wordless officers.

Robinson's anxieties grew with each passing minute. Had he misjudged the difficulty of getting up the cleft? He felt the strain beginning to cramp his neck muscles as he watched the line of the dark bluff against the star-strewn sky.

"How long a climb did you estimate it was?'' came Edgehill's quiet question.

"I couldn't really judge, sir. It appeared to be at least a hundred and twenty, perhaps a hundred and fifty feet. There looked to be plenty of handholds and ledges through the glass. But he's doing it for the first time, and in the dark. He might...''

"Quiet! Listen!'' Pollett's hissed interjection was urgent.

Robinson stiffened and listened, as did the men in both boats. For an instant it seemed as if there was no sound at all. Then faintly, very faintly, it floated to them.

"Cheerin', sir. From the Frenchman'', said O'Brien.

"So it is, by God. Wonder what the Frogs have got to cheer about in their pickle?''

"They enjoy their brandy, sir'', offered Robinson.

Pollett grunted. "Bloody peculiar nonetheless.''

For the moment they listened to the distant voices, until O'Brien's gravel voice broke in.

"Signal from above, sir.''

Robinson looked up. After a moment he saw the faint ruddy glow of a lantern waving back and forth. Tinker had reached the top.

Pollett had seen it too. "Good man! All right, then. Redoubtables, get your seaward grapnels out. Pass the lines for the boats.''

The men worked busily in the darkness, passing lines across to Robinson's boat and lashing the two craft together. Grapnels splashed into the water further out.

The lantern circled twice, then three times from overhead.

"Heads up in the boats. Line coming down."

The end of Tinker's light line dropped into the water beside the boats and was quickly hauled in.

Edgehill coughed delicately. "Very well, lads. Shore party and marines, one at a time up the bluff. Use the line for a guide. Marines, sling your firelocks."

Pollett touched Robinson's sleeve. "You'll go up to do the firing. Captain Edgehill will command once up there, so mind your manners."

"And you, sir?"

Pollett shook his head. "I can't lad. Took a privateer's ball in the arm some years back. It won't hold me. I'll be here waiting. Up you go!"

"Aye, aye, sir. Sorry, sir." He knew Pollett was itching to scale the bluff and lead the attack himself.

"Go, damn you!"

One by one the seamen and marines detailed for the climb set off up the precarious route, guided by Tinker's light line. The barefooted seamen, used to vertical climbs, were less upset at the prospect than the booted marines. Soon the last man was stepping off the slippery, weed-strewn lip of the shore, and the party began working up through the rocky cleft in almost total darkness, hands feeling for each hold. The only sounds were the heavy breathing of the straining men, the clink of musket butts and accoutrements against the rocky outcrops, and the rattle of loose stones freed by searching hands and digging toes.

Leading them up, followed closely by Captain Edgehill, was Robinson, who was wondering somewhat wildly whether he would ever overcome his habit of suggesting schemes that invariably ended with the risking of his own life.

Almost as soon as the climb had begun it became for each man involved in it a personal nightmare of varying intensity. For Robinson and many others of the panting, trembling men, the saving grace of the darkness was that it made it impossible to see down. For the seamen, used as they were to teetering high above the deck on the intricate network of spar and shroud, the uneven course of the cleft taxed their nerve to the fullest. For the stolid marines, it was an unspeakable trial that only their pride and enormous discipline was forcing them through.

Robinson heard nothing from Edgehill, below him. He wondered if the marine captain's breath was coming in the same shaking gasps as his own. The voluminous skirts of his coat were constantly fouling around his knees, and although he had hitched his cumbersome waistbelt around to the small of his back, the hanger scabbard clattered and banged against the rocks with every movement. Robinson wished he could have begun the climb in nothing save his breeches.

The fissure was thankfully well-endowed with ledges and projecting shelves, and as he climbed he found his hands naturally seeking out the best grip, his knee or back pressing without thought against any point where support could be found. Slowly, placing each foot in turn, he worked his way upward. Below him he could hear the clink and scrabble of the men following, punctuated by the occasional oath.

At one point a man halfway down the climbing group lost his footing and began to fall, his bleat of fear choked off immediately as the brawny arms of the man below him closed round him, holding him until balance and a foothold returned. The climb resumed.

Then, before Robinson expected it, Tinker's shaggy head was outlined against the stars and the sailor was hauling him like a sack up over the edge of the bluff.

"Good on 'ee sir. Fair climb for a gennulman."

"Thank you, Tinker", puffed Robinson. "Damn your insolence."

Robinson felt his heart pounding against his rib cage with almost frightening violence, and a red glow seemed to show at the edges of his vision. He noticed for the first time that his upper legs were trembling uncontrollably.

"Where have you tied on the line? Is there some kind of solid point we can anchor lines on?" he said.

Tinker disappeared into the depth of some broad, low bushes some feet back from the bluff edge.

"In 'ere, sir. Bowlin'd to a right tough old root, she is. 'Twill hold all rights, I'd say, sir."

Robinson took off his hat and wiped his streaming forehead

with a sleeve cuff.

"Good", he said, somewhat hoarsely. "See to helping up Captain Edgehill, will you?"

The marine had in fact already made his way over the bluff and was carefully watching the progress of the rest of the party. Robinson felt a touch of annoyance at noticing that Edgehill hardly seemed to be breathing at all, while he himself was still gasping and wheezing like a fishwife.

One by one the men struggled over the lip, the white gaiters of the marines showing pale in the starlight. They unlimbered their muskets and stood about looking uncertainly at the shadows inland until a word from Edgehill set the sergeant to spacing the men out in a loose perimeter around the arrival spot. Robinson heard the slide of steel on steel as the marines fixed their bayonets. The sound sent an involuntary shiver up his spine.

He turned his attention to the bluff edge again. Tinker was helping Petty Officer O'Brien over the lip, the latter man swathed in a coil of heavy manila line. Within ten minutes the remainder of the men had followed, and O'Brien had set them immediately to laying out his line and that carried up by another seaman, first making them fast to the stout root tangle Tinker pointed out.

Robinson touched his hat to Edgehill.

"If you'll permit, sir, I'll begin bringing up the materials from the boats."

"Yes, by all means", said the marine.

Robinson called over his petty officer. "O'Brien, make the signal to Mister Pollett's people that we're ready, will you? We've not a moment to lose."

"Aye, aye, sir."

An instant later Tinker was leaning out over the bluff edge, swinging his small lantern. Almost immediately O'Brien's seaman heaved the free coils of the two lines over the edge, the root tangle popping and creaking as the lines snapped taut to their full weight.

A tug several moments later indicated that the men in the boats had secured the lines to the two timbers to be used in hauling up the coehorn.

"Lines lashed on, sir", said O'Brien.

"Very well. Haul away."

The petty officer spat on his hands and hitched up his broad leather waistbelt. "All right, buckos, down slack! One to six... Heave! And heave!"

Slowly the lines were hauled up, tug-of-war fashion, the sound of the spars thumping against the bluff face sounding from below.

"Come on, you lot o' damn sowjers, heave!"

After a few minutes of work the timbers emerged over the edge of the bluff. O'Brien set several men to work at once laying the beams out in a broad V, lashing the crossed ends together to form a sturdy bipod.

"Right. Now what winger carried up them blocks?"

Two men came forward, each unlimbering a large, single-sheaved block. O'Brien set them to splicing an end of one of the manila lines to one of the blocks, then reeving the line through both blocks to make a workable tackle. The block to which the line had been spliced was then tied sturdily on at the apex of the bipod.

Robinson glanced out to sea. Shimmering on the water, the warm and inviting glow of the anchored squadron's lights seemed an immense distance away. He shivered again.

O'Brien's men finished the sheerlegs with a crude topping lift looped over the head of the assembly. They had shoved the timbers around so that the open end of the V faced the cliff edge.

O'Brien turned to Robinson. "'Legs is rigged, sir."

Robinson cast a quick look over the assembly, although he trusted O'Brien's judgement and seamanship without question.

"It looks all right." He nodded. "Very well. Stand the thing up and begin paying out the tackle. Tinker?"

"Sir?"

"Flash for 'block descending', or whatever, will you?"

Tinker's lantern waved four times over the bluff lip.

Under O'Brien's direction the sheerlegs were wrestled closer to the bluff edge. Then, having braced the feet with several flat boulders, the men heaved the assembly up to the vertical, holding now to the lift as they canted the legs out over the bluff edge gingerly. While several men held the strain on the lift, its end was securely lashed on to the root tangle.

"Right. Stand clear o' the lift. You Jones, and you, Shaw. Lay aholt o' them larboard and starboard stays and don't let go of 'em!"

O'Brien had rigged stays to either side of the bipod as well. This would keep it from swaying to either side as the mortar was hauled up.

"Weight the hook, Jenkins. Stand to the fall. Pay away... steady, now...no bloody rush, lads..."

With a heavy rock ingeniously slung on its hook for weight, the lower block of the tackle sank out of sight toward the boats below. For several minutes the men paid out the line until it suddenly went slack.

"Hold the strain." Robinson nodded as O'Brien reported, "She's down, sir."

"Very well." Robinson scratched at a new flea bite he had discovered under his waistcoat. "Eyes peeled for that flash, there, Tinker!"

A moment later Tinker called that he had seen a lantern flash from below, signalling that the small but heavy little mortar was ready to be hauled up the bluff.

Robinson mentally crossed his fingers and nodded to O'Brien.

"Take up the strain!" barked the petty officer. "Come on, Jenkins, you whoreson, stand to it! You're a bloody King's 'ard bargain, you are! Heave! And heave!"

The blocks of the tackle squealed as the heavy weight of the mortar lifted off the boat floorboards far below. Robinson trotted to the bluff edge and after an anxious look at the sheerlegs peered into the darkness below. He could see nothing but the faint light of the boat's lanterns.

"Heave...heave..." The blocks squealed on to O'Brien's chant. The line of men on the falls worked silently, their feet spread in the dry, rocky soil for balance.

Suddenly the mortar appeared above the bluff lip, swinging slowly on the hook. The bronze of the piece gleamed dully in the starlight.

"'Vast haulin'!" O'Brien's orders went on. "Stand to the

lift. Bring 'er vertical, now...careful, Allen, you great looby... 'Vast! Hold'er there! Pay away...lower..."

With a thump the mortar and its blocky carriage set down on the bluff top.

It took fifteen minutes more to send the tackle back down and haul up the bundles of gun tools, buckets, shell bomb cases, and the carrying poles to move the mortar about. At last O'Brien reported that everything was in carrying order. Robinson turned to Edgehill.

"Ready to proceed, sir."

Edgehill took off his tricorne and settled it at a determined angle on his neatly queued wig. "Very well, Mister Robinson. Let's go and find the Frenchman, shall we?"

Robinson had O'Brien form the seamen up in a squad, the mortar carried like a sedan chair between two rows of the bigger men, and the tools and other paraphernalia apportioned out among the others. Edgehill's sergeant called in the marines from their perimeter line and formed them in two files ahead of the seamen, with a nimble man posted well to the front as a scout.

After a check of the sheerlegs and a glance below at Pollett's boats, Robinson moved up to join Edgehill at the head of the column. He nodded at the marine.

"Well, then", said Edgehill, "let's be off. Party, to the front...march!"

The men stepped off, with a few uncertain lurches from the mortar bearers until they got the feel of their load's swing. The marines settled in to their normal parade plod of seventy paces to the minute, which was well suited for feeling their path over the uneven ground.

Robinson had been caught a bit unprepared for the suddenness of Edgehill's command. He drew his sword, for no other reason than that it seemed the thing to do, and trotted to catch up with Edgehill. Behind him, the marine sergeant at the head of his men set his eyes on the white flash of the officer's breeches and simply followed them.

Even in the dark, however, the men could see well enough to avoid any large obstacle, and Robinson felt a sense of relief that the ground was fairly level and not difficult to walk over. The column wandered along the bluff close to its edge, keeping to the open, gravelly spaces and avoiding the inky patches of undergrowth. The shoes of the marines crunched along on the dry soil, and now and then a barefoot seaman caught a toe and swore. O'Brien hovered about the rear of the little column, fearful for his precious mortar and the powder, keeping the silence with a curt word or two.

Edgehill was letting the marine scout pick the route ahead, watching only that he did not stray too far inland. Robinson could make out the shape of the tasselled mitre cap and the ghostly gleam of the white gaiters winking amongst the low scrub. From time to time the man's bayonet reflected a tiny blue spark of starlight.

Then the marine was suddenly looming larger before them.

"Inlet's 'bout twenty yard ahead, no more, sir."

"Halt", said Edgehill.

Robinson took off his tricorne. He was wringing wet with sweat.

Edgehill motioned to him and the two officers walked forward to where the ground seemed to vanish away before them into darkness. Robinson inched to the edge of the yawning black chasm and looked down.

There below them gleamed the single light of the French corvette's anchor lantern.

Robinson clamped his tricorne back on his head and sheathed his sword. He turned and called O'Brien quietly forward from the party of men.

"There she is, O'Brien. Our target."

The petty officer nodded, looking down at the small light below them.

Edgehill sniffed at a small scented handkerchief that had materialized from his sleeve cuff. "You may carry on, Mister Robinson. Open fire as quickly as you can. Sergeant Hall?" This to the sergeant at the head of the marine files. "Set out a picket, please. Fifty-yard perimeter. And send Mister Robinson your best marksman."

The sergeant slapped his musket in salute and began detailing off his men quickly and quietly.

"Carry on breaking out the tools and materials, O'Brien", said Robinson. Then he turned to Edgehill. "How did you know I'd want to speak to your best shot, sir?"

The marine officer's wink was just visible in the gloom. "Did a bit of artillery training m'self once. Please carry on."

The same marine who had acted as the column's scout halted in front of Robinson, his musket held stiffly at the Present.

Robinson touched his own hat cockade in reply. "So you're the crack shot. What's your name?"

"Private Price, sir."

Robinson gestured to the inlet edge. "Ease arms, Price. Have a look again at the French vessel down there."

He walked with Price to the cliff edge. "What do you estimate her range from here?"

Price scratched his head under the tall cap. "Dunno, sir. Can't rightly make out 'er shape too well in this gloom." He peered again, resting on the long Tower musket.

Then he said, "It's nought but a guess, sir, an' that only."

"How far?"

"Line o' sight ball shot, 'bout five hundred yard, sir. If you'd musket to do it. Not likely with an old Bess like this 'ere, sir." The marine shook his head.

"Very well, Price. Thank you. Carry on." The white gaiters vanished toward the other marines.

Robinson looked again at the light. Just faintly he could make out the dimmest outline of a hull. Yes. Perhaps it was about five hundred, but no more.

He rubbed his brow and considered the little mortar, which O'Brien was having set down about thirty feet from the bluff edge. The mortar was permanently fixed in its carriage at an elevation of forty-five degrees. He tried to remember the complexity of figures involved in calculating the range of the little piece. Extreme accurate range of the big thirteen-inch mortar in *Sylph* was about 1750 to 1800 yards. Anything beyond that put the shell in the air over twenty seconds, and only God knew then where it would land. The little coehorn might range the five hundred yards in eleven...no...twelve seconds at the most.

Robinson sucked on a tooth. But the little corvette was in fact a target below the horizontal. He would have to calculate a theoretical horizon and mentally plot a projectile path aiming not for the ship but for the point where an accurate ballistic path would cut the the imaginary horizon.

The lieutenant's head began to ache. He cursed the weakness he always had with figures. Luckily O'Brien was already laying out the gun tools and would see to most of the other tasks. He forced himself to concentrate again.

The horizon. The shell's path. They would cut at three hun... no, three hundred and twenty-five yards apparent range, more or less. Robinson winced. It was an approximate figure, perhaps too much so. That would give a time to apparent target of perhaps eight or nine seconds, which, for the small shell bombs, would call for a charge of..."

"Petty Officer O'Brien?"

"Sir?" came the reply in a hoarse whisper.

Robinson walked over to the mortar, now surrounded by the waiting crew. A good distance back two more men hovered over the charges in their leathern buckets, and a little pile of shell bombs.

"I'll have a ranging charge of two pounds. And break out the plumb line, two stakes and a mallet."

Robinson took the stakes and mallet from a seaman and walked back to the inlet edge. As close as possible in a line with the ship's light and the mortar, he tapped one of the stakes into the soil. Squatting down, he picked out an irregularity on the further side of the chasm, where the bluff descended steeply to form the spit, choosing it so that a mental line between it and the stake would have touched, as near as he could judge, the corvette's anchor light.

Keeping his eye on the irregular mark on the inlet's far side, he moved back carefully until he stood just in front of the mortar. Here he squatted and tapped in the other stake, looking along to see that it lay in a line with the feature he had picked out and the first stake. He was surprised at how much he could see by the light of the star-filled sky.

Then, he stood behind the mortar and held up the plumb line centred on the mid-line of the mortar's muzzle. With low commands he had O'Brien's crew handspike the little mortar around, inch by inch, until he aligned as far as he could by eye the two stakes and the plumb line.

Robinson sighed. It would have to do.

He doffed his hat to Edgehill, who had been watching from nearby. "We may fire when you wish, sir."

"Please proceed at once, Mister Robinson", replied the marine.

Robinson nodded to O'Brien. "Very well, then."

The petty officer spat and stepped to beside the mortar. "Take heed!" he intoned, in the time-honoured opening command of all naval gunners.

With curt orders he worked the crew through the loading of the little mortar. Robinson intervened only once, using a small clasp knife to nip the shell bomb's beechwood fuse at the mark for an eleven-second burn. Finally the ventsman unslung his heavy horn and primed the vent, after which he picked up the smouldering portfire and looked at O'Brien.

O'Brien knuckled his forehead to Robinson, who was standing with Edgehill some yards to one side.

"Ready, sir."

Robinson licked his lips. "Fire as you please."

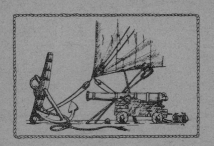

SIX

The brass oil lamp in the tiny midships cabin of *Écho* swayed gently with the slow motion of the ship to its hawser. Paul Gallant lay back in his cramped box bunk and stared at the weak glow, trying to calm the pounding of his heart and the discomforting tingle in his bowels. In an odd way, the rational part of him felt calm, and controlled, but below this he felt a seething cauldron of emotion threatening to burst through the veneer of reason.

Again and again the same nightmarish images swirled through his mind. He saw in horrible clarity an inferno of flame engulfing the buildings of Louisbourg, the lurid light of the fires bright against the night sky. Then he was seeing Philippe's farm on the Miré, the bodies still on the ground as the buildings smouldered around them.

Gallant looked at his hands, which were trembling. Lying here with thoughts like these will solve nothing, he thought. Get on deck and do something, you fool!

He rose and picked his coat up from where he had dropped it across the small sea chest beside the bunk, and after slipping it on, clamped his tricorne on his head.

At that moment the watchboy's thin call rang out, and the slap of feet along the decks and up companionways signalled that Béssac was mustering the men on deck, in the after waist about the the great head of the capstan.

Ducking under the beams, Gallant left the cabin and went on deck, where he was greeted by an amiable Béssac who was rubbing his hands together in anticipation.

"Ah, enseigne! A fine night for an escape!"

"Why, yes indeed, Béssac."

The marine clasped his hands behind his back in the position he favoured in public and made every effort to make his own voice sound calm. He wondered if the mate would notice the cold sweat running down his temples.

Gallant moved to the rail. Béssac was positioning the men about the capstan, the heavy bars being slipped into place and the men posted behind them shoulder to shoulder, in more numbers than would have been normal for raising the anchor. A scuff of feet on planking behind Gallant indicated that Bédard, the best helmsman, was moving to the wheel.

Perilly's few remaining men were busy dropping a grapnel from the longboat, and the lantern-lighting youth was already shinnying up its jury mast.

Gallant licked his lips. "Bon. Let's light that lantern, eh?" He cupped his hands. "Proceed, Perilly!"

Perilly, standing on the foredeck, nodded and then snapped his fingers, once. It made a hollow, popping sound that echoed back from the inlet walls. Aloft, dangling from a bosun's chair in the foremast rigging, a seaman blew out *Écho*'s anchor light.

"Come on, come on", muttered Gallant under his breath.

A split second later the new lamp atop the longboat's mast flickered into life.

"Good! All right, Béssac. Stand to the capstan. Take out the pawls and then break out the larboard anchor!"

In a few minutes the thirty-odd men at the capstan bars were straining to hold the weight of the anchor cable by main strength, their feet slithering and slapping on the deck. Forward, Perilly hung over the bows, watching the great hook rise dripping from the black water.

Gallant glanced at either side of the inlet. *Écho* was not moving appreciably in any direction.

Perilly hissed from forward. "A cockbill, enseigne!"

"Bon. Hook on the cat tackle and haul her home. Hold the strain on that cable!" Gallant's voice was tinged with excitement.

Perilly's men forward stopped their rapid hauling. "She's catted up, m'sieu'!"

"All right. Now nip the messenger to the starboard cable. Stand ready to take the strain, there."

Gallant's heart slammed against his ribs. He licked his dry lips again and looked out at the distant English lights. Here we come, Messieurs les rosbifs, he murmured to himself. He felt an overpowering urge to yawn, and wished in the bargain he had gone to the heads earlier.

"Pass the niplines. Take the strain." On Béssac's orders now, the men leaned into the capstan bars, bunching their muscles for the coming effort. The cable made a few protesting crackles as the pressure was applied.

Gallant tapped the rail. "Ready, there...ready..."

The men tensed. Gallant felt he could hear their short, tight breathing.

"Haul!"

The men threw their weight against the bars, cursing as their feet slipped on the deck, now spotted with the sweat running from their bodies. The cable groaned and creaked as the men struggled to drag it in.

Béssac was everywhere, nimbly hopping around the labouring circle of men. "Hold that strain! Now, push! Into it with your backs! One step! And another! Move ahead!"

The men cursed and fought the bars. Their bodies bent forward, they strained against the weight of the extended cable until they felt their tendons cracking. The best they seemed able to do was hold the capstan against the heavy drag of the cable's weight out through the hawse. Béssac fumed and raved.

Then, slowly, the capstan began to turn. The men took one step. Then another. And two more.

Béssac pointed up at the bluff walls beside them. "Look, m'sieu'! We're moving!"

The corvette was indeed inching forward, almost imperceptibly. Gallant spun on the helmsman.

"Steer small!" he hissed. "Your course is for the inlet mouth, as close to the spit as you dare. But ground us and I'll cut out your heart!"

The spread-footed helmsman flashed a quick, gap-toothed smile, nodding vigorously.

The men were moving slowly now around the capstan, their laboured breathing and occasional grunts revealing the intense pressure they were applying, made all the more difficult without the steady and supporting click-click of the capstan pawls.

Gallant glanced up at the mastheads, moving slowly against the canopy of stars, then looked astern. The anchored longboat with its brightly glowing decoy lantern was already a good fifty feet astern.

"Steady...steady. Starboard a point...ease it over." Gallant was watching the helmsman with a hawklike attention.

Écho was slipping through the still inlet water toward the mouth with hardly a sound other than Béssac's voice. The mate was urging on the capstan men, who were walking slowly but steadily now around the great drum, the cable slithering in through the hawse and tumbling into the cable tier like some monstrous slime-covered snake. The nippers, the several small boys who kept the capstan line seized to the cable by darting in and out with their hand lines, chattered excitedly at the sight until a bark from Béssac silenced them.

Gallant bit his lip. The inlet mouth was scarcely two hull lengths away.

He cupped his hands at Béssac. "Béssac! That will do! Belay that and stand to the sweeps! We shall cut the cable in an instant! Perilly?"

The second mate's voice carried back from the foredeck.

"Axes ready, enseigne!"

"Bon!" Gallant watched the approaching spit head, gauging the speed and distance of the ghosting corvette to the open water.

"Stand ready!" he warned. "Ready...ready..."

He slapped his palm on the rail.

"Now!"

Béssac's men left the capstan bars with a rush and surged down the companionways with a thunder of bare feet. The thick cable now lay inert on the deck as *Écho* overran it. Several sharp, chopping blows sounded on the foredeck, and then the freed end of the severed cable slithered with a splash into the water.

Écho was gliding along at a good three or four knots, her momentum carrying her along with little diminution after the men left the capstan. Gallant watched in fascination as the low black mass of the spit slipped silently toward them.

He moved to stand close beside the helmsman. Their eyes, and those of every man on deck, were on the fast approaching inlet mouth. A rumble below decks marked Béssac's readying of his cumbersome sweeps.

Gallant's scalp began to tingle at the ghostly silence that fell over the gliding ship once the noise from below faded. His ears rang with the pounding of his blood. Would they never be through the inlet mouth?

Below, Béssac's panting men stood poised at their places on the sweeps, eyes feverish with excitement, watching the mate who stood at the companionway foot waiting for Gallant's word.

Ten yards. Five. Then none.

They were out in the channel!

Gallant leaned over the rail and hissed at the open companionway mouth. "Pull, Béssac!"

With a squeal and rumble of wood on wood the great sweeps reached out from the corvette's side and took their first slow bite into the black water. A few men at the looms slipped and struggled with the heavy weight until Béssac's penetrating voice established a steady rhythm. With regular beats the heavy spars began to dip and rise as the men swung to and fro with them.

In a moment Béssac reappeared on the quarterdeck, poking Gallant in the shoulder with a gnarled thumb. "Look at that, enseigne. You were right. By the Sweet Virgin, it's moving us!"

The mate jabbed the thumb at the distant English riding lights.

"And the English are still none the wiser, I'll trow!"

Gallant grinned, trying to still the excited shaking in his limbs.

"God grant you're right, Béssac! And grant we'll succeed!"

The mate clamped a hand on his shoulder.

"Succeed?" He nodded. "I feel it in these old bones! We'll be out of this mess in a few ticks of my watch! And it's thanks to your..."

Astern of *Écho* the night was rent by the blast of an explosion and a bright yellow flash that threw the faces of the astonished men into garish relief.

Gallant stared, his stomach a piece of cold stone, as a towering plume of glowing water leaped up from the anchorage in the inlet, and the decoy lantern on the end of its spar toppled into the phosphorous-flecked wreckage of the longboat.

"God in Heaven!" whispered Béssac.

High on the bluffs, Petty Officer O'Brien cleared his throat and spat.

"Blow on your match," he intoned. Then, "Fire!"

Down arced the portfire.

There was a brief pink spurt from the vent and then the mortar fired with a bright flash and a thump that set Robinson's ears ringing. In the brief instant of light he had seen the members of the mortar crew, O'Brien, Edgehill, and even the distant marine pickets frozen in their poses like statuary.

As his eyes recovered from the flash he looked up into the night sky over the corvette. For an instant a tiny red streak showed as the shell peaked over the top of its path before plunging down.

A moment later there was a brilliant flash on the surface of the inlet, almost directly on the position of the corvette's light. It was followed by a sharp detonation and a ghostly, vertical plume of water. The flash of the burst lit the inlet and threw the sharp furrowed faces of the bluffs into stark relief for a split second.

Robinson gasped, momentarily stunned. Behind him one of the mortar crew swore incredulously.

"What in bloody hell!" burst out Edgehill.

"It's gone! Sir, the ship's gone!"

O'Brien ran forward to the inlet lip. He turned back to Robinson, his voice cracking in disbelief.

"The bastard's escapin', sir! To seaward!"

Abaft the huge mainmast timber-bitts on HBMS *Redoubtable*'s spar deck, Lieutenant William Meade stood stifling a yawn and dividing his attention between the vocal complaints of the duty boatswain's mate and the more personal mutterings of his stomach. He had missed dinner through making the arrangements for the Commodore's conference, and his innards had begun to mount a belated protest.

He had just begun a reply when the flash of an explosion caught the corner of his eye. As he swivelled to look shoreward, the dull thump of the detonation reached his ears.

The duty boatswain's mate punched one hamlike fist into the other. "Our lads, sir. They've opened fire on the Frog!"

"Yes. It would appear." Meade tugged at one of his cuffs. "Send a man below to Mister Franklin's cabin at once, and ask him to come on deck, with my compliments. And call the marine drummer."

The boatswain's mate knuckled his forehead and almost immediately collared a seaman from a jabbering knot of watchmen at the rail, sending him scuttling under the half-deck.

Franklin, *Redoubtable*'s First Lieutenant, appeared a half-minute later in shirtsleeves, hat askew, hauling on his coat as he came.

"What the devil's the matter, Meade? I was asleep!" His tone was almost petulant.

Meade grimaced slightly. For some time he had considered Franklin little better than a worthless nincompoop, and found being civil and respectful to him very tedious indeed.

"Mister Pollett's people ashore have opened fire on the Frenchmen, it appears, sir. Only one round as yet."

"What? Already? The hell you say!"

There was considerable activity around the two officers as the duty watchmen emerged from various hideaways the men habitually took to during the quiet night hours of an anchor watch. High overhead the lookouts in the tops were yelling across to one another.

Meade swore. "Master at arms! Keep those men silent! And shut the mouths of those chattering jays aloft!"

In a few moments the curses and cuffs of the master at arms and his corporals had quieted the excited seamen. Almost as the hubbub subsided a second flash winked shoreward, followed by another muffled thump. This time the flash came from high above the shoreward bluffs.

"A second round. Bloody high, though, what?" said Franklin.

"Yes, sir. Too high. I wonder what..."

The wink of Robinson's mortar was visible this time, sparking from the dark mass of the shore. Several seconds later the third shell burst, again high in the air over the inlet.

"Deck there! Deck there!" From high in the foretop one of the lookouts was shrieking down at them.

"Speak, man!" called up Meade through cupped hands.

The lookout's voice was cracking with excitement.

"A ship, sir! In the flash o' them bombs! A ship outside the inlet, makin' for sea, sir!"

"Are you sure?" Meade's hairline tickled.

"Aye, sir! It's the bloody Frenchie!"

At that instant Robinson's fourth shell burst low over the inlet, and silhouetted in the instant's glare of the shellburst Meade saw the dark shape of a ship's hull, well out from the inlet.

"Good Christ, he's right!"

A slap of feet behind him indicated the boatswain's mate had returned. Meade glanced at Franklin, but the latter was fussing with an overabundant knot of lace at his throat.

"Send below for the Commodore, Atkins, and have..." began Meade.

"That won't be necessary, Mister Meade, I am on deck. What the blazes is going on?" Fitzsimmons was in his vest and breeches.

The two junior officers raised their hats to him. Meade spoke after glancing again at Franklin, who was looking vacantly off shoreward.

"Lieutenant Robinson's mortar has opened fire, sir", he said exasperatedly. "Four rounds. The first on the surface, the rest aerial bursts. Foremast lookout reports a ship outside the inlet, standing out toward us."

"Standing out? What, under sail?"

"That's not clear, sir."

Fitzsimmons scratched his chin. "My word. Could it be? I think you'd best beat to Quarters, Mister Franklin."

"Aye, aye, sir", said Franklin, and began looking about as if he had lost a coat button.

Meade nodded to the boyish drummer, who had by this time panted up, his cap askew. "Beat To Quarters, lad."

The regular thud of the boy's drum brought an almost instantaneous response from below decks in the multi-layered bowels of the *Redoubtable*, as its familiar beat penetrated to the far corners of the ship.

Heart of oak are our ships

Heart of oak are our men.

Redoubtable's complement numbered some four hundred men and boys. Nonetheless each had a task, whether large or small, to which that drumbeat sent him. The beat had scarcely begun when the remainder of the ship's marines began falling in on the forecastle and quarterdeck, muskets at the shoulder, dressing their ranks with stiff shuffles, the brass buckles of the buff crossbelting catching the light from *Redoubtable*'s lanterns.

Lights were passing rapidly to and fro along the levels of the ship as the gunner's mates carried the heavy lanterns, or "glims" to each gun position from the storesman's tiny locker. Boys scuttled about sprinkling bucketfuls of wet sand on the decks to provide traction. The off-duty watchmen clambering up the companionways from below flung their lashed hammocks into the nettings which circled the upper deck, affording a kind of barricade. Aloft, the topmen were carrying up extra line, blocks, tackles, and tool boxes, while others were out along the lower yards, slinging them with chain lifts to prevent them from crashing disastrously to the deck during an action. Great nets were set up, slung over the upper deck to catch the falling debris from aloft which gun damage might bring.

At each gun the gun captains slung their large priming horns over their shoulders and told off men of their crews to readying the gun tools, wetting the sponges, setting up the breechings and side tackles that controlled the motions of the guns, and lighting the slow matches that hung in their notches over the match tubs. Each captain looked to his own T-shaped linstock which would hold his match, and took from the darting powder boys the leathern buckets which held the first round of paper cartridges for each gun.

To an uninitiated observer, it would have resembled a scene from some infernal mine, as the orange glow of the glims spilled over the hunched and half-naked forms of the seamen, shining off shirtless torsos glistening with sweat from their exertions, and glinting from earrings or the polished metal of the gun tools. The men bowed and served the obscene humped forms of the guns almost as supplicants to a deformed idol, a threatening picture increased by the claustrophobic lowness of the deckhead and the fierce light in the eyes of the men.

Fitzsimmons had left the gunports open and the guns run back, but set up for action. As they arrived at their respective batteries on each deck, the ship's officers gave the order to load and run out. The order was repeated by each gun captain, and the crews sprang to action. Powder charge, wad, ball, wad, the whole rammed securely at each step, then the vent primed and the handspikes taken up, ready to lay and train each gun. Already from here and there on each deck came the squeal and rumble of guns being run out, the crews straining on the side tackles. The whole of this complex effort went on with few words being spoken as the men bent to their tasks. The only voices to be heard were those of the gun captains, and occasionally, an officer.

On the upper deck, Meade touched his hat to the Commodore. "If you'll pardon me, sir, I'll tend to my guns."

"Carry on, Mister Meade, by all means."

Meade hurried below to his battery of twenty-four pound guns on the second deck. As he vanished down the companionway another mortar round exploded high in mid-air shoreward.

Franklin was calling up to the lookouts aloft, shouting to be heard over the noise of the preparations. "What can you see now?"

The reply was faint. "A ship all right, sir! Heading out... sweeps!"

Fitzsimmons peered over the rail, a frown creasing his forehead.

"My God. Can he really mean sweeps?"

Then, very faintly, against the quick flash of another burst from Robinson's mortar, the Commodore made out the dark mass of a ship. A mass that carried sticklike legs to either side, like a water beetle.

Almost simultaneously, the gun captain of the nearest quarterdeck nine-pounder pointed shoreward and called out.

"There, sir! The Frog's out there, bearin' right abeam on us, sir!"

Indeed he is, said Fitzsimmons to himself. He's come out of his hole. And the fool appears to be rowing out.

"He appears, he appears to be...ah...under oars, sir", said Franklin, beside him.

Fitzsimmons shot him a glance. "Quite", he snapped.

The Commodore sensed the air with his nose. Not a whisper of a breeze. Perhaps the fellow was not such a fool. *Redoubtable* was unable to move, while the corvette was making way toward the open sea.

Very well, he thought.

"It would appear our landing party were giving us those aerial bursts as a warning, Mister Franklin. However, we shall need to think quickly if we are not to be left empty-handed once again. Lower your boats that remain. Strip some of the gun crews to do it if you have to. I want us to be able to turn about our cable if the need arises, by spring or otherwise. And I want it soon. Do you follow?"

Franklin nodded. Fitzsimmons could see that the man was pale and was sweating profusely.

"Very well, then. Carry on, please."

Fitzsimmons sent a hovering midshipman for Meade almost as Franklin left, and the former arrived within seconds, having seen to the running out of his guns.

"Sir?"

"We appear to have a problem here, Mister Meade. The corvette is out, under sweeps, it would appear. I think that she might pass through our line within fifteen or twenty minutes if not sooner. Certainly no more than that. As the current here is putting us with the shore abeam, we must put her under fire before she can reach any of the gaps in our line."

Here Fitzsimmons pointed to *Vigilant*'s lights over the bows. "The gaps are too wide for my liking, and under these night conditions she might well break through out of gun range to seaward before we could hole her or bring down her rigging. Do you see?"

"Of course, sir", Meade nodded. "I never would have expected her to pull out, sir."

Fitzsimmons gave a small, mirthless laugh. "Nor I, Mister Meade. But there she is, and I dare say she might be managing a good two or three knots in the bargain."

Franklin reappeared. "Boats are away, sir. The kedge is being towed out in one. I gather movements in *Vigilant* and the other ships indicate they are preparing for action as well."

"Good. Saves having to fire that damned swivel. I suggest, Mister Franklin, that you stand to your boats and await my orders. In the absence of Mister Pollett I will assume command of *Redoubtable*. Have the sailing master report to me."

"Sir." Franklin's pale face was void of expression. He touched his hat perfunctorily and left.

The Commodore swung to Meade once more.

"Your battery of twenty-fours on the starboard side will be our best chance to get her, until we can swing about fully. Particuarly your forward guns, if he intends to pass between *Vigilant* and ourselves. Stand to your battery and commence on my signal, will you? I suggest as well that you load with chain or bar shot on the second and succeeding rounds. Very likely we'll be firing blindly in this damned dark!"

Meade hurried below to the lower gun deck, where he commanded the long battery of sixteen twenty-four pound guns that stretched along one hundred and sixty feet of the starboard side.

As he passed forward of the tiny enclosed gunroom to the battery, the faces of his gun crews, lit theatrically by the glims, turned expectantly his way.

"Bar and chain shot", he called, "after the first round. Captains, stand ready to fire on my signal." He drew his hanger and paced the line of guns, eyes flicking over details of the equipment and tackles.

The gun captains hefted their linstocks and blew on the smouldering matches, keeping them brightly glowing. The crews waited motionless around their guns, one or two here and there making some last minute adjustment in the placement of a tool. A few men were tying broad bandanas over their ears as a precaution against the tremendous pressures the gun blasts would put on their eardrums.

On the quarterdeck, by now fully dressed through the efforts of his fussing manservant, Fitzsimmons stood talking with the quiet and bespectacled ship's surgeon.

"Is your pit all in order, Doctor Sansom?"

"I certainly hope so, Commodore", replied Samson. "My loblollies have learned their trade fairly well, so I imagine the little lads'll have it waiting when I go below."

A slight midshipman with a choirboy's voice trotted to the Commodore and gravely raised his hat in salute.

"Mister Franklin's compliments, sir. He's encountered problems and says he'll not have the spring down under ten minutes. He says he's sorry, sir."

Fitzsimmons winced, then acknowledged the lad with a nod before turning back to Sansom.

"Good God! Ten minutes! The fellow might be clear through us by then!"

The doctor adjusted his spectacles. "Where in fact exactly is this vessel you wish to engage, sir? I'm afraid that I see nothing at all!"

Fitzsimmons waved a hand off to landward.

"In there, damn it. In there, and pulling her way out, if you can believe it, in what appears to be a try at slipping through us to the open sea."

The Commodore walked to the rail and squinted into the darkness shoreward.

"She believes we can't see her, and for the moment that's true. But she'll find we are awake, at least. And if she gives me the chance within the next few minutes, she'll feel my broadsides, by God! I'll not put chaos into His Majesty's plans in the Americas and my own bloody career because I let that minnow and her message get away!"

He spat into the sea. "Not damned likely!"

SEVEN

Ashore on the bluff overlooking the inlet, Robinson and Edgehill watched the movement of lights on the anchored English ships, and tried once again to make out the shape of *Écho*, plotting mentally her track from where the last shell burst had illuminated her.

Petty Officer O'Brien appeared at Robinson's elbow.

"That 'un was the last round, sir", he said.

Robinson sighed. "Very well, O'Brien. Tell the lads they did well. I think you'd best pack up the gear and the mortar. It'll be a difficult descent to the boats, and judging by the state of things we may have to run all the bloody way back!"

"Aye, aye, sir", said O'Brien, and hustled back to the waiting gunners. Sergeant Hall was already forming his marines into two files.

Robinson paused for a moment, and then looked at Edgehill. "Do you think it worked, sir? Do you think they saw the Frenchman coming out?"

Edgehill took off his tricorne and ran a hand over his brow. For the first time since the landing a note of strain sounded in his voice.

"Haven't the slightest, Mr. Robinson", he sighed. "Haven't the slightest."

Then he added, "God knows I certainly hope so. We have spent quite enough time pursuing that fellow!"

On *Écho*'s gun deck the effort of working the heavy sweeps was beginning to take its toll of Béssac's men. Facing forward, the line of seamen on each spar thrust it away from them, hands intertwined in the rope loops passed around each sweep, shoulders set against the wood. Then on reaching the end of the stroke they straightened, pressing the spar downward to waist level and shuffling backwards. Béssac's steady chant controlled the steady and even rowing which so far had prevented any team from becoming entangled with the next.

Even without blades, the makeshift sweeps were moving the corvette along slowly but steadily. But the work was backbreaking, and here and there men were beginning to miss steps and stagger on their feet.

Gallant slid down the companionway from the upper deck to meet Béssac's questioning look.

"How much further, enseigne? Is there no hint of a breeze? These men cannot last much longer. And what of the shooting we heard?"

Gallant shook his head. "The English know we are out. There are lights moving all over their ships. They must have managed to get a mortar or some small piece up on the bluffs. I think they were trying to alert the other ships with the last rounds."

"Mon Dieu!"

The marine went on. "The English may have seen us, but there is a chance that they cannot see us now in the darkness. In any case it's too late to worry. I'm steering us for the biggest gap in the English line."

He held up two spread hands.

"You've got to keep the sweeps going for at least ten or fifteen more minutes. If there is a breeze it'll be out past the English."

Béssac's face set into a grim expression. He nodded.

"All right. They'll do their best."

When Gallant regained the quarterdeck he pointed out to the helmsman the gap he had selected in the line of English lights.

"Là", he said in a low voice. "Just to starboard of the largest one. Steer dead on the gap!"

Gallant looked up at the night sky. Over the few minutes that *Écho* had been free of the inlet, a high cover of cloud had closed over the stars, thankfully rendering the darkness now almost total. He could barely make out the helmsman by the faint, oily light from the binnacle lamp. There'll be wind under that cloud, he thought. But how long away?

Alongside, the slow thresh of the sweeps was holding its even beat. The cook and the few men not aloft or on the sweeps stood at the rail in motionless silence, watching the rows of lights ahead draw steadily nearer. The largest gap, between the second and last ships, now bore dead ahead.

Gallant's throat was as dry as parchment. He swore under his breath, not a little in self-contempt.

Béssac's voice at his elbow startled him.

"Well, enseigne, we will know in a few moments if they know where we are, eh?"

"How can't they?" Gallant laughed briefly, and without any humour. "Sweet Virgin! You think we can actually hope to get through them? Splashing along like this?"

The mate laughed. "Tiens! You needn't be so pessimistic. We have no choice now in any case, n'est-ce pas?" He shrugged. "They may not have seen us in the shell flashes. I am afraid that will give us away, as much as the noise we are making!"

Béssac pointed toward the water. Each stroke of the sweeps lit glimmering pools of blue-white phosphorescence that sparkled and then faded into a glowing path astern of each line of sweeps. With no star or moonlight, and the corvette's own lights extinguished, the eerie glow seemed to be of almost beacon strength.

Béssac spat manfully over the rail.

"We'll be under that largest Englishman's bows in five minutes, not more", he said.

Gallant found it difficult to think of a reply. His hands felt cold and clammy. The lights of the last British ship already seemed to be looming far above the corvette's bows. The only thought that seemed to have any form in his mind was the feeling of drifting into the coils of a great, glowing snake.

Suddenly the night was split by a fiercely bright ripple of flashes along the line of the largest vessel's lights, and Gallant's chest felt the hard, punching concussions of heavy gunfire, accompanied by an unbelievably loud banging. Before the marine could move, a low howl filled the air, followed by a tremendous splash that leaped up on *Écho*'s larboard side, spattering Gallant and the others on the quarterdeck with a shower of spray.

Gallant wiped the back of his hand across his mouth.

"They've begun!" He turned to the helmsman, who was crouching behind the wheel. "Stand up, stand up! Steer five points to larboard!"

A second ripple of flashes leaped out from the English line, and again the painful concussions thumped into Gallant with the force of physical blows. The hideous low moan sounded in the air again, but now also came a shock to the deck below the marine's feet, and a splintering crunch. Something ripped at his arm, and the belaying pin he had been holding vanished from his grasp. The air was suddenly full of the noise of falling blocks, groaning rigging, and the clang of metal.

Then to his ears came a spine-chilling sound, like nothing he had ever heard, except perhaps the scream of a rabbit at death. It came from the gun deck.

Béssac's resonant voice pierced the cacophony. "The first blood! They've drawn first blood!"

Perilly suddenly materialized out of the gloom forward. He wiped a sweaty face with one sleeve.

"Enseigne, we've lost the mizzen topsail yard. Most of the shot is going high, thank the Virgin! The mizzen topmast seems to be untouched. Wreckage went right over the side."

"And from below? What of the men below?"

"I don't know, sir."

"All right. We'll need to rig a new yard."

Perilly shook his head. "Very little I can do in this dark, m'sieu'."

Gallant turned on him savagely.

"I know, damn you! Don't you think I know that?" Then, catching himself, he said, "For God's sake do what you can."

The marine found himself suddenly calm. A portion of him seemed detached and remote, and he was looking at the deadly rows of English lights with an icy clarity. He felt sure that he would die.

The next broadside came a split second later, and by a seeming miracle no rending blows smashed into the corvette. The low moaning, which Gallant realized with a start was the sound of the English shot passing overhead, brought no quivering shock of impact and the crash of falling wreckage. The ghastly screaming from below decks had faded, and ahead the bows were continuing to turn.

Gallant moved to the rail and looked at the glowing swirls around the sweeps. The spars still lifted and dipped, slower now, more uneven. But they still threshed, and the corvette continued to slide toward the gap.

There might be a margin of hope yet. He swung to face toward the helmsman.

In a terrifying sequence which lasted no more than a few seconds, but which Gallant would always remember as an eternity, a ragged broadside burst from the second English ship on the far side of the gap, as he spun on his heel.

In the flickering gun flashes that lit the corvette's deck Gallant saw Perilly's head vanish as if by magic, the dark blood pulsing out in a jet from the trunk as it collapsed loosely forward on the deck. As it fell, a seaman standing next to him was slapped violently backwards against the mizzenmist foot as if by a great hand, and sprawled sideways to the deck, his arms flailing limply.

Gallant felt bile, burning and bitter, surge into his throat. In the next split-second, while the nightmarish image was still seared into his brain, Gallant was stunned by a white light that exploded in his head, and he felt himself being lifted and tossed like a rag doll across Perilly's outstretched legs into the quarterdeck scuppers. In the instant before blackness swallowed him he realized that the low moaning of the shot reminded him of something.

Bees, he thought. Huge, cruising bumblebees.

"Gallant! For God's sake wake up, enseigne!"

Béssac's voice penetrated the fog in his brain. His eyes snapped open. His head was ringing like an anvil under a smith's hammer.

He tried to sit up and gasped at the lancet of pain that shot through his head. Béssac was fumbling with some sort of bandage on his head, and an exploring hand Gallant put up came away with something hot and sticky. His mouth was fouled with bile, and he felt worse than he had ever felt in his life before.

"You've taken a splinter, enseigne", said the mate. "Not too serious. This will staunch it up." Béssac's voice was low and rasping.

Gallant peered into the gloom around him, hearing now the cries and shrieks of wounded men, the clatter and crash of wreckage being chopped free and flung aside.

Then he remember that ghastly scene in the gun flashes.

"Perilly!"

Béssac's powerful hand gripped his shoulder. "Perilly's dead. Let me finish this, will you? The English will be firing again any moment!"

Gallant's head whirled, and he felt weak and sick from the pain of his wound.

"Are we still underway?" he said with difficulty.

"Yes. Barely. The casualties are everywhere."

The marine struggled to sit upright. He caught Béssac by the arm as the world canted crazily before his eyes.

The flashes of the English guns lit the night again, the crash of the reports seemingly only a few feet away. Even as the concussions punched into them, Gallant and the mate were crouching low to the deck. Again the howl of a shot. Again the thunderclap of a ball striking home and the rending crashes that followed.

And more screams.

Béssac started to his feet. "They're killing my ship!" His voice was hoarse and full of rage.

Gallant grabbed at the burly mate in a vain attempt to restrain him, but was thrown off with a push of the thick muscled arms. Béssac shook a fist toward the winking tongues of flame, oblivious to the noise of the guns, the howling shot, and the repetitive crashes and splinterings going on around them.

A quick, hot gust of air hit the two men. In the next instant the night was transformed into brilliant day. A huge fireball, its billowing mushroom form laced with black, sprang into being where a moment ago the second English vessel's broadsides had been vomiting death at *Écho*. With a roar the shock wave of the blast slammed into the little corvette, snatching the breath from the astonished men and thrusting them back as if from a physical blow. Slowly the great ball of flame rose and faded into the inky night sky.

All around him, his ears still ringing from the sound of the blast, Gallant heard bits of wreckage splashing into the sea, some thumping and clanging on to *Écho*'s decks. Bits of burning fabric and wood drifted down, leaving little glowing paths as they fell.

The English guns were silent.

"Béssac! Sweet Mary, she blew up!" She must have blown her magazine!" cried Gallant.

Béssac was standing with his mouth ajar. Behind them Gallant could hear Bédard, the helmsman, still clinging to his wheel, muttering in a low stream of curses.

Almost like water thrown on a fogged windowpane, Gallant's mind suddenly flashed into clarity.

"That's it, Béssac! There!" He pointed over the rail. "Through there, where she lay! The Englishman that exploded, man!"

Béssac seemed stunned, immobile.

Gallant felt a reckless savagery course through him, and he seized the burly mate's shirt front, shouting at him.

"The sweeps, Béssac! Get them going again! We'll go through there!"

"But the English!"

"The English are not firing, can't you see? They must be dazed, or damaged, or simply even stupid, but they're not firing! We've got to get underway!" He shook the big mate, like a terrier with an oversized rat.

Something seemed to fall into place inside Béssac. With an assertive grunt he made for the companionway leading below.

Gallant wavered on his feet, and put a hand to his brow. The pain in his temple almost made him retch once more, and he gritted his teeth, fighting the nausea back.

He turned and felt his way aft to the wheel, where Bédard still stood gripping the spokes. The deck was littered with pieces of debris and rigging, and once his toe thudded into something soft and yielding. He shuddered involuntarily and pressed on.

Below, he could hear Béssac's baritone rising now above the cries of the wounded and the noise of clearing away the wreckage. There seemed to be men forward on the upper deck, helping the wounded below, working to clear wreckage away. In the dark it was hard to tell.

Bédard was looking at him wordlessly, his face a pale spectre in the gloom.

Gallant swallowed and forced a calm tone to his voice. "Can you hold her, matelot?"

"As firm as a Toulon trollop, m'sieu'", said the man. His voice was shaky, but there was a determined note in it.

"Good. See the gap in the English lights? Where the blast took place? You'll steer for that as soon as we get underway again. Cleár?"

Gallant licked his cracked, dry lips. God, he was thirsty.

A mute nod from Bédard.

"Good."

Gallant's heart was pounding against his ribs, and his eardrums hummed in the stillness. Why the devil were the English not firing? A good two minutes had passed since the explosion, and the English broadsides had not resumed. Dead in the water as *Écho* was at that moment, she would have been a doomed ship at this range, even given the darkness.

The marine suddenly noticed that a few feet in front of him, Perilly's headless trunk lay in a widening inky pool on the planking. It seemed such an abominable waste, and such an absurd one.

He swore. If only the ship would move!

A slap of bare feet behind him spun him round to face a panting seaman whose hands were swathed in bloody bandages.

"M'sieu' Béssac says to steer, enseigne. He says the sweeps will move again now."

"Thank God!" breathed Gallant.

Even as he spoke, the marine heard Béssac's voice launch into a rolling cadence, punctuated by oaths and encouragements. Unevenly, the sweeps swung outboard from where they had trailed in disarray against the ship's side and began to thrash the black water. Gallant felt the deck move under his feet.

"Steerageway, enseinge!" Bédard's voice was stronger now, as if the motion of the ship had given him renewed strength.

"Bon. Now steer for that damned gap!" Gallant's hand brushed by accident against his bandage, and he clutched at the rail for a moment until the weakness and nausea passed.

Now the sweeps were lifting and falling regularly, setting the phosphorescence twinkling, the shuffling of the men's feet and the squeal and thump of the makeshift locks carrying up to Gallant's ears. *Écho*'s bowsprit swung toward the gap in the English line, and the corvette slowly began to glide forward through the darkness again.

The stout, aproned figure of Guimond appeared up the ladder from the waist, and the carpenter knuckled his brow to Gallant.

"If you please, m'sieu', with Perilly dead I undertook to clear away the wreckage and the wounded. Is M'sieu' Béssac killed as well?"

"No, Guimond. He's below, with the sweeps." He looked keenly at the man, and felt a part of him ease with relief, even in the midst of their danger. Thank God the carpenter had taken the initiative he had, as an unspeakable chaos would have resulted otherwise. Even now groups of men were moving swiftly around the corvette, feverishly chopping at the trailing remains of the mizzed topsailyard's rigging, flinging debris over the side, and carrying the pathetic forms of the wounded men below.

The carpenter grunted and turned to go. Then he looked back at Gallant.

"I was a boatswain in l'*Affriquain*, enseigne. I can handle it. You and M'sieu' Béssac just get us out of all this!"

Gallant looked for a moment at the carpenter's retreating back. God knows if we will manage that, he thought.

The lights of the English loomed so near that Gallant believed he could hear the shouts and tumult of frantic activity aboard the largest ship.

Activity that included the unmistakable sound of the clicking pawls of an anchor capstan.

Guimond's voice boomed out of the darkness forward.

"Enseigne! The English are warping around! They can't get us over their bows, so they're trying to warp around!"

Gallant leaped to the forward quarterdeck rail and shouted down toward the open companionway leading to the gun deck.

"Faster, Béssac! We've got to move faster!"

Gallant looked up, and a chill ran down his spine. A break had opened in the cloud cover overhead, and in the dim starlight he could see the great canted arm of *Redoubtable*'s bowsprit looming high above the larboard bow. They were passing dangerously close aboard her, and the huge sprit might foul in their rigging as they passed.

The marine moved quickly back beside the helm.

"Starboard two points! Another! Steady on that, or we'll ram!"

Bédard grunted with exertion as he spun the broad oaken wheel, his hands slapping on the spokes. "I have her, enseigne!"

Gallant's heart was pounding so furiously in his chest he wondered if he could bear the tension much longer. If the English opened fire now...

The noise of activity from the towering black hulk of the English sixty-four was clearly audible over the thrash of *Écho*'s sweeps. Voices shouting orders.

And the ominous squeal and rumble of gun trucks.

"Sweet Jesus", whispered Gallant. They were almost at point-blank range.

Écho's bows, a small white ripple showing beneath her canted cutwater, were now only a scant hundred yards from the Englishman. Gallant closed his eyes. In the next moment or two it would be all over. The English shot would sweep like a storm over the corvette, shattering the ship and mangling their bodies, ending the whole affair in a screaming bloody chaos.

Gallant's nostrils tingled at a sharp, overpowering stench of gunsmoke. He opened his eyes.

Écho was enveloped in a thick, stinking miasma that blotted out every vestige of light. The cloud reeked of gunpowder, but of other things as well. Scorched wood and cordage. Burnt canvas. Bilge stench, oil, and heat-scorched tar. And the sickening aroma of burnt flesh.

Bédard's voice whispered beside him. "Holy Mother of God, what is it?"

"The cloud, Bédard. The cloud from the explosion! It didn't dissipate! There's no wind to break it up!"

Écho's sweeps maintained their steady beat. Through the blackness Gallant could hear shouts and calls from the English ship. The corvette was not only completely hidden from whatever light there might have been, but the cloud would muffle the sounds of her passage, making it difficult for the straining ears of the Englishmen to locate its direction. They might break through to seaward yet!

Gallant stood close beside Bédard.

"Careful, now. Make as few corrections as possible. We mustn't lost a point to either side until we get clear of this!" His voice was low, as he made an effort to control the racing excitement within him.

Bédard nodded. He was breathing heavily.

A dim flash lit the darkness off to their left, and the ear-jarring bang of a twenty-four pound gun firing very near slapped at them. Gallant winced, bracing himself for the smashing impact of the shot.

From somewhere astern he heard the shot splash into the sea, and heard the shouts of the English gun captain, the squeal of another gun's trucks as it was run out. He bit his lip. They were firing blindly into the dark, which gave them an even better chance for survival.

Gallant started as Béssac materialized again without warning beside him.

"Sweet Blood of Christ, enseigne, this is a godsend!" he whispered hoarsely.

The marine rubbed his brow. "Béssac, how much longer can those men of yours row?"

"Hah! Five minutes. Maybe less. They're ready to drop where they stand."

Gallant swore as another round from the English vessel shattered the night, making him flinch involuntarily.

"Somehow, you've got to keep them at it. The English are feeling for us with ranging shots, and I think we must have already slipped past their bows. We've got to get out of gun range to seaward before this cloud disperses!"

The mate spat. "They need rest!"

Gallant slapped the rail with frustration. Around them, Guimond's work party had stopped in their tracks, mesmerized by the thick, eerie cloud that enveloped them. The steady slosh of the sweeps still sounded alongside.

Gallant turned back to the mate, fighting for self-control. "If we can…"

Béssac put a tarry palm on his shoulder. "Wait!"

"What?"

"Wait, please, enseigne!" Béssac was tense and breathless, as if he were straining to hear a distant tune.

"Béssac!"

The mate grabbed his arms. "There! You feel it? You feel it?"

Gallant shook his head, then stiffened.

A tickle of wind on his cheek. A faint, delicate coolness, settling in over *Écho*'s stern.

"Sweet Christ, please!" breathed Béssac.

Gallant's hairline prickled. Now the coolness was stronger, more distinct.

"Béssac! Make sail! We've got to make sail! This'll carry us right out!"

Gallant cupped his hands, shouting forward.

"Guimond! Do you hear, there!"

The startled carpenter appeared out of the dark.

"Enseigne?"

"Delay that work you're doing. Get those men below up on deck. Cut the sweeps free any way you can. Jettison them if necessary. We're going to make sail!"

Gallant turned to Béssac and swallowed hard. Now came the plunge.

"Vite, Béssac. Headsails and topsails!"

Béssac flashed a grin, gleaming and animal in the dark.

"Oui, enseigne!"

Within the instant Béssac's voice was propelling men up the ratlines. The exhausted men who had driven the sweeps staggered on deck only to be hustled aloft, the mate's appalling blasphemies ringing in their ears.

Gallant found himself rapidly pacing the quarterdeck, his hands clenched behind him, watching the gloom lifting and details becoming visible in the starlight. He tried to avoid thinking what might happen if he made one slip, gave one stupid or fatal order.

"Loose topsails!"

High overhead, the men inched out along the footropes and cast off the stops on the furled canvas which was tightly clenched to the topsail yards. Released to the force of gravity, the mighty sheets of canvas dropped with a crack and bellied almost at once to the gentle breeze from astern. Gallant heard as if in a dream the rigging creak to the first pressures from aloft, and felt the deck cant slightly beneath his feet.

Off the larboard quarter, a series of rippling flashes split the gloom, followed by the roar of a broadside. The English must have known *Écho* had slipped through the gap, and were firing now to seaward.

Gallant tensed, then shook his head in thankful wonder. Not a hit. Not even the splash of a near miss.

Then he realized that the English were still firing blindly. The gradually fading cloud of smoke was being driven along with the corvette out to sea, cloaking their motion still.

The wind was freshening rapidly. Water gurgled and rushed along the corvette's counter, and she began to roll slightly.

"Loose headsails!" called Gallant.

The pale triangles of jib topsail, jib and foretopmast staysail rose like spectres up the stays to the steady, rhythmic hauling of the men at the halyards. Gallant felt the ship shudder beneath him, as if a quiver of excitement passed through it.

"Course to steer, enseigne?" said the helmsman.

"Steady as she goes for the moment, Bédard. Just watch the leeches, if you can see them. I want her to draw every cup of wind she can!"

Bédard grinned. "Oui, enseigne!"

Béssac's voice carried aft from where he was seeing to the trim of the topsail and headsail sheets. It suddenly rose in volume.

"Enseigne! We're breaking out of the cloud!"

In the next minute the slowly accelerating *Écho* moved clear of the cloud of reeking smoke from the explosion out into a star-filled night. Low on the eastern horizon, off the larboard bow, a beet-red moon hung bloatedly above a band of glowing copper running across the sea toward the ship

Gallant swung round. Astern he could make out the humped outline of the coast, and closer, the grey mass of the slowly dispersing cloud. Of the English anchor lights, three or four were visible.

A cry came from the maintop lookout. "Deck there! The English are making sail!"

The marine ran up the slope of the quarterdeck and peered aft past the broad gilt face of the stern lantern. Yes. The lights were moving. The English had hove short, broken out their anchors, and made sail in very short order indeed. The chase was on again in earnest.

The wind had been freshening all the while, and Gallant's eyes caught the small white flashes of the first breaking crests on the sea. Below him the rudder thumped and creaked in its gudgeons.

He turned forward. "Béssac!"

The mate appeared beside the mainmast fiferail.

"Can you put the courses and topgallants on her?"

"Bien sûr! She'll carry them easily, enseigne!"

"Very well", said Gallant. "And we'd best put two men on the helm, eh?"

"He's already on his way M'sieu'!" Almost as Gallant turned to look shoreward again, the second helmsman was arriving to join Bédard, and men were scrambling aloft.

Gallant smiled. Béssac knew his ship well.

He glanced up. The wind was steadily rising, and he spread his feet to steady himself. There was no way of knowing how long the corvette could carry on without reefs. They would have to push the little ship to its limit.

Bédard and the other helmsman were elbowing each other and grinning. Gallant noticed that happier voices sounded here and there among the men, even the exhausted rowers from the sweeps. A spirit came over a vessel released from the land and once more at sea.

Gallant sighed. His muscles ached with tension, and he suddenly felt terribly tired. The thought of his cot in the small and airless cabin swam through his mind, and he shook it off.

The loss of the mizzen topgallant yard had not seemed to affect the speed of the ship too greatly, and *Écho* was moving lightfootedly before a good quartering wind, boring out to the southward. The corvette was rolling in a gentle corkscrewing motion as the steadily growing swells caught her fine on one quarter and boiled past her. As the stern rose Bédard put the helm up slightly to counter the broaching motion. Then, as the ship sank into the trough, he would spin the wheel back to catch the yaw to the other side. This he did again and again, endlessly, in a beautifully controlled meld of man and vessel. Aloft, the taut bellies of the sails were warmed with peach-coloured tints from the rising moon.

Béssac looked for a long while shoreward, listening to the sea sounds, before speaking.

"We have a good start on them, enseigne. It'll be daylight before we have to worry about them, if this wind holds."

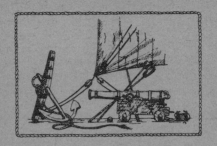

EIGHT

Gallant awoke with a start, a metallic taste in his mouth and his eyes smarting as if from driven sand. For a baffling instant he had no idea where he was.

"Enseigne! Wake up, m'sieu'!" Béssac was bending over him, his voice hoarse, his hand shaking Gallant's shoulder, his face thrown into high shadow by a small lamp in his other hand.

"Yes, yes, Béssac, enough!" said Gallant testily. "I'm awake!" It seemed to the marine that this had all happened before. He sat up and rubbed his face, trying to clear the fog. His clothes were still damp, and smelled like a sodden dog. He felt utterly ghastly. "What in God's name is it?"

"It's morning, enseigne."

"What!" The fog vanished immediately.

"I managed to keep us out of gun range of the English all night. But they've closed the gap now!"

Gallant swung his legs over the edge of the cot, feeling for his shoes. "What the devil did you mean by letting me...?"

"You were like death, enseigne. No one could have wakened you."

130

The shoes were clammy and heavy. Gallant swore.

Béssac went on. "You'd best come on deck, enseigne. I took us into the African coast for shelter, and I think we've found that shelter, if I've planned rightly. But there's something else..."

Gallant could hardly believe his ears. What had the man done? Were they trapped in some dusty cove awaiting hordes of marines rowing in to get them? He was wild to get up on deck.

"When did you bring us here?" he cried, ducking out the cabin door.

"Last night, enseigne. We had no choice, eh?"

"What do you mean?"

Béssac spread his hands. "After I relieved you the wind increased and the English spread more sail. With that damaged mizzen we don't have our usual turn of speed. So I had to do everything to lighten us. Everything went over the side. Even our sea chests."

Gallant paled for a moment until a pat on his stomach reassured him that the despatch was safe in its belt around his waist.

"Everything?"

"Almost", said Béssac. "I kept a gun and some powder and shot. You never know."

"What course did you steer?"

"I just kept her on a dead run, enseigne. Anything else and the English would've run us down. Besides, I had reasons for taking us in here."

Gallant shook his head. "Sweet Christ! Africa!"

"It saved us, enseigne!" Béssac's shoes thudded after his up the companion ladder.

Gallant scrambled out on deck and became immobile. He was thunderstruck at what he saw about him.

"What in the name of God!" His voice trailed away.

Écho lay rolling slightly in a light swell, the blocks aloft and the slack canvas slatting and banging to and fro. They were a short distance off a sunbleached, rocky coast, its heights looming uncomfortably near in the hazy morning sunlight. But the shoreline was not what sent a shudder along Gallant's spine.

"They're Moors, enseigne", said Béssac quietly. "Algerines. This is the Barbary Coast."

From where Gallant stood with the mate on the quarterdeck there seemed to be at least twenty fleet-looking, oared gunboats closing in on the corvette. They were long, low craft, the single black muzzle of what appeared to be a twelve- or eighteen-pound gun gaping above each boat's bows. Amidships there were four rows of oarsmen, their heads either shaven or bound with multi-coloured scarves, the bodies glistening as they bent and strained in swift unison on the oars which lifted and flashed in the sunlight. In the stern, above raised platforms, enormous blue and green banners streamed from tall staffs, banners bearing gleaming silver crescents. Under those banners stood knots of heavily-armed men, many bare to the waist. On their heads were large, pumpkin-shaped turbans surmounted in front with long feathers and twinkling with jewellery. Their faces were dark and fierce, and many of the men wore broad, upcurving moustaches. About their waists the men wore wide sashes of red, gold, purple or white, into which wicked-looking daggers were thrust, and here and there a heavy pistol. On their legs they wore billowing pantaloons, which for the most part were of a brilliant scarlet. Their feet were either bare or shod in soft boots whose toes curled up peculiarly. Sunlight glinted from the curved blades of the swords the men carried loosely in their hands.

Gallant finally found his tongue. "Béssac, have you gone mad?" he growled. "You've sentenced us to death!"

"Not just yet, enseigne", replied the mate, with a cryptic smile. "Watch and see."

The mass of boats was parting, and the larger body turning past *Écho* toward the English vessels behind her, which Gallant now saw for the first time since coming on deck.

Béssac spat over the side. "Hmph! I knew the English would not be anxious to take on those gunboats. They're putting about!"

Gallant was looking aft. The pursuing Englishmen had uncomfortably closed the gap during the night's chase and were now just over a half-league astern. The big sixty-four and its smaller consorts were wearing round gradually to the northeast, turning their flanks to the corvette. Béssac evidently was right. They had given up the chase for the moment.

Gallant tugged at his neckcloth, which rasped on his unshaven chin. He eyed the approaching gunboats apprehensively. "Béssac, I hope to God's glory that you know what you're doing. The English seem to be doing the most sensible thing for my money!"

The mate shrugged. "I think the little banner I've hoisted may help us, enseigne", he said, jabbing a thumb heavenward. "I think we'll be all right. I've got to make sure I get a message through to the Dey, the ruler here. That's all."

"That's all? And if we can't?"

"Simple, enseigne", said Béssac, walking forward. "We get our throats cut!"

Gallant scarcely heard him calling to the topmen, ordering the clewing up of the courses. He squinted aloft at Béssac's banner, but could only make out a limp blue rag with odd markings in white, like aimless scrawls. He looked at the rocky coast behind the approaching boats, his heart beating harder than he would have liked. Where was this place?

Écho was footing ahead slowly, and Béssac came aft again, looking calm and unruffled. "Look there." He pointed inward toward the scene which was slowly appearing beyond a headland.

"Islands", said Gallant. "There appears to be a bay or harbour with islands in the middle. And is that a city behind?"

The mate nodded. "The islands give the place its name. *Al-Jazair*. We call it Algiers. In the old days the Moors had those rocks thick with guns to protect the harbour. Probably still do. There's a jetty that joins 'em to the shore."

The captain of the foretop hailed down. "Lead gunboat's about a cable off, messieurs!"

Gallant watched the gunboats, which were closing in now on the corvette's bows. Their oar blades were slowing. The men on the platforms were staring at *Écho*, pointing with their swords at Béssac's little banner.

The men of *Écho* were tense and silent, looking anxiously aft at Gallant and the mate. The marine was trying to look calm and found himself wondering if Béssac's assurances were going to be the last thoughts he had as a Moorish scimitar cut into his skull.

The nearest Moor boat suddenly held water with both banks of oars, the foam gleaming whitely around it as it stopped its progress. Then, as one bank of oars held water, several sharp strokes on the other side in response to a bark from one of the afterdeck men swung the gunboat broadside to *Écho*.

Gallant touched Béssac's elbow. "What's he doing?"

"Sign of wanting to speak. He's shown his flank as a salute."

Écho was barely making way now, her sails hanging with scarcely a motion. The men aloft in the tops and on the yards were motionless, as watchfully still as the men below on deck, their eyes on the Moorish boats. One by one the latter ceased rowing so to not overtake the lead vessel.

A tall Moor in brilliant scarlet pantaloons and turban stepped forward from the group on the lead boat's afterdeck, cupping his hands. His voice carried clear and ringing across the oily, undulating water.

"La illa ha il Allàh!"

Gallant whispered at Béssac. "Do you know what he's saying?"

"Yes. It's Arabic. You might say it's sort of a challenge. We must give the right reply," said the mate through his teeth.

Béssac called back, flinging his arms wide.

"Rasulahu! Mah'met resul Allah! Nah'noo Ashaab!"

Gallant started. A broad grin had split the face below the scarlet turban. The men standing around him had raised their arms over their heads and given a short, barking shout. Gallant noticed that the other craft stopped their progress out toward the English vessels and turned back as the shout carried to them. Several of the other boat crews were echoing the shouts.

The marine looked sharply at Béssac, appreciation in his eyes. "All right, Béssac. Just what in Hades did you say?"

"Very little, really", said the mate, with a shrug. "They made the Universal Call, that there is no God but Allah. I replied as any good Moslem would, saying Mohammed is his Prophet. And I said we were friends in the bargain.''

The red turban was gesturing shoreward, toward the harbour. It was obvious *Écho* would have to work in and anchor. Not that they had any choice, thought Gallant.

The oars were dipping again, and as the corvette glided slowly into a broad half-moon bay, curving to a distant headland, the gunboats were ranging themselves all about her. Gallant was fascinated by the glitter and colour of the crews' dress and the disciplined rhythm of the barebacked oarsmen.

''Those are no mob, are they, Béssac'', said Gallant to the mate, pointing at the gunboats.

Béssac clucked his tongue. ''Ho! You can be certain of that, enseigne!'' He cocked a thumb toward the distant English. ''The English, no less than we, know that. As long as we can get in and anchor, there'll be little chance they'll try and get in to get us. If I can get some kind of message to the Dey, I hope we'll get a sanctuary.''

Gallant added another note of astonishment to his appreciation of his mate. ''Where did you meet the man, this 'Dey'? And how did you pick up Arabic, of all things?''

A shake of the shaggy head. ''I'd best not start the tale now, m'sieu'. Too long in the telling. Besides, we must get to anchor.''

Gallant sighed. The mate proved in each new crisis to be an ever more surprising character, and an unpredictable one, for all his sturdy outward simplicity. ''Yes, all right. I suppose you know where the anchorage would be, as well?''

''Yes. I anchored here five years ago or so. That leading boat captain is pointing that way. There. Just to the right of those two tartans.''

''Two what?''

''The ships with the big lateen mains'ls. It'll be about a half-cable off the nearest tip of the outer island.''

With the wind weak but steady from astern, they were running gently into the anchorage with little effort. There should be enough way on to swing into the wind before we drop anchor, thought Gallant. They were about fifteen minutes from the point Béssac had indicated.

"I think we should take in the t' gallants as well, don't you, Béssac? You know this anchorage, but it seems to me we'd be better to take in sail now. Give ourselves more time to think our way in, eh?"

Béssac grinned. "You're right, enseigne."

As Béssac's orders began booming out Gallant was surprised to see the gunboats veering off, all except for that bearing the brilliant turban. It had dropped back into the corvette's wake and was pulling slowly along some hundred yards astern. The corvette had rounded the western headland of the great bay as the gunboats had converged on her. Now she was sliding into the calm, glassy waters inside, the bay appearing to be almost perfectly circular. On the eastern and distant southern shores of the crescent Gallant could see the white gleam of scattered buildings, and low white-washed walls above which clumps of palm rose. But this paled compared with the breathtaking view on the western and southwestern curve of the bay.

Here, rising from the shoreline behind the low islands they bore on was a broad triangle of dazzling white terraces, set over with domed or flatroofed buildings clustered in an intricate maze up the slopes of green hills. From here and there amidst the pale mass of the city the tall spires of what Gallant later learned were minarets rose like ivory fingers into the sky. The city seemed widest along the shoreline, where a series of long quays and jetties were packed with every conceivable form of Arab sailing craft, whose names Gallant would come to know in later years: the *tartans*, and *dhows*, *sambuks*, *feluccas*, and a strangely shaped but ubiquitous little lugger. From the harbour edge the city narrowed as it rose to the apex of the triangle up the hill slopes, to a massive and intricate assembly of buildings and spires that appeared to crown the entire city.

"That's the *kasbah*, up there", said Béssac unexpectedly at his elbow. "And see that largest peak in behind? The central one? That's *Djebel Bouzarea*. All those hills are known as the *Sahel*, or part of it. They run parallel to the seacoast all along here."

Gallant remarked to himself on the beauty of the place. The *Sahel* hills were mantled with a light, hot haze that turned their grey-green bulk into watered shades of purple and orange. A shimmer of heat hovered over the city itself, although the air was not that hot on Gallant's face. The fairylike spines of the minarets and the terraces and domes below them seemed to float lightly above the hillsides. Before the masses of brightly painted hulls that crowded the docksides Gallant could see several craft making sail in the gentle wind out of the bay, the winglike lateen sails dwarfing the low hulls, the worn canvas glowing with an odd luminosity in the strange light.

The city was walled, and along the coast roads in either direction Gallant could see neat cultivated fields and groves, the white dots of moving figures, and here and there a dusty cloud marking the passsage of horsemen or a group of carts.

In spite of his apprehension Gallant could not deny a certain feeling of anticipation. Algiers and the Barbary Coast were so entirely foreign to his experience that he found himself impatient to get ashore. Then he remembered rather abruptly that there was still no guarantee that they would get ashore without slit throats.

To seaward the English vessels were well out toward the indistinct, hazy line of the horizon. The sea out there was almost colourless, so that it was hard to tell where the pale brilliance of the sky blended into the flat, unruffled water surface, which was of almost the same colour. The three ships themselves were masked by the low-lying haze, so that they appeared like watercolour sketches faded and bleached by sunlight until they were a pale, somewhat unreal shadow of themselves. They were almost two leagues away now, sails hanging flat and listless in the near calm.

Béssac reappeared from forward, scratching a vermin bite under one arm. The glare off the sea, the distant city and the myriad points of metal about the ship had narrowed his eyes to tight slits.

"About five minutes to anchorage, enseigne."

"Good", said Gallant. "I suggest we clew up all but the foretops'l. We may not have to bring round into the wind after all."

Écho moved silently now, the fluid ripples under her bows

in the still sea gurgling softly. Gallant began now to notice the full intensity of the heat as land air began to reach them. He felt his coat. It was almost bone dry.

The islands were quite near now, and Béssac had not been mistaken about the Moorish gun positions. From embrasures set deep into heavy stone walls the dark snouts of bronze long guns gaped seaward toward the ship. The whole outer face of the nearest island seemed honeycombed with similar gunsites. What a deathtrap this harbour would be for a becalmed ship, Gallant thought. He whistled softly through his teeth.

Bédard had appeared to take the wheel. As Gallant paced slowly aft again, looking at the gunboat pulling along slowly astern, the young man caught his eye, knuckling his brow.

"Your pardon, enseigne?" said the young man hesitantly. "Are we to go into a Moorish prison? The men were wondering."

Gallant looked at him, feeling sympathy for his worry. "There's no talk of prisons yet, Bédard. We hope to find sanctuary here for a time. It was this or the guns of the English sixty-four." He smiled as sincerely as he could. "We'll come out of this all right."

Bédard thanked him, looking at least partially relieved. The man's concern was certainly understandable, thought Gallant. If my officers had sailed me into a Moorish port unannounced I'd have thought they'd lost their minds!

Béssac came aft again, his eyes fixed on the trailing gunboat.

"More messages from the children of Allah, the All-Seeing", he muttered as he passed Gallant.

Red turban was jabbing shoreward with his scimitar, the blade gleaming evilly in the sunlight. He was shouting as the gunboat pulled up close under *Écho*'s counter.

"Ut'hul min hinah! Ut'hul min hinah!" His voice rang out powerfully over the splash of the oars and the rowers' low chant.

Béssac nodded, showing an enormous theatrical grin. Gallant, who was now standing beside him, contorted his own face into a smile and casually asked through clenched teeth, "What now?"

"Nothing, really. He seems to want us to land over there, at the centre of the dock area. I'd say near that big Egyptian *dhow* alongside there."

The gunboat sheered off, bearing its load of resplendent ruffians shoreward. Gallant watched them move off with respect in his mind. The Moorish craft in numbers would be a formidable foe in calm seas. One error in gunnery and a European ship would be at bay surrounded by agile little craft disgorging hordes of fanatic boarders. Gallant felt an involuntary shiver at the thought. Somehow there had been an aura of cruelty about the dark expressions of the gunboat men. A struggle with them would be a ruthless one, and to the death.

"The *'dhow'*, as you call it. How do you know she's Egyptian?"

"Her prow", said Béssac. "A big angled stempost, like a Persian Gulfer. The Egyptians like that hull."

Gallant scratched at the stubble on his chin. He was willing to take Béssac's word for it.

The bow lookout called aft. "Coming up on the anchorage marks, messieurs!"

"Very well." Gallant looked at the mate. "What marks?"

Béssac, who had fished out his pipe, jabbed it off to either side. "There. And there. Keep the guerite on the island's centre bastion dead abeam, and those two minarets in line with that double dome and the big building up the slope more or less in transit."

"More or less?"

Béssac shrugged, a thing he did often and eloquently. "Very little tide here, enseigne. Good gravel bottom. All you need." He looked forward, stuffing his pipe, again unlit, into his pocket. "Actually, we're about a hundred feet off it. Time to do it."

"You're the expert on this place. Perhaps..." Gallant began, but Béssac was already halfway down to the waist.

Through cupped hands Gallant ordered the remaining canvas clewed up. Even as the sails crumpled up to the yards, the anchor party were busy forward. Béssac paused a moment, watched the marks line themselves up, then barked an order.

The heavy anchor dropped with a splash into the sea, and as the hawser paid out through its port in the eyes of the ship the corvette swung gently to its cable, its progress stopped. Within a few minutes the hands aloft had finished furling and stopping the canvas, and were slithering down lines and stays to the deck to join their fellows in gazing with some awe at the scene ashore. It was not lost on them that they were anchored in the home grounds of some of Christendom's most pitiless and feared enemies.

Gallant took off his hat and experimentally touched his bandage again, only to have it peel off in his hand. The wound's scab was small, and he decided to leave it exposed to the air.

Béssac came aft again, squinting at his anchor marks as Gallant tossed the bandage over the rail.

"Well, then", said Gallant. "Here we are more or less anchored in the jaws of the lion. We presumably should get ashore, if that bonhomme in the peculiar underwear meant what he said."

Béssac cocked his head. "He meant what he said, all right, enseigne."

"But I wonder. You say you must get word to the Dey to ensure our saving our necks, correct?"

"Yes."

"Is there any way you can think of to get that message to him? You seem to know these people."

Béssac puffed. "That boat captain was an officer of the Dey's household guard, so I think we'll make it ashore, all right. The mob wouldn't try to get at us unless he let them. They may have an escort for us. I don't know."

"So we could row ashore and simply be cut to pieces."

"Yes. It's possible."

"My God."

Gallant touched the wound absently, about to speak again when Béssac put in, "Again, I think that officer would prevent it. He may be making his report now, and I'm sure the whole city saw us and the English. Besides, it will prick the Dey's interest to meet these Europeans who spoke Arabic to his gunboat."

"So that's when you think we might make our asylum plea?"

Béssac nodded.

"Bon", he said, feeling not a little peculiar once again. "We'll row ashore in three groups. You and I will go with the first group. Guimond with the second. Akiwoya with the third, but he's to return aboard, keeping some other men, perhaps his gun crew, as a watch aboard."

Béssac was a few moments later supervising the lowering of the jollyboat, the men responding quickly to a welcome order for work to break the growing tension. It gave them something to think about rather than the gun muzzles in the island fortifications or the brilliant nearness of the Moorish city.

Gallant spoke briefly with Akiwoya and outlined a simple anchor watch system. The jollyboat was to be held ready at all times. At any sign of a direct attack on the ship from the English to seaward, the gunner and his men were to pull for shore. No last-ditch, wasted defence.

"And you, m'sieu' ", asked the African, when Gallant had finished.

"Béssac and I will be ashore, Akiwoya. We're going to try and get us asylum here, hopefully until the English let down their guard and we can escape."

Akiwoya nodded slowly, and then looked Gallant in the eyes, softly repeating a phrase in an incomprehensible language.

Gallant's eyes narrowed. "What the deuce was that, man?" he asked.

The African smiled. "Just a blessing, enseigne, in my own tongue. From my...religion. You French call it Voudou."

Gallant shivered. He knew what the word meant. "A blessing for what?" he said, his lips dry.

"For the safety and long life of a good man, enseigne. For you."

Before the marine could reply the dark, muscled form was vanishing down the midship's companionway. Gallant looked for a long moment at the gleaming city. An unease tightened the back of his neck, and he had the feeling of looking at an anthill. He had never been in a Moorish city in his life, although he had tasted the Tropics in the Caribbean. There the towns were indolent clusters of planters' and traders' buildings, thronged with the white men who owned the land and the white and black men they owned as well. Thronged, but somehow not pressed. From this city before him he sensed pressure; humanity shouldered together to mingle sweat and blood, excrement and cooking smells, death and birth. Somehow he felt rather than heard the shouts, yells and hubbub of narrow streets, something he would have identified as "Eastern" had he known that term. He knew as he looked at the white domes and minarets that he was entering an environment completely foreign to his own experience and training for the first time in his life. As aware as he was of the danger that lurked in the city, he felt irresistably drawn to it.

As he considered these thoughts his nose twitched as a vaguary of the wind carried a breath of the land breeze to the corvette. The scent was indescribable, although had Gallant the time to spend he might have identified some of its parts. The deep reek of animal urine and ordure, and the sicklier aroma of their human counterparts; oils; leather; smoke from uncountable cooking fires; spices and herbs; rotting fruit and vegetables; coffee; charcoaling meat; the heavy perfume of flowers; a tang of thousands of work-sweaty human bodies wrapped in heavy sheep wool and soaked with the odor of mutton; the dust and chalkiness of masonry and whitewash; and throughout and over all this the lush, too-sweet smell of tropical decay.

"Boat's ready, enseigne."

Béssac's voice pulled the marine back to awareness. He smiled at the mate, somewhat self-consciously.

"Yes. Thank you, Béssac."

He swung down to the crowded boat, having decided to leave what little possessions he had left in the corvette. If they faced a long stay ashore, he would have to make do with what he had on. Arriving in the presence of the Dey with a sack over his shoulder would not be conducive to dignity, which he felt obliged to maintain. There was always the chance they would be able to return to the ship. As he settled in the boat he turned to watch the corvette slowly dropping away.

Akiwoya was aft on the quarterdeck, alone by the wheel, watching them pull away. Guimond's party were assembling by the rail. The ship looked trim and functional, yards square and tightly furled, the new wood of Guimond's repairs blending in smoothly with the hull's contours. He felt a tug of homesickness for her as they left; she had become a home to him as much as it had to the crewmen, and the sweat of labour and blood of war that had soaked into her decks was now partly his own.

Gallant squared his hat on his head, low over his eyes against the glare, and looked ahead. They were passing now through anchored Arab vessels, whose high sterns and canted cutwaters silently related the ancestry of the corvette's own sleek lines. The hulls were rough and splintery, and as they passed close aboard one which Béssac identified as an Iskandariyan *boum*, Gallant was amazed to see its planking was sewn together with tightly laced fibres of heavy rope. The enormous yard of the *boum*'s lateen mainsail was merely two slender trees lashed together, butt to butt overlapping.

The marine blinked as the boat rounded the *boum*'s counter. A thin, dark crewman wearing a loosely wrapped white garment was perched on what passed for the chain platform, the garment hitched around his waist and his thin backside thrust out over the water. He looked blankly at the passing boat and the upturned faces and carried on with his business, which was defecating productively into the sea some fifteen feet below him.

The men in the boat snickered, and beside Gallant Béssac grunted in amusement and shook his head.

"An East Indian, that fellow. Maybe an Indus River man. They drive the Moors crazy with their habits."

Gallant scratched his chin. Understandable, he thought.

They were approaching the quayside now, the smell and noise of the city becoming stronger. The quay was crowded with other small craft, their crewmen swarthy, muscular men wearing snug little caps and pantaloons fashioned, it appeared, by wrapping a colourful cloth several times around the body before passing the free end through the legs to hitch into a belt at the waist. The faces were dark and deeply cleft, with sharp, close-set glittering eyes that put an involuntary chill up Gallant's spine. The boatmen halted their work and watched wordlessly as *Écho*'s boat drew near.

There was a worn, uneven set of stone stairs that led down to the water's edge, and Béssac put the boat alongside them, the bow and stern men stepping out on to a step which was barely awash, Béssac and Gallant an instant behind them.

The stairs were littered with rubbish of every description, most of it organic and most of it decaying. Gallant almost fell headlong halfway up as he stretched to avoid the putrescent carcass of a wharf rat almost as long as his forearm.

But nothing prepared him for what awaited at the top of the stairs.

"Irham nyeh, ya sayedi! Irham nyeh!"

Almost as Gallant's shoes touched the top step a chorus of shrill cries and moans rose from the lips of a mass of ragged beggars which moved on the two men from about the quay. No two seemed the same in size or shape; no two seemed even to move in the same way. Their appalling deformities and diseased bodies crawled, hopped, slithered and humped toward them in a nightmarish scramble, the tiny forms of children among them. Gallant blanched. At the sight of one hideously deformed old woman whose anguished face peered up at him from a body like nothing so much as a crab, the marine's stomach heaved.

He gritted his teeth, fighting off the retching, trying to look away, back at the sea, at Béssac. The mate was yelling in Arabic, waving with his hands, the toes of his heavy shoes thudding into a struggling body here and there.

Gallant looked back at the horrified and sickened faces of the corvette's men, bunched on the stairs behind him.

Sweet Saviour, what kind of place is this? he thought wildly.

A gutteral scream jerked him round in time to see a bloody scimitar slice down into the packed mass of beggars, drawing a spurt of crimson into the dust of the quay and a wail from the throats of the wretches. They panicked, struggling pathetically to escape to either side from the swords of the men literally cutting a path through them. Gallant watched, aghast, as a group of men in bright uniform like the gunboat crews scythed the beggars out of the way, moving toward Gallant and Béssac. Those beggars who managed to scramble out of the way with but a cut or two from the whistling blades were fortunate; not so fortunate were those the men hacked down where they crouched. They flung the bloody, thrashing bodies to one side almost before the gurgling screams of the dying ceased.

A moment later a tall Moor, apparently an officer, strode through the laneway his men had made, to halt with a look of interest and surpassing arrogance on his features. Oblivious to the moans and piteous cries around them, his men were wiping their blades on the rags of their victims and sheathing them, looking about calmly as if they had merely been shifting bales of hemp.

Gallant willed himself with enormous difficulty to keep an impassive expression on his face, although his hands behind his back were bunched into white fists. He drew a deep breath and prayed the Moor would address Béssac first, as he felt certain there was no sound he was capable of uttering at that moment.

The Moor did turn to Béssac, speaking as his men quietly surrounded Gallant and the mate and the knot of corvette men behind them. Béssac and the Moor began a spirited conversation which appeared to be a series of challenges from the officer and shoulder-shrugging explanations from Béssac. The latter's command of the rich Arabic was apparently fluent, for both men spoke rapidly and with no discernible hesitation or block in communication.

Being deaf to any meaning in the words allowed Gallant to fix his attention on the officer, in no small part to avoid contemplating the ghastly human wreckage that lay on all sides. With grim awareness he noted that the busy work on the quay had resumed, seemingly oblivious to the brutal killings.

Gallant gritted his teeth tighter. He felt a premonition that the butchery of the beggars might be merely a beginning.

The Moor officer was a tall and striking figure in a large purple turban in the now-familiar pumpkin style, decorated with a magnificent ostrich feather clamped vertically in place over his forehead by a large brooch that glittered with jewels in the sun. His hair was hidden by the turban, but his brows and a neatly pointed beard were jet black, matching the flashing eyes inset under a wide and intelligent forehead. From his shoulders fell an ankle-length robe of grey-white, hooded and wide-sleeved, which was thrown back over his shoulders. Below scarlet pantaloons soft leather boots tipped with small bells protruded. In the broad leather belt about his waist a curved dagger and wicked-looking Miquelet pistol were thrust. Altogether the image was of a warlike and determined leader.

The conversation came to a halt and the Moor stood back with arms folded, watching hawklike as Béssac turned to Gallant.

"Well?" said the marine, his voice a little thick.

Béssac looked at him with eyes flashing warning.

"Enseigne, keep your face blank as we speak, whatever I say. This man would kill us without a thought."

Gallant raised his chin ever so slightly. "Yes. We've seen that."

"Literally, what he says is that we infidels, unclean unbelievers in Allah, are excrement upon the surface of the sea and are defiling the city of His Most Untouchable Perfection the Dey of Algiers, the Chosen of Allah, Sword of the True Faith, and the Deliverer of Death and Torment to the leprous souls of the Unbelievers. He spits in our mother's milk."

Gallant pursed his lips. "How very colourful."

"We deserve nothing less than…"

The marine raised a hand. "Very well, Béssac, spare me the imaginative threats. Can we stay here? What does he say about sanctuary or asylum?"

"Nothing. It would appear our lives are to be spared for

the moment, at least, due to the boundless mercy of His Perfection, who has taken to loathing the English lately. We will be permitted to grovel at his feet and reveal what reasons brought our worthless selves to this place. He also recognized that banner I had us fly, as I hoped."

Gallant pursed his lips again and glanced at the Moor, who was beginning to show impatience.

"Béssac, you're positively eloquent", he said, smiling broadly. "Very well. What next?"

"We're to be given quarters. You and I separate from the others."

Gallant looked hard at the mate. "What does that mean for the men? Where'll these fiends put them, man?"

Béssac shook his head. "J'n' sais pas, enseigne. We really have no choice anyway."

He glanced at the Moor. "We'd best say yes, right now, m'sieu', if we want to see the next minute alive."

Gallant searched his mind desperately for some argument they might use to demand the men be kept with them. The Moors very likely had interest only in Gallant and Béssac. He felt certain that if they were taken away the men were as good as slaughtered or enslaved.

"Béssac", he said in a low but urgent tone. "We've got to figure out some way to keep the men with us!"

Béssac spread his hands. "I know, enseigne! But do you think we have any..."

With a snarl the Moor officer waved his men in. Before he could move Gallant felt his arms seized in a steely grip, and he was propelled between two burly swordsmen along toward the inner city. He twisted around once before being shoved on again, but it had been enough to see that Béssac was being frog-marched right behind him, and that the men of *Écho* were being roughly herded in another direction.

The men holding Gallant kept moving, setting up a fast pace. The Moor officer strode ahead, his cloak billowing dramatically behind him. Gallant stumbled as he forced his feet to move quickly, sensing that if he fell it would be blows that would drive him to his feet again. His hat was still clamped firmly on his head, for which he was thankful, for he oddly hoped it would help protect his head from forthcoming blows as well as the brilliant sun.

His escorts were burly, bare-chested men in the same wide sashes and pantaloons of the gunboat men. Both appeared to have their heads shaven beneath the bulbous turbans, and both wore large, curling moustaches. The deadly scimitars hung from the sashes. The fingers gripping his arms were steel-hard, and he knew he could not have broken that grip even had his life depended upon it. He tried to keep a cool head and concentrated on keeping his feet under him.

They were being rushed up a terraced street; one that went along again and again from short steps at intervals of several paces. It wound up through the centre of the city, a tight and claustrophobic little channel pressed on both sides by the whitewashed walls of the shops and houses. The light was dim and streaked, cut off from the narrow slice of sky overhead by carpets, washing, multicoloured laundry and tattered sheets covered with the same peculiar curved script Béssac's little banner had borne, all hung across the narrow street above head level. In some places ill-made, screened galleries hung out from the upper floors of the buildings, almost joining where they met. The fronts of the houses on the street had dark doorways, with a low step or two before them; the shops literally had no fronts, being simply raised somewhat and open to the street, the tightly packed rows of fruit or vegetables or a myriad of goods open to view. Goods hung from hooks beside doorways, piled across big wicker baskets and clay urns, in some cases spread out on bright cloth on the narrow street surface itself. Through this passed a gabbling torrent of people, jamming the shops, haggling at full voice with owners, clustering in the doorways and squatting in tight circles before particularly inviting displays.

The crowd parted like water before the officer and his party, and Gallant only glimpsed in a blur the hundreds of faces that passed inches from his own. The standard garment of those he could study appeared to be humbler versions of the officer's cloak or robe. Some were brown; most were grey or off-white, and a few were striped. Small urchins with shaved heads wore them; bearded old patriarchs in red felt caps and little turbans wore them. Some were spotless. Many were filthy, reflecting the refuse and stinking waste the passing hundreds ground underfoot constantly. Gallant was no stranger to filth in the streets, for even the mud and cobble lanes of his own Louisbourg were a dumping ground for the wastes of the houses along them. But the sheer awfulness of the slop he now squelched through was the worst he had known.

It struck him rather wildly as they rounded a sharp bend that he had seen no women. But then he looked again at the smaller, quick-moving figures among the men that were sheathed in black from head to toe, like Spanish penitents, their faces vaguely sensed behind squares of gauze in their hoods. Why the devil do they hide their women? he thought. thought.

After a good fifteen minutes of this march, plunging on upwards through seemingly endless streets, all of which seemed identical, Gallant began to feel his legs weakening. He had heard Béssac curse once as he fell, and knew his mate was still behind him. His chest was heaving and his lungs burned. God, how much longer!

Almost in response to his silent question the officer ahead turned down a darkened laneway, savagely kicked a snarling dog out of his path, and halted at the laneway end before a tightly woven lattice gate through which pinpoints of light were visible.

Gallant and Béssac were pulled up to a halt. Gallant was breathing heavily and could hear Béssac's wheezes behind. A quick glance at one of his captors revealed the latter was not even breathing deeply, and was returning his glance with a look of the most humiliating contempt.

The officer exchanged some succinct Arabic with someone inside the lattice. A heavy bolt was thrown back, the lattice swung open, and the Moor officer stepped back into the darkness of the archway.

Before Gallant's eyes could adjust to the bright daylight

beyond the gate he felt himself flung through the archway with startling force, and he thudded painfully on his face on a hard, gravelly surface. An instant later Béssac grunted as he landed beside him. The lattice slammed shut.

Gallant lay for a moment gathering his wits, listening to Béssac mutter a series of inventive curses on the origins of their departed escorts.

Then he rolled over and got to his feet, picking up his hat and brushing off his coat. He looked about him. Beside him, Béssac sat up, straightened his own battered hat and then froze, jaw agape, as he rose.

"Sweet Blood of the Saints", said the mate.

The two men were standing at the end of a long rectangular courtyard, bright with sunlight, on a walkway of small pink stones that led to the edge of a shimmering pool of water, parting to border the pool down both sides to the far end of the courtyard. The pool had a low wall of polished white stone, and its waters were an exquisitely clear aquamarine over the white tile of the pool bottom. A simple vertical jet of water leapt up from the centre of the pool to mist away in the still air, the droplets forming a tiny rainbow. Around the edge of the courtyard were placed carefully tended shrubs and low trees bearing blossoms of incandescent hues or hung with oranges or lemons. On all sides of the yard save that with the lattice gate, tall smooth columns of white stone rose to semi-circular arches. Behind these columns was all cool shadow, with doorways leading into the pale pink building walls. Above the arches the stonework bore intricate designs in the same odd flowing script as Béssacc's banner. The sounds of the city and of the dark, narrow streets through which they had been brought were inaudible, and all that could be heard was the splash of the fountain, and the delicate chirp of a songbird hidden somewhere among the trees.

Gallant brushed off his breeches and pushed his hat to the back of his head. He looked at Béssac.

"Very well, my friend", he said. "You're the expert on this damned place. Now where are we?"

Béssac shrugged, then pointed with his chin toward the far end of the courtyard.

"Enseigne, I haven't a clue. Maybe he'll tell us."

"Who?"

Gallant squinted down the yard, and saw the figure of a man move out of the shadows of the columns and walk lightly toward them.

At first glance he thought he was looking at the brusque officer of the escort. Then he realized this man was slighter and somewhat shorter. His clothes, too, were evidently not military. Above pale yellow pantaloons he wore a white, silken-looking coat which reached up close around his neck under a neat black beard. The inevitable sash was yellow and carried a small bejewelled dagger sheath. The man's turban was decorated with a single long white feather, held by a silver brooch bearing a blood-red ruby in its centre. He walked with one hand behind him, and the visible hand was laden with rings. Tiny bells on the man's white boot toes gave a soft tinkling sound as he walked.

"*Ah-lan wa-sahlan!* Good day, gentlemen, good day! How flattered we are to have you visit our shores!"

Gallant and Béssac exchanged a quick glance. The man had shifted into pure, perfectly accented European French.

The Moor stopped before them, bowing slightly and touching with a graceful gesture his breast, his lips and his forehead.

"*As-salaam 'alaikum.* May peace be upon you. You may address me as Hussein, at your service, messieurs", he said, "advisor to His Most Merciful Serenity the Dey of Algiers, may the peace of Allah be upon him!"

Gallant threw another look at Béssac, pursing his lips slightly. Then he swept off his tricorne and made the courtliest bow he could muster. "Enseigne Paul François Adhémar Gallant, of His Majesty's Independent Companies of Naval Infantry, your servant, m'sieu'", he said. Béssac, who had never learned how to bow like a gentleman, and who would not have even had he known how, briefly raised his hat and bobbed his head.

"*Wa'alaikum as-Salaam!*" he said quietly.

Hussein flashed a dazzling smile. "Such beautiful Arabic!

Wa-llaah! I am in awe. But you must be exhausted! Famished! We'll attend to that at once!'' He clapped his hands toward the archways. ''And I imagine your escort here through the *suq* was'', and here he laughed lightly, ''somewhat impatient?''

Gallant paused, thoughts of duelling in his head. Fence with him. Parry these charming probes.

He smiled graciously. ''Military men understandably have their duties to perform.''

''How well spoken!'' Again the gleaming smile. ''It gives me great pleasure to see you understand such things, m'sieu'. But then of course, you are a soldier yourself.''

Gallant's expression was appropriately modest. ''Merely a junior one of no importance, m'sieu'.''

''Oh, tut tut. The colony troops of King Louis in the Americas are every bit as necessary to him as any infantry in Flanders.''

Gallant twitched not a facial muscle, but inwardly started. Hussein had identified him with ease as a colony officer rather than a dockyard or shipboard one. Very likely he knew things of much greater seriousness than the uniform cut of French troops. Gallant realized he would have to tread carefully indeed.

''You are most kind, m'sieu','' he said.

''Not at all. But you must replenish yourselves. Here, please do me the honour of sharing a small morsel or two with me. I am for one quite ravenous!''

As he spoke, three servants padded into the courtyard, bearing large wingback wicker chairs which were deftly slid in behind the three men. A fourth servant whisked a delicate table into place before the chairs, and a fifth appeared bearing a tray with a silvery urn and three small cups.

Hussein folded himself smoothly into his chair, gesturing for the two men to sit. A servant poured cups of something hot and dark from the urn, offering it round. Gallant and Béssac exchanged a glance as they held the steaming little bowls before them.

Hussein laughed, showing his teeth. ''Gentlemen. Please allow me.'' He drained his cup and set it down, when it was immediately refilled by the hovering servant.

"You really must not think we would bring you all the way up here simply to poison you, would you?"

Gallant smiled. "You will forgive us, m'sieu', but a certain caution is instinctive, as you will understand."

"By all means." Hussein leaned back in his chair, folding his hands and regarding the two men over his fingertips.

Gallant sipped at his cup. It was a sweet and powerful coffee, with a heady aroma that drenched his nostrils as he drank.

"Turkish", said Hussein. "Do you like it?"

Béssac, who was finishing his second cup, said he had never tasted better in his life. Gallant agreed that it was a refreshing and delicious beverage.

"Splendid", said Hussein. "Drink as much as you like. The servant will refill your cup until you shake it." Hussein demonstrated a little wrist-twitching motion of the cup before setting it down.

At length a more businesslike look came over his face. "There are a few questions I think we should now have answers to, gentlemen", he said smoothly.

"Your masthead banner, for example. I presume you know it is one of the battle standards of the Tunisian oar galleys and that it carries a rare and very specific quotation from the *Qu'ran* emblazoned upon it. I wish to know how it came into your possession. You do not even appear to be a ship of war."

Béssac drew a cuff across his mouth and shifted back in his chair.

"The banner is mine, *sayèd*," he said quietly. "It was a gift to me from a friend and comrade in arms. A Muslim."

Hussein's eyes narrowed. "Explain, if you will."

"Years ago I was serving in a French *xebec* which was attacked and taken by a Moorish galley, after we had been storm-driven to just off Djerba. The Moor shot out from under the guns of the fortress at Houmt Souk and was upon us before we could move."

Hussein nodded. "Ah, yes. *Borj el Kbir*. I know it well. Please go on."

"We were almost slaughtered to a man. I escaped death only by luck and a fatal-appearing wound. I came round as the battle fever abated, and they made me prisoner, eventually chained to an oar in the same galley.''

Gallant's eyebrows twitched in surprise. But then, the mate had said nothing about serving in a Moorish galley.

"Three days later, after I had been put to the oars, we set out from Ajim and were set upon by two Neapolitan galleasses. The fight was brutal, and they were flying the red flag of No Quarter. We rammed and sank one of them, but the other boarded us. A ball shattered my irons and I found myself on the afterdeck, with the Neapolitans everywhere. I decided for some reason that my life was more likely to continue under the protection of Allah, so I seized a blade and joined the galley soldiers. At one point our commander fell and was about to be piked by a mob when I skewered one lout and fell over the commander to protect him from the rest.''

Béssac unconsciously arched his back slightly. "That cost me a dirk in the back. But we won the battle.''

"*Wa-llaah*! I am impressed. And thereafter?''

"We became friends, the commander and I. I stayed with him for two years and eventually became his chief lieutenant. I believe we were...as close as brothers, *sayèd*.''

Gallant caught himself gaping at the mate. He was trying to picture the improbable image of Béssac in the service and full regalia of a Moorish corsair. It was not easy.

"The banner?'' said Hussein, quietly.

"When I finally came to ask that I be allowed to rejoin a Christian vessel or port, he consented, and wrapped me in that banner, which he said had flown above us the moment I saved his life. He said it would repay the debt to me on his behalf, some day.''

The mate fell silent.

Hussein looked at him steadily for a moment, as if to digest the story.

"And it has, my friends'', he said presently. "Had you not flown it, the waters before the guns of the *Al-Jazair* would have been your grave.'' His expression brightened. "But this, of course, explains your mastery of Arabic, M'sieu'..."

"Béssac."

"M'sieu' Béssac. And what of your business in these waters?" The dark eyes turned to Gallant. "What would justify your little vessel's pursuit by these Royal Navy warships, enseigne?"

Hussein's languid gaze had turned steely-hard as the question ended.

Gallant felt a small shiver run up his spine. There was not an ounce of pity or compassion in that stare; merely the highly concentrated energy of a ruthless and logical mind. The marine held that stare and returned it.

"You were not, I think, merely tempting the Royal Navy a little too much on one of your usual routes."

Gallant thought quickly, smiling to gain another moment. From the brutal reality he had seen beyond the lattice he knew this civilized questioning could lead to something far more direct and far more fearful. He sensed that to keep Béssac alive now meant he would have to keep his story simple and direct, and without hint of intrigue.

"It is a plain enough tale, m'sieu'", he said, trying to look every inch the inexperienced and slightly simple junior officer. "M'sieu' Béssac's vessel was bound to Marseille from Louisbourg, Isle Royale. I was ordered to accompany it and upon reaching Marseille, to proceed to Paris and report on the situation at Louisbourg. There I would receive further instructions.

"Our plight at Louisbourg is desperate, m'sieu'", he went on, a sudden recklessness taking hold. "The English have beseiged us and may at this very moment be pouring over the walls of the city. And it is not just that we are trying to report this fact as mere servants of France. Our homes are there. Our families. The fall of Louisbourg would mean not only the end of France in America but the end of our lives. All of us, my crew included!"

"Your crew?"

"They are Acadiens almost to a man, m'sieu'. You can see the urgency of our mission. I must report in time so that His

Majesty can respond with aid, in time to save Louisbourg from the English!''

Gallant leaned forward. ''Hence, m'sieu', I beg of you, if it is possible for you to aid us in sheltering or eluding the British and continuing on this mission, which is so important to...''

Hussein held up a hand. ''Patience, enseigne, patience!'' he smiled. ''Therefore you carry a message which contains merely a cry for help from an endangered outpost, so to speak.''

''Yes. My task is merely to deliver it.''

''And?''

''And nothing, m'sieu'. In truth it is all I know'', said Gallant, as earnestly as he could. He sipped his coffee, avoiding for a moment the Moor's gaze.

After a moment Hussein spoke. ''I see. I presume, of course, that your ship's papers will indicate that you were in fact bound for Marseille. A detail we can clear up in short order.''

Gallant winced inwardly cursing his own forgetfulness. The papers would show *Écho* listed for the Biscay. Hussein might assume they had pirated the vessel, which made it and them fair game for quick disposal; he might also conclude that they were involved in some clumsy attempt by the French ad-mirauté, or even the British to prod Moorish defences, in which case a highly unpleasant fate awaited them.

He swallowed down a sudden tightness in his throat.

Hussein turned to Béssac. ''I want to know some further details concerning your banner, M'sieu' Béssac. Such a gift to an infidel is most extraordinary even given your friendship. I wonder if you might tell me who the commander was?''

Béssac scratched at his chin as he replied

''Ibrahim ibn al-Habib Al Hached'', he said.

Hussein sat up with a start in his chair. ''What? This is the man?''

''Yes. Do you know him?''

Hussein smiled, a somewhat rueful and oddly disappointed smile.

''He is the brother of he whose city you see about you. He is full brother to the Dey.''

Gallant felt as if a bar that had been pressing across his shoulders had been lifted, and that he could see the colours and textures all about him in greater clarity. What incredible luck! He found it hard to believe that the canny mate had not known this all along.

"But this changes, things, gentlemen. Changes them very much indeed." Hussein's eyes had lost the disappointment, and he rose from the chair into the graceful salute he had used to greet them. *"Al-hamdillaah!* How fortune has its way! My sincere apologies for the abominable reception you were given and your conduct here through the city. Rest assured the men responsible will be severely dealt with!"

"But..." began Béssac.

"And you will of course forget my impertinent and tactless questionings of your personal affairs. I am sure that the Dey, Allah's peace be upon him, would wish the savior of his true and favoured brother nothing but hospitality and the freedom to depart as speedily as he chooses."

Hussein's glance took in Gallant. "Of course this extends to his comrades and associates as well." He rose swiftly. "There are things to attend to. You must be housed in proper quarters. The Dey must learn of your arrival. There is no time to waste!"

He bowed again.

"Gentlemen, if you will do me the honour of waiting here while my servants attend you, I shall leave for a few brief moments to see to these things." He strode for the archways.

"Hussein!" called Gallant, who had stood up.

The Moor spun round.

"Our crewmen from the corvette, M'sieu'. Can their needs and quarters be seen to?"

Hussein bowed deeply once more. "To hear is to obey. It shall be done, you may rest on it." Then he was gone through the archways, the bells on his toes tinkling after him.

Gallant and Béssac looked at one another and at the slow grin that spread across each other's face.

"Sweet Mary", said Gallant. "Why didn't you tell me all this, Béssac?"

"I didn't know if it would work, enseigne. I wasn't sure of the Dey's identity, for one thing. I was truthfully hoping we'd get by on the strength of the banner. I thought the Dey's brother would be a bonus, if it was the right man. Thank God it was!"

Gallant shook his head in amazement. Again their luck had held. He found himself thinking that soon there might be a chance to get back to the ship, and perhaps reprovision her. After a time the English would tire of hovering along the coast, and contrary winds might drive them off. The *Écho* could be well to sea and beating northward for Marseille or Toulon before the English..."

Hussein had reappeared, holding his hand out invitingly.

"Gentlemen. If you'll follow me, please."

NINE

Gallant tried to shift his legs to a more comfortable position on the broad silken cushion, uneasy in the cross-legged tailor's squat that was obviously called for. Béssac, he noticed, had hunkered down with ease, and was busy picking steaming morsels out of the large bowl that had been set before them. He swore silently and tugged at his breeches.

Both men were seated along with perhaps a hundred resplendent Moors in a vast hall that appeared to function as a sort of throne room and feasting hall for the Dey, whose bejewelled magnificence shone from a raised platform at the far end of the chamber. The decor about them was much the same as they had seen in the apparently endless series of rooms Hussein had been leading them either in or out of all afternoon: broad, tiled floors spread with exquisitely worked carpeting, high, vaulted archways and ceilings held aloft by delicate columns, all of this alive with intricate designs in mosaic and tile, geometric patterns in some cases almost beyond the eye's comprehension. And everywhere, cool archway vistas of the distant *Sahel* or glimpses into treed gardens alive with delicate fountains.

The hall was obviously of central importance, for the Dey himself reclined on the cushioned dais under heavy sweptback draperies that suggested a pavillion. The broad couch that bore him was so cushioned that the robed figure appeared almost lost in a sea of silken billows. To either side and before the couch a collection of lesser creatures lolled, so that the effect to Gallant was almost that of a retinue of archangels bearing aloft the central figure of a saint, in a Christian religious work. The pyramid thus formed was gently washed by the breeze from a great feather fan which was slowly and steadily swung overhead by an enormous and very black servant.

Gallant glanced at Béssac, who was helping himself again to the bowl. Gallant's one taste of the meaty little items therein had almost scorched his mouth beyond recall; he was beginning now to find the spices more tolerable, and the gamey meat at least something his stomach could seize on. Thankfully there was fresh fruit as well to cool off with. The mate had been bantering in expressive Arabic with Hussein until that worthy left, and now with several of the finely robed guests around them, leaving Gallant with little else to do but study their surroundings, and think over the past few hours' activities.

Hussein's startling change of demeanour from polished interrogator to equally polished host had been remarkable enough. No less remarkable had been the luxurious suite of chambers he had led them to; open, spacious rooms in cool tile and white, brightened with flowers and fruit on the low, unobtrusive furniture, with balconies off which long vistas looked out over the city rooftops to the harbour and sea beyond. With a pang Gallant had seen the small shape of Écho, familiar and appealing, and far out to sea distant white spots that marked the hovering English vessels.

There had been a chance to wash from steaming bowls carried in by the wordless, wraithlike servants who had followed from the garden, and a chance to shake some of the sea grime from their clothes.

Then, as Gallant was tying back his queue, Hussein had arrived after a brief absence, again all smiles and smoothly oiled hospitality.

"How fortunate you are, gentlemen!" he had said, indicating that they were to follow him again. "His Most Serene Perfection is feasting this afternoon in celebration of the capture of a Neapolitan merchantman. You will join his guests and enjoy yourselves before I present you!"

Gallant sipped at the little cup of coffee that reappeared constantly at his elbow. He found himself wondering if there was anything in particular he would have to explain to the Dey; would the man be a smiling, benign ruler who left such unpleasant trivia as interrogation to his aides? Likely not. The dark, bearded face with a long patrician cast to the nose at the far end of the hall was more likely that of a shrewd and ruthless intellect. He would have to watch every word, and every gesture, for clues to the man's character. There was no question on the matter: they must receive permission to return to the corvette and slip away northward.

He started as a cluster of musicians who were seated to one side of the dais suddenly struck their instruments at once, as if to announce something of importance. Gallant shifted on his cushion, pushing his hanger around from where it had been pressing on his hip.

The musicians had two small hand drums and a larger one, a peculiar one-stringed instrument played with a bow, and several deep-bodied lutelike instruments.

Béssac suddenly nudged him, speaking through a food-stuffed mouth. "Ho! Listen to those ouds! You're in for a treat. It'll probably be dancing. Has to be seen to be believed!"

"What? What kind of dancing?"

"Quiet!" the mate hissed. "It's starting!"

The musicians were swathed in the usual white robes and wore, like the guests, simpler variations on the pumpkin turbans. With a flourish they struck into a rhythmic, staccato tune set in a minor key, the drums pumping out a steady, intricate beat below the rapid plucking of what Gallant supposed were the ouds.

Then the marine caught his breath. A hanging veil at the far end of the huge room had been swept back, and a girl leaped lightly through the arch to sink down on to widespread knees, her arms held out in supplication to the couch of the Dey.

Gallant blinked. Except for a massive gold belt that looped low around her hips and hung down before her in long, braided tassels, the girl was naked.

The Dey made the most imperceptible twitch of one hand. The girl was still for several moments, until at last her shoulders began to shake slightly back and forth to the insistent tempo of the music. Her head was thrown back, and her hair, which was black and shone as if it had been treated with oil, hung in rich waves to the small of her back.

Béssac was grinning. He nudged Gallant again. "What did I tell you, enseigne, eh?" he whispered.

Gallant nodded mutely.

The kneeling girl had lifted off her heels now, twining her arms above her head and beginning to sway her hips from side to side. Her breasts, which were full and uptilted, swung gently with the motion. Her tawny body had apparently been oiled as well, and as she moved its smooth curves glistened like a seal. She swept her hair up over her head and let it cascade down, opening now her dark, shadow-edged eyes.

There was a guttural murmur from the watching men and the musicians bent to their task with fervour. Gallant noticed out of the corner of his eye that the men nearby were tapping feet or fingers to the building music.

The girl rose sinuously to her feet, and Gallant saw that she wore two small anklets of golden bangles that chinked each time her feet moved, in time with the rapid patter of the drums. She began to move forward, each step ending with a lift of her hips in a smooth motion to either side. Her arms were winding like snakes about each other, and she beat a counterpoint to the steady *chink-kachink* of her anklets with a pair of tiny cymbals fastened to the fingertips of each hand.

As she danced, the girl would sway to one side and the other, and then spin into a whirling turn that sent the tassled belt and her streaming hair swinging about her body. Every part of her seemed alive to the driving, burgeoning flow of music, so that it appeared to Gallant that for every note and beat of the musicians' hands there was an answering motion to some part of that shining, coppery torso.

The men were calling to her now, some raising cups to her in toasts, a few trying playfully to catch the whirling belt as she swept by. She laughed at them, a warm, liquid sound, white teeth flashing as she spun into another and another turn.

Gallant was gazing at the girl. He had never seen a woman that moved with such pantherish grace and abandon. The girl's back was to him now, and he grinned and looked down when he caught himself wondering how it would feel to trace with his hands the line from her small waist over the rounded hips and down the beautifully muscled legs.

He felt his loins stir. God help me, he thought. I wouldn't have the strength to resist the passion of these people.

He looked up with a start. The girl had stopped in front of him, barely arm's-length away. He could see that her body was wet with sweat mingling with the shining oil, her upper lip dotted with tiny drops of moisture. She stood lightly on tiptoe, her hips swaying smoothly from side to side, and he watched in fascination as her breasts began that maddening swing she had begun the dance with. Gallant tore his eyes away from her dark nipples only to look up into the girl's eyes and see a teasing amusement there. He laughed and looked down, the heat in his face burning.

Without warning the girl stopped her dance and knelt down before him, lifting his chin with one hand. For a long moment she looked into his eyes, her own glowing with a strange tenderness. A small smile crossed her lips.

Then she gently and quickly kissed him, the pursed cone of her lips sweet on his, the soft tips of her breasts brushing against the hands he raised in surprise. Before he could move she had sprung away from him, catlike, and was gone through the archway, the tinkle of her anklets echoing back into the hall.

A great shout went up from the men, and cups were raised in Gallant's direction. Several men nearby were roaring gusty phrases at him, slapping their thighs and grinning broadly. Not a few fixed glittering, envious gazes on the speechless marine.

Beside him, Béssac was roaring with laughter, and Gallant seized his elbow, in the process finally finding his tongue to speak.

"Béssac! Damn it, what's so hilarious!"

The mate could hardly talk for laughing, and his eyes were filled with tears.

"You! You've just been kissed by the Dey's favourite dancer! Hussein told me about her! Men come here for years and never get a look from her! And you...the first time!" He dissolved into another gale.

The mate walloped him on the back. "It means", he hooted, "my young pup, she'll come to your bed, if you want her! You could have her tonight!"

"What?" Gallant was astounded.

"Yes, you! Tonight! Béssac rolled back on the cushions, convulsed by another wave of laughing at the expression on Gallant's face. "Our Lion of Acadia!" he roared.

Gallant's recollection of the rest of the meal was none too clear, although he knew that it went on for several more hours into the evening, and that along with endless courses of unidentifiable food which Béssac greeted with joyful recognition there were other entertainers: jugglers, a heavy-set pair of wrestlers, and more than one dancer who whirled and shook to the music of the seemingly inexhaustible little band. He watched it all and experimented with the food halfheartedly, always finding himself thinking again of the girl's kiss, the warmth of her lips, the animal grace of her movements.

Then Hussein was before them, gesturing Gallant and the mate to follow him to the foot of the dais.

Gallant rose, wincing as his cramped legs protested. He hitched his hanger around to its proper position, gave a perfunctory tug at his jabot, and followed Béssac and Hussein down the length of the hall toward the pavillion.

The Dey had risen from his sea of cushions and stood coolly observing them. The deep orange sunlight shafting in from the colonnaded balcony lit his figure dramatically, firelike glints showing in the jewelwork of the Dey's robe and turban.

Hussein stopped somewhat unexpectedly at a distance from the dais and bowed deeply, which Gallant was careful to copy. Hussein opened his arms wide, as if in appeal, the rich Arabic flowing in smooth eloquence from him, turning now and then to indicate the two Europeans. At one indication of Béssac the Dey's chin lifted in a short, quick motion, the dark eyes taking on a new glitter.

Again, the almost imperceptible twitch of the hand. Hussein moved aside, and the Dey stepped down and strode in a commanding manner to the two men.

Gallant met the dark stare evenly, until at last a small smile twitched one corner of the Dey's mouth, and his attention swung to Béssac. A deep, melifluous voice phrased lengthy questions at the mate, and Gallant heard Béssac's replies, calm and fluent. From time to time a question would go to Hussein, whose replies were quick and intense. It seemed to Gallant that the Dey was in some ways a larger, somewhat more aquiline and dignified version of Hussein, alike in an oddly cruel handsomeness, poiseful bearing, and an aura of unsentimental intelligence that had no trace of softness about it.

Gallant felt his palms moisten. When would the critical questions be asked?

Without warning, the Dey seized Béssac in a powerful embrace and kissed the burly mate on the cheek. Hussein beamed as the Dey took a step back toward the dais. Then he listened attentively as the Dey turned, showing even white teeth as he pointed languidly at Gallant and said something which ended in a chuckle.

Hussein replied, bowing very low once again and warning the two Europeans with a glance that the interview was at an end, and that they were to do likewise. The two men aped him, backing in a half-crouch several paces down the hall before turning to walk to the far end and out into the passage beyond the archway.

Hussein said nothing until they reached the apartments. The chambers were darker now, lit by the last fading rays of the sunset behind the hump of the *Sahel*.

Béssac had hardly pushed the latticed door shut when Hussein spun to them, hands alive with expressive gestures.

"*Wa-llaah!* The One True God has put His mighty arm about you, gentlemen! The Dey has taken you into his heart, particularly you, M'sieu' Béssac; You need have no fears about your shelter here under the omnipotent arm of His Excellence!"

Gallant found that images of the slaughtered beggars on the quayside arose in his mind whenever Hussein's flowery accolades of the Dey were forthcoming. He had a feeling that the one undying quality of His Excellence was a cruel unpredictability.

Still, Gallant told himself, the asylum seemed granted. He had what he had sought, apparently: a chance to reprovision the ship, refresh the men, perhaps even obtain some guns for the corvette before confronting the English again.

But why did he have that uncomfortable tension in the back of his neck?

"And as for you, enseigne, the conquest you made of His Magnificence's favoured *ra'aasa* did not go unnoticed!" The dark eyes glittered again. "Out of his boundless generosity he has decided to give her to you."

"I beg your pardon? said Gallant.

"She is yours, my young friend. A wondrous jewel." Hussein leered elegantly. "A toy for your dalliance. You may use her as you wish. She is, shall we say, an expert in the delights of Heaven. You may make sport with her, or you may of course kill her, if that might amuse you", went on Hussein.

"Kill her!"

"Naturally", said Hussein, languidly. "She's but a slave, and a woman at that. It's for you to decide." He sighed. "A delightful prospect, indeed. I envy you."

Gallant was unable to say anything in reply. Hussein ignored the thunderstruck expression on the marine's face and turned to Béssac, pulling two velvet pouches from the folds of his coat. These he tossed on a nearby couch. Then he reached again into the front of his coat.

"To protect you both during your stay here you must wear about your necks these pendants." He pulled two light chains from his coat, chains which bore small silver medallions. "They mark you as under the special protection of the Dey. No man may harm you, under pain, of course, of a most excruciatingly painful death. With these you will have the freedom of the *suq*, the *bazaar* — the city, in short."

Hussein indicated the pouches. "From his private coffers he provides you each with a small purse with which to amuse yourselves, or if you wish, purchase supplies for your vessel. You will, of course, be quartered here as his guests. You'll find the purses contain the equivalent of five hundred *louis* each."

Béssac whistled softly. "Mon Dieu", he breathed.

"Please." Hussein radiated hospitality. "It is but a small token of the much he owes you for the saving of his true and beloved brother."

He strode to the door. "Rest well, gentlemen. You have but to pull this cord and my servants will appear, night or day." He raised a finger to Gallant. "The young woman will be here shortly. I would recommend, M'sieu' Béssac, a visit of yourself to the seventh archway to your left along this hall. That is, if your mind and body would appreciate the soothing attentions of several of Allah's most entrancing creations, Praise to His Name! They expect you, of course "

In the next instant he was gone.

Béssac dropped a big paw on Gallant's shoulder. "By the Virgin, enseigne, we've struck true Inca gold here! Look at this purse!" He hefted the bag of coins and whistled softly again. "I could get you ten batteries of nine-pounders for this!"

"Yes", said Gallant after a moment, a thoughtful look on his face. "In fact, one might say it's almost too good, wouldn't you say?"

"What?"

"Too good, man! As if they wanted us to put our guard down, to relax. As if something was being planned."

Béssac looked the marine squarely in the eyes. "Enseigne, your caution is a good thing. It'll keep you out of a lot of trouble, no doubt. But I know these people! The Dey owes me something, because I saved his brother. It's a point of honour with them. I know!"

"All the same, Béssac."

"Look, ensiegne", the mate cut in, "how helpless are we now, eh? They could have slit us from stem to gudgeon as soon as we stepped ashore! They don't need to intrigue to get us off our guard. A couple of those lads who frog-marched us up here could do for us in two minutes."

The mate was only pointing out the obvious.

"You're probably right. I still somehow feel a bit uneasy." He picked up and hefted the other pouch. "It's still too pat."

Béssac shrugged.. "Enseigne, good fortune is good fortune. I for one am ready to accept it. And to make the most of it!"

The mate leered comically as he moved to the door. "After that meal, I'm game for some 'soothing attentions', all right. It's been a long time since I enjoyed those!"

Gallant smiled. "All right. Maybe I am just seeing shadows."

Then he froze, Hussein's words coming back to him. "Béssac!"

The mate stepped back in through the door. "Enseigne?"

"That girl. The dancer. God, man, she'll be here in a minute!"

"So, enseigne?"

"Damn your eyes, Béssac, what do I do with her?"

Béssac winked. He stepped out the door, his voice echoing back in amusement as he went off down the hall. "Hah! A sturdy trooper like yourself ought to be able to think of something, m'sieu'!"

Gallant swore, and ran his fingers through his hair. Events were coming too thick, too fast. There was almost too much to digest, to consider. He needed time to think, to plan. Were they really out of danger? What would *Écho* need to get to sea again? Would the English be hovering out there just beyond the horizon? Was the Dey planning some hideous treachery, and merely toying with them now?

Gallant flung off his coat and tossed it carelessly on the couch. He drew his hanger, and taking a handkerchief from his waistcoat pocket, began absentmindedly to polish the blade, as he did so pacing up and down the room. He began to go slowly over the events since their arrival in the harbour, looking for some kind of inconsistency. No doubt Béssac was right; the Moors were merely repaying a debt, and *Écho* would soon be on her way again with no harm done.

Behind him, the lattice door rattled. He spun on his heel, the sword blade whistling as he turned.

The figure of the girl who had danced before him, hidden now in a full red cloak, was flung through the doorway on to the floor of the apartment.

God's teeth, thought Gallant. Don't these people ever simply walk through doorways? His heart began pounding at his temples, and he looked at the girl, who was still crouched on the floor, staring at him with a wide-eyed, fearful expression. The expression made her face look younger, less harsh than he remembered it from the hall.

"Well. So here you are", he offered, his tongue feeling thick and unresponsive. He took a step toward the girl.

"Oh, God...No...please...!" The girl shrank back, pathetic fear in her face. She had spoken in English.

English! Gallant's surprise was so great that only after a moment of gaping at the girl foolishly did he look down and see that he was still carrying the unsheathed sword, its gleaming point centred on the girl's throat. He tossed the weapon quickly on to the couch behind him, and turned his open palms toward her.

"Don't be afraid. Please don't", he said. There was little doubt what the girl thought he intended to do. Damn their black Moorish hearts! It touched something inside him to see the helpless fear in the girl. Something that hated to see it. "I won't harm you, Mademoiselle."

The girl's voice was faint, almost a whisper. "You won't kill me?"

Gallant shook his head.

The girl's face lost some of the fear. But it had none of the teasing amusement that had sweetly mocked him in the dance. Or had that, too, only been part of the dance?

Gallant rubbed his brow, thinking for a moment. His heart still beat violently against his ribs.

"You speak English", he said, in as gentle a tone as he could muster. "Why?"

"My mother was English. She was taken by the Moors." Her eyes had not moved from his face.

"Your father?"

"Killed. When they took our ship. My mother was set to work in the kitchens here." The girl seemed so small and slight, now, her black hair tumbling over the red-cloaked shoulders, her hands slim and white-looking on the tiled floor.

Gallant reached out his own hand toward her. "Come. Stand up, little dancer." He smiled. "Do you have a name?"

Her voice retreated into its whisper. "Abigail."

"Abigail. You really must believe that I won't harm you. Was I not almost a child in your hands, back there in the hall, during your dancing?"

The corners of the girl's mouth tugged upwards, and she nodded.

"You were anything but afraid in there", he said.

She looked up, shaking back her hair in a way that touched a sweet pain in his chest. "It's not the same...in there. That's all part of the dance. Part of the acting I used to do."

Gallant turned slowly and walked to the far end of the chamber, to the archway that opened onto the wide balcony. He looked out over the domed and terraced roofs, touched now with the bluish light of the rising moon.

Can these people be this cruel? he thought. Would I really have had the choice of killing this girl? For my own amusement? He shuddered.

It was not Gallant's first encounter with evidence of the appalling blackness that human beings sometimes wallowed in. He had seen torture, ill-treatment, callousness, rough brutality; all of these were a part of life, and particularly of the age he lived in. One steeled oneself to them, the way a hunter desperate for food steels himself to the piteous thrashing of a dying animal. But the reality that this girl might have been sent in to be put to death simply as an amusement for a favoured guest of the Dey was almost more than Gallant could accept. It was monstrous and cowardly, and all his hatred of bullying and cruelty rose in his throat.

The girl's voice broke in. "I believe you."

He turned, surprised. She was standing now, looking at him steadily, her hads folded demurely before her.

"I believe you won't harm me", she said, as if for emphasis.

Gallant nodded.

"But you must want something else..." She tugged at one shoulder of her robe, and it dropped away about her hips. She cupped the beautiful breasts and lifted them toward Gallant. "I am very skilled..."

The girl's hypnotic sensuality caused his heart to race, and he felt a surge of desire course through him. But he heard his own voice, strangely foreign, replying.

"No, Abigail." An image of the Dey's face, amused and mocking, flashed through his head.

"I wish nothing from you", he said.

"But I am yours!" The girl was trembling slightly.

Gallant looked hard at the girl, his heart pounding in his ears. Fighting the urge he felt to reach out and crush her in his arms was another emotion, a sudden rage at a world, or at least a society in which this girl and others like her could exist as toys for the amusement of men whose cruelties he had already witnessed.

His eyes travelled over the curves of the girl's body. He could not be a party to her exploitation. He would not play the Dey's vicious little games. And neither could he accept owning the girl, as familiar a thing as slavery was, even in his own distant Louisbourg.

He was sure now of what he would do. He reached forward and drew the girl's robe up over her breasts.

"I can't own you, Abigail." He shook his head curtly, looking into her eyes.

"You are free", he said. "You are no longer a slave. I free you from it, as God is my witness."

The girl stared at him, uncomprehending.

"You are free, Abigail", he said again. He shook a handful of coins from Hussein's velvet purse and, reaching out, took one small hand and closed them within it.

"Take these and go", he said.

For a breathless instant the girl's large, dark eyes were fixed on his with a wild light kindling in them. A half-sob caught in her throat.

Then, before Gallant could speak, she was gone, her cloak's red swirl flashing, the tinkle of her anklets dying as she ran.

Gallant turned back to the balcony and stared at the moon, a feeling of desolate loneliness stronger than he expected rose in his throat. For a moment he cursed his idiocy, his priest-warped sense of principle that had made him send away the girl when now every fibre of his being ached for her.

He remained staring out at the night sky until the day's fatigue finally overwhelmed him, and he stripped off his clothes and the despatch belt to fall on the couch. There he tossed and murmured in a troubled half-sleep as the darkness of night deepened over the sleeping city.

High above the moonwashed roofs, a peregrine swung in a broadening arc, catching in its broad wings the faint updrafts of air rising from the streets below. The still evening air was crystalline and clear, and the bird's great eyes could have seen, had she cared, far out to sea to the faint twinkle of the stern light of His Britannic Majesty's Ship *Redoubtable*; or she might have angled her glide with a cant of her wingtips and swooped silently down the long, stepped slope of the city roofs out over the dark water of the harbour, where she might have wheeled above the mastheads of the *Echo,* whose unlit decks were paced by a watchful Akiwoya.

She chose instead to swing upslope, kiting silently round the slender tower of a minaret, her *che-reek* echoing from the white tile and stone that glowed pale and ghostly in the moon's light. Stars shone in carelessly flung splendour overhead, but the bird treasured only the moonlight, watching until it gleamed from a flying beetle rising into her path, and then swooping to pick the creature out of the air with a snap of her hooked beak as she turned toward the pale orb of moon, chirupping in satisfaction.

The same spreading moonlight revealed not only its prey to the circling bird, but, far below her, spilled across the balcony and into the chamber where Paul Gallant lay, shafting along the walls, spilling over the chair where his clothing was draped, gleaming from the naked blade of the hanger where it lay on the floor.

And it revealed the slow opening of the latticework door, and the small, robed figure that stepped noiselessly in to stand in the shadows, watching the marine as he slept.

Gallant stirred. Something within him was calling him, prodding him, pulling him up out of the deep pool of sleep toward the light of consciousness. Something primeval, some wary self-preservation that sensed a presence, pushed his protesting body up, woke his mind to sudden and chilled clarity and a ringing danger alarm.

With a lithe bound Gallant was off the couch, scooping up the hanger, crouching now to defend himself against the intruder he sensed in the shadows.

"Who?" he hissed. "Who is there! Speak, or by the True Christ, I'll gut you!"

A small figure moved into the light. A figure in a long red robe, with dark tumbling hair.

"Sacristi!" Gallant swore.

"Will you always greet me with sword in hand, my *djinn*?" Her voice was a soft whisper.

"Abigail!" For a moment he was unable to think of words to say. Then he remembered his nakedness, and reached for his breeches.

She moved to him, her hand on his arm stopping him. "Don't dress."

Through the pounding of his heart, which suddenly seemed to have come to life, he heard his own voice say, "What heathen thing did you call me?"

"My *djinn*", she laughed. "None but a spirit would have

done what you did. Sent me away. Released me.''

A deep, heady fragrance from her, warm and animal, reached his nostrils. He imagined the coppery form moving under the heavy folds of her robe.

"By Christ, you're beautiful!" he said.

He took her hand, her eyes shining now. The moonlight fell through the lacy trellicework that edged the balcony, casting an ink and ivory pattern over her. With his free hand he twisted the brooch at her shoulder, and the robe fell free of her body to the floor.

Sunlight was shafting in from the balcony over the head of the couch. Gallant woke with a start, blinking at the glare. He rolled over and found an empty pillow where the girl had lain.

Late in the night they had awakened to another spell of passion, to lie awake after in the darkness, talking. Slowly she had told him her story: the horror or her capture at the age of ten, when the Genoese merchantman bearing her father and his family out to his post at the court of the Two Sicilies had been taken by the Dey's gunboats, and her father butchered on the deck before her eyes; her mother's slavery and eventual death in the kitchens, and her own imprisonment in the Dey's palace where she was drilled for eight years in the art of the dance and the pleasuring of men. How she had almost become an Algerine, but cherished deep inside the flicker of hope for freedom and escape.

He sat up quickly, looking round the apartment. His clothes were still in disarray over the chair. The hanger lay on the floor.

The breeze in through the windows was warm and delightful on his skin, and he took a deep breath.

At the other end of the apartment Béssac's unmistakable bulk lay across the other couch, bare feet protruding from the covers. The mate was snoring, slowly and sonorously.

Gallant looked again at the empty pillow beside him and noticed for the first time the tiny golden circlet pinned to it. He held it in his palm, watching the sunlight glint from it.

"She left you a little token, eh?"

Béssac's hearty boom startled the marine. He looked up to see the mate wallowing up to the surface of the covers. Béssac's eyes were bleary, and he scratched his chest, yawning hugely. He was still fully dressed, with the exception of his shoes.

"You look as if you just rolled in", said Gallant.

Béssac snorted amiably, scratched his thatch. "Faugh! My mouth feels like it's lined with mole hair."

"I take it you found the seventh archway."

The mate nodded slowly, grinning sleepily. "In spades", he whistled. "Such women! I had almost forgotten." He padded over to the hanging cord and gave it a vigorous yank."

Gallant lay back in bed, smiling at the ceiling. Abigail's smell was still in his nostrils, the sound of her whispers in his ears. Sometime in the night she had slipped away without his knowing. It was possible he would never see her again, he thought.

The servants had padded in with a breakfast tray, to which Béssac addressed himself with a will. So lost was Gallant in his thoughts that he listened only half-heartedly to the mate until breakfast had been disposed of and both men were dressed for the day.

Gallant's mind was in turmoil. As it had since the moment when the despatch had come into his hands, his heart and mind were filled with the iron resolve to see it delivered. An iron resolve overlaid with the growing anxiety that somehow it was already too late, mixed with a refusal to believe that was true. Now Abigail had stepped into the scene, her passion and beauty sweeping in like a sudden wave over a sand beach he had carefully organized and patterned to his purposes. Driving *Écho* to her goal, pushing Béssac and the crew to their limits were all part of the ultimate goal, the purpose : getting the despatch through. And into that task Gallant had poured all his passion and resolve.

And now a small and beautiful girl whose touch and feel was like fire in his blood was overturning the ordered determination in his mind.

Gallant bit a lip.

The mate was clamping his salt-stained tricorne on his head.

"And a little Moroccan did something I didn't think possible. Mon Dieu, she'd fill her mouth with hot water and then... By Saint Peter enseigne, it's too fine a day to blather on like this!" He was hefting Hussein's bag of coin. "We've still got these to dispose of. What do you say we go down and wallow in the market of this city of anti-Christ. This time without a bloodthirsty escort."

Gallant flicked the talisman he had hung round his own neck. "Don't forget this."

"Sacristi, no. I almost forgot, can you believe!" said the mate, pulling the little chain from the bag.

"What should we look at first, then? Talisman or no, is there a place we can start without getting our throats cut? And where can we get ship's stores, eh?"

Béssac nodded. "The *suq*. The market, where everything goes on. You'll never forget it, enseigne. And it'll be the place for me to track down chandler's supplies."

"Very well", said Gallant. "I'd feel better if I knew how our men ashore were doing, and how Akiwoya was getting on."

The two men walked down the long, cool hallway, their heels echoing in the arched spaces overhead. Béssac led them through an interconnecting maze of colonnaded cloisters and sunlit plazas until finally they reached one of the latticed gates. A swarthy sentry in the yellow pantaloons squinted at the talismans before unbolting the gate, and the Europeans passed into the press and hubbub of the narrow streets.

TEN

The morning became for Gallant, when he tried in later times to pull it from his memory, a shifting kaleidoscope of colour, light and smell. For two or three hours the men moved through the crowds, stopping to stare and finger the goods in the endless shops and hawkers' stalls that filled every available corner. Gallant often simply stood aside while Béssac haggled volubly with the occasional vendor, buying nothing in the end but coming away looking pleased. Gradually they worked their way down hill toward the lower city, and after the initial confusion Gallant was beginning to be able to pick out what looked like a worthwhile purchase, and what did not. Gallant found he was walking as he did on the deck of the *Écho*, hands behind his back, body moving now not to balance against the heave of his ship, but to pass through the flow of robed humanity with a shifting step here, a turned shoulder there. Their Christian dress brought sharp, startled, and often hostile stares, but the glittering little medallions and Béssac's river of Arabic seemed to turn aside any hint of true ugliness. Gallant was beginning to enjoy the stroll, glad of the chance to study and wonder at the profusion of goods that filled the shops and even hung from the spaces overhead. Some of the intricate workmanship was even at a quick glance akin to artistry. It was a wonder that such care and concern was being spent on the most humdrum of items. That small kettle in the next shop, for example: engraved in intricate interlocking scrollwork.

"Paul! Paul!"

Gallant spun round, startled.

Behind them, in the midst of the shifting crowd of Moors, some kind of commotion had suddenly occurred. Figures were bobbing, heads ducking, voices being raised, robes flashing white in the shadows as their wearers scampered out of the way of whoever was forcing his way through.

One of the burly gunboat swordsmen appeared, his sword drawn, pushing bodies aside to clear a path for the small, hooded figure trotting behind him. "Paul! Oh, Paul!"

The marine gasped. "Abigail!"

Red robe billowing, she ran into his arms, gasping for breath. Her massive escort eyed Gallant and the wide-eyed Béssac for an instant before sheathing his blade and folding his arms to wait.

Gallant kissed her hot, flushed cheeks, and lifted her chin. "What is it, girl? What are you doing here?"

She clung to him, panting for breath.

"The ships! The...English ships! They're coming in toward the harbour! Hussein. His men are looking for you!"

"Coming in? To attack?" Gallant shot a look at Béssac.

The girl nodded, her hair falling about her face. "Hussein is sure of it. I overheard him. The Dey has ordered out the gunboats. To fight the ships. Hussein said you and your men could take your chances to get clear away in the confusion. His men are trying to find you and tell you!" .

Gallant gripped her shoulders hard. "My crew. Did he say anything about my crew beside that!"

Abigail winced at his strength. "They're all released, and back on the ship. And Paul, you must take me too!"

Gallant waited to hear no more. "That's it, Béssac. We get to the ship. Now!"

He spun back on the girl, "Do you think I'd have left you behind! Come on!"

"Yussef!" Abigail began, looking back at her hulking escort.

"What about him?"

"He's my protector. They cut out his tongue. I can't leave him!"

"Who says you must?" said Gallant, grinning crookedly at the huge Moor. "We can use muscle like that. Come on, you too!"

In seconds they were rushing down the terraced streets toward the harbour, arms linked, Yussef's huge bulk to the fore, shouldering a path through the crowd. The mobbed bodies made their progress slow and maddening until, without warning, Yussef vanished off to one side into a narrow alley.

"Follow him!" Abigail cried out.

With the girl gripped between them Gallant and Béssac dodged and weaved after Yussef's broad back for what seemed like hours through a serpentine maze of shadowed, rat-infested and stinking passages, conscious only that under their feet the path sloped ever downward.

"Mother of God, how much further!" puffed Béssac.

Then they were out, the sunshine brilliant and delicious, a breeze suddenly on their faces, heavy with the coolness and fishy stench of the sea edge.

Gallant blinked, eyes smarting from the glare, aware now of the mass of fishermen and dockworkers who were massed along the seawall edge, chattering and pointing seaward.

"Oh, Paul! Look!" said Abigail, her grip tight on his arm.

Almost as she spoke a booming thunder rolled over them, a sharp series of detonations echoing and re-echoing off the city walls and the hills inland. The thunder of naval guns.

"Mon Dieu!" muttered Béssac, unheard.

Aligned out in the neat formation of a Vernet canvas were four European warships, their British ensigns bright and challenging in the sun. Unmistakably it was the same squadron that had pursued *Écho* thus far. The ships were in a tight line, incredibly close inshore to the islands, moving swiftly and magnificently along before the northerly wind.

The large sixty-four and her smaller consorts were sending broadside after broadside into the island batteries behind which *Écho* lay in partial shelter. Already immense clouds of white smoke from the cannonading were beginning to tower into the sky, rising over the city. From the smaller shape of a bomb ketch, slightly farther offshore and moving slowly under clewed sails, gouts of heavy smoke erupted from its mortar well, followed by thumping detonations on the battery ramparts. And the batteries were firing back with fervour, pink flames winking back seaward at the stately line, tall and ghostly geysers from their shot leaping up beside the tan British hulls.

Somewhat closer inshore a long, ragged line of the Dey's gunboats were rowing vigorously out to intercept the ships, their oar blades flashing amidst the splashes of the British shot, hoarse cries from their crews barely audible. Here and there a bow gun was barking, wreathing its boat in a quick shroud of smoke.

The heavy pall was drifting inshore, and Gallant could see it swirling now around the brave, small shape of the corvette at her anchorage. But it did not obscure the flicker of movement on *Écho*'s deck, and the tongue of flame that lanced out from her side toward the British line.

"Good man!" Béssac spat into the dust. "Akiwoya's got a gun working!"

Gallant jerked his attention away from the mesmerizing panorama and looked around, biting his lip. "Where in Christ's name are the rest of our lads in all this?"

Béssac was pointing. "There! By the ship! Sacristi, they've got to her already!"

Gallant squinted and then swore luridly. Close aboard *Écho* was the ship's boat. And scrambling up her side were the figures of the corvette's crew.

Abigail gripped Gallant's arm and pointed toward the near angle of the quay. "Paul! What about one of these boats?"

Gallant followed her point to a small, lateen-rigged craft tugging gently at its lines. His eyes widened. No one was near the boat.

"Sacristi, my sweet, yes!" He tapped Béssac on the arm, indicating the boat. "What is it, Béssac?"

Béssac glanced quickly at him. "A *sambuk!* Fast little boat. She's thinking we should...?"

Gallant nodded, rubbing his hands on his breeches. It was obviously the one thing they could try

The boat was a miniature version of the big *dhows* and *feluccas* cluttering the roadstead. From its single mast was slung the same enormously long boom, a single triangular sail furled round it. The deck seemed open, although it was hard to tell from this angle. He could see that the craft had a small-boat's tiller bar, and a beamy hull with good freeboard. It was very like the handy boats Gallant had used as a boy to explore the corners of the rugged and treacherous Cape Breton coast.

Gallant gathered Abigail close against him. "Hang on to my arm and don't let go! We're going to have to run like the possessed for it!"

Abigail nodded, her lips tight.

Béssac casually picked up a short, sturdy chunk of wood, unnoticed by the jostling fishermen all around them whose eyes were still fixed on the action seaward. The British line was now dead abeam of the island battery, and was pummelling it with a fearful storm of shot.

Then Yussef gave an almost imperceptible nod. Abigail between them, Gallant and Béssac began to sidle through the crowd toward the boat. Yussef moved ahead, a path silently opening for the gleaming steel of his blade.

They were five yards from the boat when a lone fisherman, squatting beside it on the quayside, looked up, brows wrinkling in surprise. He began to rise from his squat when Yussef was on him with a bound, cuffing him flat with a swipe of one hamlike fist.

"Now!"

The three raced past Yussef and the sprawling fisherman toward the *sambuk*. Behind them Gallant heard a few shouts of alarm and anger from the crowd.

He glanced over his shoulder to see a man, then another,

break from the crowd and run toward them. A rock hurtled through the air, then another. The second struck Abigail's head with an audible sound and she sank, suddenly limp, in his grip.

With a curse Gallant swept her up in his arms, a fierce anxiety for her hard in his chest. "Get aboard, Béssac!" he barked. "I've got her! Yussef! Come on!"

With desperate strength Gallant leaped across to the rope-strewn deck, laying the girl quickly but gently down to one side of the great furled mainsail. Béssac was feverishly hunting for the lashing point and coil of the halliard, a stream of rich Acadien curses pouring from his lips.

Yussef sprang lightfootedly aboard, and with a grunt he seized Béssac's hand and placed it roughly on a coil to one side of the mast, jerking his other thumb upward.

"Good man!" breathed Béssac. "Help me cast off, Yussef!"

"For Christ's sake, man, come back!" cried Gallant.

Yussef had snatched up a boathook and leaped back on to the quay. Gallant and Béssac tore at the lashing, Gallant's hands working almost on their own as he bellowed at the Moor.

Then he saw what Yussef had seen. Two other fishermen, wicked-looking long pikes in their hands, sprinting along the quay toward them, faces distorted by snarls.

Damn these lines! Gallant and Béssac threw their weight on the halliard, the heavy yard stirring from the deck and beginning to squeal aloft. Sweat stung Gallant's eyes, and he felt his muscles crack with the effort. Slowly the yard rose until the broad face of the lateen was rippling loosely in the wind. Gallant stumbled aft to the tiller, scooping the sheets into coils as he went. He looked around wildly for Yussef.

He gaped as he saw Yussef parry the thrust of one of the fishermen, then drop the man with a club of the boathook's butt end. The second man stared at Yussef for a split-second, then dropped his pike and ran.

"Yussef! Sacristi, man, get aboard!" roared Béssac.

The breeze, offshore now, was pushing strongly at the sail,

and the lateen yard was thankfully riding on the leeward side of the mast. Béssac scrambled aft and hauled in the heavy lee sheet until the big sail filled, and the boat strained forward against its lines, eager to move.

Yussef came at a run to the bow line, and with a sweep of the boathook cut it from its piling.

"Leave the other, Yussef!" yelled Gallant, little caring that the Moor could not understand him. "We'll cut the stern line from on board!"

Gallant ducked involuntarily as a tremendous hissing column of spray leaped up scant feet from the *sambuk*, his ears suddenly opening to the colossal thunder in the air. The noise was almost beyond comprehension. The British line of ships had tacked smartly and were pouring an avalanche of fire from their opposite gun batteries into the island and the harbour as they glided on the return pass, the Algerine gunboats harrying after them, small terrier shapes in the sunlight.

Yussef sprang for the boat and tumbled on the deck, teeth bared in a savage grin.

"Good lad!" hooted Béssac, and added a phrase of Arabic that stretched the Moor's grin even further.

An arrow hummed by Gallant's ear and smacked into the sea. With a bound he was at the stern line, wrenching it free.

The *sambuk* leaped ahead instantly and Gallant dove for the tiller, grasping it just before the stern swung into the rough pilings. A second later and the boat was clear of the quay, water hissing round the rudder as it gathered speed into the harbour.

Gallant crouched, feeling the pull of the rudder, checking by feel the strain on the jam hitch he had put on the sheet. He glanced astern in time to see a last arrow drop into the wake, the bowman's shrill and venomous curse carrying across the water. The *sambuk* was alarmingly fast on this point of sailing, and within a few minutes the staring, shouting faces on the quay were mere shapeless blobs.

The *sambuk* surged across the harbour, Gallant threading his way recklessly through the anchored hulls, ignoring the roar and blast of the cannonfire, heedless of the gigantic columns of spray that were leaping up everywhere.

Béssac had crouched by Abigail, covering her with his stained seacoat. He cursed and spat as a near miss from one of the British shot drenched them with a sheet of spray.

"Courage, mon ami!" Gallant cried. "We're almost there!"

Béssac spat again. "To where?" he roared back. "The ship or Hell?"

The *sambuk* stormed on, and then suddenly *Écho*'s side was looming in front of them, and the *sambuk* thumped against the corvette's wale, the noise and smoke enveloping them now. Shouts of recognition and joy rang down from the corvette. Yussef gathered up Abigail's small form in his arms and suddenly found twenty pairs of willing hands propelling him up the side of the ship. The same hands seized on Gallant and Béssac and hauled them roughly up the battens and over the rail to the deck.

As his feet hit the planking Gallant heard a roar go up from the Acadiens, and he grinned back at the grimy, open faces, their eyes shining with the excitement of the fight and the joy of seeing Gallant and the mate again. But there was no time for reunions, if an escape was going to take place.

Gallant knelt quickly by Abigail, who was still cradled in Yussef's massive arms. Her face was still and beautiful, her lashes long against her cheeks. But thankfully her cheeks had colour, and there was no blood to be seen.

He looked into Yussef's broad face. "She's got to be taken below, Yussef. Below, understand?" He gestured to a seaman standing nearby. "Take her to my cabin. This man will show you. Guard her there."

He looked deep into the Moor's eyes and understanding registered there. With effortless strength Yussef rose with Abigail, carrying her with infinite tenderness, and padded after the man Gallant had pointed out.

Gallant spun on the waiting, anxious faces of his crew.

"All right, listen to me! We'll slap backs later! Akiwoya, silence your gun and get your men aloft!" He glanced at the sterns of the British ships, which were at the far corner of the crescent harbour, preparing to wear about for a third pass, the pass when the cutting-out boats might come in after the corvette. If *Écho* made sail now and angled for the farther, south-east corner, the escape might work! "We've got a chance of getting out of here!"

He spat over the rail. "Béssac!"

"Here, enseigne!" boomed the mate.

"Take her off the wind, Béssac. Cut the cable, and let the anchor go! The wind's out of the nor'west, so take her out due on sou'east! And cram on every scrap of canvas she'll carry!"

With a joyful roar the hands scattered to their positions for getting underway. Axe blows rang out forward, and even as the tail of cable splashed into the sea the big headsails, hauled tautly aback, were swinging the bows off the wind. *Écho* rolled slightly as she turned, the rigging aloft shaking as the canvas slapped and boomed. Then, blocks squealing, the yards swung round, a silence falling over the taut, straining bellies of the sails. The English guns had ceased their roar briefly as the ships wore about, and once again Gallant could hear the sweet music of the sounds of his own ship: the chants of the haulers, and the slap of bare feet on planking; the creak and groan of the rigging working against the pressure of wind and sail; and the building swish of the sea water along the corvette's side and under her counter.

"There, Béssac", said Gallant to the mate, who had reappeared at his side. "By the lee of the island battery. Get through that and we might be half a league at sea before the English are back!"

Béssac pulled his hat low over his eyes and folded his arms. "D'accord, enseigne. That's where we'll take her!"

Gallant ducked down the companionway and stepped in through the door of his cabin. On the small settee Yussef had lain Abigail down, still covered with Béssac's seacoat. Gallant gently lifted the coat off and, stripping the coverlet from his own little box bunk, covered her with it. Her face was soft and exquisite in repose, and he found it almost impossible looking at her to see there the face of the wanton dancer in the Dey's great hall. He saw instead the shining light in her eyes as love had possessed them, and the bravery that shone from them on the quayside. He had known her very little more than a matter of hours; had spoken at all with her for any length only in the dark of a lovers' bed; and realized he knew almost nothing about her.

Then he looked up at Yussef, whose eyes were looking at his with intelligence, and now, with sympathy. He smiled, and Yussef smiled back. The Moor knew.

"Yes, Yussef", said Gallant. "I love her too. I hardly but know her, yet I love her." He looked back at the unconscious girl. "I pray to God she isn't going to be lost to both of us. That stone…"

Dampening a cloth from a wine bottle he wiped her brow, and poured a little of the dark liquid on her lips and temples. There was little else that could be done for her at the moment, unless, somehow, someway, they could find a surgeon.

"Care for her, Yussef", he said. "For both our sakes!"

There was a clumping outside the cabin door and Béssac looked in, frowning at the look on Gallant's face.

"Will she be all right, enseigne?"

Gallant shook his head. "Christ in Heaven, Béssac, I don't know." He stroked her forehead gently. "It may just be a temporary swoon, but I'm not leech enough to know. If she keeps still…"

Before he had time to finish the deck canted suddenly underfoot, and overhead the men heard the boom of luffing canvas.

"What in the Name of God!" cursed Béssac.

A young seaman appeared breathlessly at the cabin door.

We're clear o' the harbour, messieurs", he puffed. "The boatswain's calling for you. We're almost a league ahead of the English squadron."

"Done it!" exulted Béssac.

"But there's another sail in sight, m'sieu'. Hull-up to nor'ard and sure to run us down in a clock's tick, says the boatswain!"

"What?"

When Gallant and Béssac reached the deck, the oaths and curses of Guimond and Akiwoya were ringing above the thunder of the lashing sails overhead.

Gallant strode quickly to the wheel.

"Helm up, man. Let her pay off."

Béssac's voice joined the chorus, sending knots of men to the braces. "Haul, there! Lee braces! Tend to what you're doing!"

Gallant looked at the compass card and the leech of the foretopsail. "Steady on south-east by east."

"Steady sou'east by east, m'sieu'. Sorry, enseigne." The helmsman looked at him ashamedly. "I was looking at that ship."

"No matter now", said Gallant. "Keep her steady as she lies now."

Béssac came rolling aft. "There's the other sail!" he said, pointing over the quarter.

Gallant turned to look, and almost immediately stifled a gasp.

"A fifth-rate. Or a frigate", Béssac said half to himself at his elbow.

Already well hull-up over the horizon, a vessel was flying along toward them under an immense cloud of tan canvas, including the first studdingsails Gallant had ever seen set. Even at this distance, a good two leagues or so, Gallant could see the boiling white of the frigate's bow wave under its dark jibboom.

"Who in the devil are they?"

Béssac squinted through a small, ivory-cylindered glass and handed it to Gallant. "She's English!" he said

"English!"

The mate was right. Behind the frigate's partially obscured mizzen Gallant glimpsed the flash of colour of the British ensign, lolling in the relatively still air before the winging gaff spanker.

"Holy Mother, look at her come!"

Gallant felt his scalp prickling. The English ship was moving down on them at a tremendous rate. This was no ordinary

Anglo-Saxon naval barge, heavy and awkward in anything but a near gale. This was likely a prize, a Spanish or French vessel taken and put on the establishment of the Royal Navy. Most of the best English vessels, in terms of performance, were of a similar background. Rumour had it the English themselves considered their own ships to have been built by the mile and cut off as required.

"A picket ship" said Béssac, through his teeth. "They must've had her cruising offshore, watching to seaward. And she must have spotted us coming out. Bad luck, enseigne!"

"Is there any chance we can get a few more knots out of her?" said Gallant.

Béssac bared his teeth and spat leeward.

"Not without crossing a royal yard, enseigne. He'll overhaul us, fair and square!"

Écho's men were lining the rail now, staring at the frigate and glancing anxiously from time to time up at the quarterdeck.

Gallant rubbed the back of his neck. A frigate such as that most likely carried anywhere from thirty to thirty-six guns, likely twelve- or eighteen-pounders, less likely twenty-fours. One well-aimed broadside from her and *Écho* would disintegrate into a chaos of collapsing rigging, flying splinters, and screaming, mangled men. A cold knot gripped his stomach.

He glanced forward. With the refitting necessary to convert her to a paying merchantman, the corvette had been stripped of her main armament. Béssac had kept only four, two six-pounders and two nines, on the upper deck. Of these, one of the six-pounders was permanently lost on the sand spit, and of the nines, one had been detrunnioned and the other's carriage smashed by round shot during the escape from the Spanish inlet.

Gallant shook his head. The corvette had but one six-pounder gun with which to reply to the murderous and well disciplined storm of iron from a British warship.

He clasped his hands firmly behind his back once more, determined to maintain a cool exterior.

One gun and its crew. Sweet Blood of the Saints. It was pitifully little, but then perhaps the Englishman would not be expecting a fight. The hidden sting might hurt the unwary attacker enough to let the corvette turn and run again, before the squadron was upon them.

Gallant shrugged, sensing even as he thought the futile absurdity of the idea. He swallowed and set his jaw. It was all they could do.

He eyed the onrushing frigate, trying to remember the gunnery lessons at the small battery on the Louisbourg quayside, the grizzled canonier in his stained red breeches pressing home the key principle of gunnery against ships, which was...

"Enseigne! She's opened fire!"

"What?"

Gallant sprang to the rail. A dull thump carried downwind from the frigate, and a twinkling white geyser leaped up from the surface of the sea, barely a third of the way toward *Écho*. The puff of bluish smoke from the frigate's larboard battery disintegrated in the wind.

"A warning shot", said Béssac, at his elbow. "He wants us to go about and heave to! But there's one break for us, anyway."

"What?" said Gallant.

"For some reason she's not mounted bow chasers. Means she'll want to get alongside to bring her main batteries to bear. We'll have a few extra moments while he tries to do that."

"Indeed? Damned small comfort that is!"

The rigging! The old canonier always pressed home that lesson, he remembered in a rush. When engaging a ship, never pound away uselessly at the hull, particularly at heavy English hulls. Dismast them, cripple them, put them dead in the water and at your mercy to make a prize, to board or rake from the ends at your leisure. Well, he thought to himself, the prize they were after now was survival. But there was the slimmest of chances.

Gallant swung around to look over the larboard quarter. The topsails and courses of the English squadron were looming closer by the minute. Damn! They'd have to turn and fight now, and hope forlornly for a chance to escape. There was no other way out.

He looked up. The wind was steadily freshening, and *Écho*'s sails were tight as drumheads. Good weather for manoeuvring and rapid movement.

Very well, he thought. It was time to bite the bullet.

"Béssac! Bring her into the wind! Starboard tack. Lay the Englishman on the starboard bow!"

Béssac's orders barked out, and the men leaped instantly to the braces, aware now of the seriousness of the situation. Their eyes turned aft to where Béssac was standing by the wheel. After a look aloft and to windward he dropped a hand.

"Helm a-lee!"

With a steep heel *Écho* swept round, the bowsprit swinging in long dipping curves around the horizon. The frenzied hauling of the men on the braces eased the tremendous thundering aloft from the luffing canvas, and within a few minutes the corvette had begun her beat up to windward, punching now into the full force of wind and swell, sails arched, clouds of spray bursting over the plunging bows to rattle on the decks and drench the hands belaying the braces.

Gallant jammed his hat more firmly on his head and squinted at the frigate, trying to make his mind work. The Englishman seemed frighteningly close, a dark, ominous shape against the silver dappling of the sun on the sea. What was the weakest part of that beautiful thing rushing down upon them? The foremast? The rudder?

The bowsprit!

Gallant sprang to beside the wheel, clutching at the binnacle for balance as *Écho* slammed into a steeving green swell, shuddered, and lifted wreathed in spume.

"Larboard a point! Another! Good! Steady there!" he rasped.

The corvette was moving well now, her canvas responding to the small corrections Béssac constantly ordered to the sheets, her sleek hull shining wet as it lifted and plunged into the hissing, blue-green swells marching down on her from windward. The full force of the wind was tearing at the figures on her wet decks, spray stinging like needles as it was driven into unprotected hands and faces.

Akiwoya appeared amidships, his muscled torso gleaming like oiled wood in the strengthening sunlight, his eyes wide and shining with excitement. Over his shoulder was slung the heavy priming horn of a gun captain.

He cupped his hands and shouted aft, over the roar of the sea. "The gun crew, enseigne?"

"Yes, Akiwoya! The six-pounder! Double shot it, quickly!"

The gunner moved forward with a catlike agility rare in a man so large, bellowing for his gun crew, staggering slightly to the heave and pitch of the wet, angled deck.

Behind Gallant the helmsman cried out, pointing to the English frigate, now moving at them at what appeared to be an impossible speed.

"Her gunports, enseigne! She's running her guns out!"

The marine swore. The frigate was driving down hard on the closehauled corvette, hoping to sweep past to weather and pummel the exposed gundeck and bilges with a hail of shot as she passed. With the greater height of the frigate the broadside would sweep the weatherdeck as well. It would be sheer slaughter, *Écho*'s helpless crew butchered where they stood by the screaming shot and splinters.

Gallant's throat was dry. He cupped his hands to shout at the top of his lungs.

"Akiwoya! Load and run out as soon as you can! Prime and stand ready to fire!"

An answering wave. Gallant watched as the gunner's straining gun crew wrestled to ready the little piece, which suddenly appeared to him such a pitifully useless answer to the doom so rapidly approaching.

He hauled himself up to the weather rail and squinted at the English vessel, trying to calculate her distance from them.

The frigate was an undeniably beautiful sight as it rushed down on them. Its tan sails were set and drawing to perfection, a trio of towering pyramids above a graceful hull. The frigate's cutwater overhauled and knifed through the translucent swells, sending spume wide to either side. Along the sides Gallant could see the muzzles of the run-out guns, small circles of red in the dark shadows of the gunports. Above her mainmast the frigate's commissioning pennant streamed forward over her bows, pointing like a lance toward the corvette. The frigate was now about a thousand yards away. In a few moments the slaughter would begin, thought Gallant. But they were going to get in one blow at least before that came to pass.

He slapped the rail.

"Now. Now we tweak the lion's tail! Stand by to come about!" His voice rose on the last order.

He glanced aloft, steadying his legs to the roll and pitch of the glistening, slippery deck. The little green burgee lay out stiffly from the fore truck.

"Ready...ready..." Then, "Helm a-lee!"

He heard the slap of the helmsman's hands on the wheel, and *Écho* heeled hard over to leeward, swooping into her rush across the wind.

"Hard a-lee, enseigne!"

Gallant felt salt bite into the cracks in his lips. The corvette plunged into the eye of the wind once more, her bows driving into each gleaming swell with a sonorous crunch and a shimmering shower of spray. The great topsails and courses thrashed and boomed with such demonic force that the deck shook beneath his feet. Foaming water sluiced in torrents down the corvette's foredeck, dragging at the struggling, drenched men fighting to hold their footing at the taffrails.

"Off tacks and sheets!"

The marine was soaked to the skin. The tang of the spray, the sharp chill of the wind, the golden glory of the sea under the now brilliant sun, combined with the enthralling thunder overhead to transport him for a moment into an exaltation akin to ecstasy. He hooted, the sound ripped away by the wind as it left his lips. To feel this, a moment before death!

"Let go and haul, there!" Béssac's voice sounded over the sea noise. "Lee braces, now, lee braces!"

Brawny, gleaming hands fastened on the heavy lines, and as the men threw their weight and curses into the hauling the thunder aloft ceased, *Écho* leaping ahead like a greyhound on the port tack.

Gallant scrubbed a cuff across his eyes and peered at the binnacle. "Larboard a point! Hold her there!"

He sprang down the ladder to the waist, crouching for a moment by the ladder's foot as a solid sheet of spray jetted inches over his head, then staggered forward along the slick, pitching deck. Akiwoya, eyes wild now with tension, crouched with his white-eyed crew beside the little gun, sheltering from the arching clouds of spray that smashed over the bulwarks.

Gallant seized his shoulder, feeling the steely hardness of the muscle.

"When I signal like this", he gasped, "take aim for the bowsprit! Try to bring it right off! You'll get only one chance, so for God's sake do it that once!"

The huge gunner spat and grinned fiercely. He jerked a short nod.

"Good luck!"

Gallant scrambled aft to the quarterdeck. Béssac was beside the wheel, shouting something, pointing forward, and as Gallant gained the weather rail he looked at the frigate.

It was almost atop them and was beginning to yaw, long dark ripples appearing in the topsails as the frigate captain tried at the last minute to close the angle Gallant's sudden turn had opened. Even as it was, if the ships did not collide in the next few moments, the frigate would roar past the corvette's ends, raking her with a deadly fire as she passed. Gallant could see figures moving on the Englishman's decks, the gleam and twinkle of brass and bayonets, the solid little clump of red of a marine squad drawn up on the foredeck. The frigate rushed in for the kill, towering over her prey.

They were an instant away.

"Enseigne!" Béssac's shout was clear over the wind.

Gallant held up his hand, waiting in agony for the right moment.

"In the name of Christ, enseigne!" bellowed Béssac.

The frigate's bowsprit loomed high abeam the corvette's own, then the cutwater, then the cathead, then...

He chopped his hand down savagely, his voice almost a shriek.

"Fire, Akiwoya!"

Gallant felt the deck buck as the gun fired, the bluish smoke ripped back around the crouching figures of Akiwoya's crew, the gun lurching back against its breeching line.

The frigate was so close aboard them that the motion of the two ships was dizzying. *Écho* swept on, a small rabbit evading the jaws of a wolfhound, and for a horrifying split second Gallant thought the shot had gone wide, with no effect at all.

Then, in that same half second, a burst of fragments sprang from the base of the frigate's bowsprit, and he heard clearly the punch of the ball's impact.

Écho slammed into a toppling swell, the deck pitching up and a stinging wall of spray driving into Gallant's face, forcing him to duck below the bulwark. He heard Béssac's shout as he slapped a hand across his dripping face to clear his eyes.

"Christ, and the Sweet Virgin, we got her!"

The frigate's bowsprit was twisting and writhing, cables and lines curling and whipping about like living things, the headsails crumpling and ballooning in tan waves over the forepeak. The wind carried the crackle of the collapsing rigging, and the hoarse shouts of the English crew. Their faces were white blobs, ducking and moving. Gallant saw one redcoated marine raise his musket protectingly over his head before a welter of rigging collapsed over him.

The frigate was wallowing, swinging her quarters to the seas, pitching so viciously that one moment Gallant looked evenly across at her weatherdeck, and the next at the dull white of the stempost rearing out of the boiling seas.

In the next instant, like the collapse of latticework under an axe, the frigate's foremast tottered forward, the curved bellies of the sails bulging obscenely as they crumpled. With an enormous crash the wreckage fell into the sea beside the frigate's larboard bow, the tangled and interwoven mass of rigging and cables trailing back up over the side. Almost immediately the vessel began to slew around, now rolling heavily in the swells, her main and mizzen canvas luffing with rippling booms.

Écho was drawing rapidly away, and Gallant saw that the wreckage on the frigate's bows was acting like a sea anchor, hauling the vessel around so that its broadsides were unable to use the point-blank range for the kill.

Gallant shook his head with wonder.

Aboard the frigate, all seemed chaos. As *Écho* widened the gap of frothed sea between the two ships, Gallant could see men scrambling in frenzied activity about her decks. Axes gleamed amidst the dark tangle of the wreckage.

Gallant squinted forward at the other English ships, as shouts and cheers began coming from Akiwoya's men and the other men about the ship.

Beside him, Béssac growled in his ear. "They're spreading stu'n's'ls, enseigne. That'll give them another knot or more edge on us!"

Gallant nodded. "All right. Show them our quarter, Béssac!"

Béssac was already cupping his hands. "Sheets and braces! Lively, you wharf rats!"

Akiwoya was moving aft over the glistening deck, his muscled torso gleaming itself like oiled mahogany in the sunlight. He rubbed his hands with gusto and cocked his head at Gallant.

"Well done, man!" called the marine.

The African's pointed teeth shone in a fierce grin. "He took that one fair and square, enseigne! Right in the gullet!"

Gallant crouched without thinking under the shower of spray that jetted up over the windward bulwark as *Écho* knifed into a white-bearded swell.

"Put the helm up!"

The corvette careened sickeningly as she fell off the wind and lay abeam briefly to the hissing swells. Blocks squealed aloft, the braces hauling the yards athwartships as *Écho* curtseyed round to leeward. The motion eased as she ran off further before the wind, the howl in the rigging dying away. Gallant sensed that like every vessel this one had a favourite point of sailing, and for *Écho* it was to run free before the wind. He listened to the hiss of the sea around the rudder as the ship began lifting her stern to the overtaking swells in a graceful figure-eight motion.

Béssac went quickly forward to direct the trimming of sheets and braces, and Gallant looked aft over the quarter. The frigate was perhaps half a league away now, the wreckage a dark clump on her bows. The only sail showing was the gaff spanker, sheeted home hard, trying to draw the bows round into the wind.

Gallant glanced at the swinging compass card. "Larboard a point. Easy, now! Not too far. Steady on east sou'east by south!"

He shuddered involuntarily, not really hearing the helmsman's acknowledgement. The sun had gone behind the low, scudding clouds that raced overhead, and his drenched clothing suddenly felt cold and heavy on him. He looked at the white pyramids of the remaining English vessels, now almost dead astern. Their forms were broadened now, with the extra curves of studdingsails reaching out to either side of the dark hulls. Pools of moving sunlight alternately glowed and darkened on the distant sails, and *Écho* herself was moving from island to island of golden light across the gunmetal surface of the sea.

Béssac had moved aft, and Gallant turned to him, his teeth beginning to chatter and an unpleasant weakness in his arms. "What do you think, Béssac? How much time have we got before they overtake us, or we fetch up on this lee shore?"

Béssac glanced over the side and then squinted at the distant ships.

"We've got ten, maybe fifteen minutes running like this, enseigne", he said, "before we're aground. And to clear that eastern arm of the bay on any kind of a reach with speed enough to keep them from cutting us off..." He shook his head. "Got to do it now."

"Otherwise it's a slow tack to claw off a lee shore while the rosbifs run down and hammer us to bits!"

"They don't even have to do that", said Béssac. "They've almost got us embayed here, and they know it. The Algerine gunboats won't come out to bother 'em in this kind of sea, and all they have to do is keep station up there to windward and wait until we run on the rocks or work up into the mouths of their guns.''

Gallant wiped the back of his hand across his mouth. "I won't give up, Béssac. Not yet. Bring her round into the wind. Reach for that eastern point!''

Within the minute *Écho* was leaving her run before the wind, bringing her bows up into the wind once again until her bowsprit pointed at the distant headland marking the eastern end of the half-moon bay. Blocks squealed as the seamen hauled through the slack in the tacks and bowlines, and braced the yards round into the full power of the reach. Once again the wind hummed and sang in the rigging, and the bows began to dash glittering necklaces of spray into the air and over the decks.

Béssac was close beside the helmsman, barking orders to the clumps of men gathered on the braces and sheet lines. Finally he grunted and turned to Gallant. ·

"That's it. Point up any further and we'll lose speed, enseigne. We'd be tacking, and they'd catch us with ease.''

Gallant nodded. He jammed his hat down lower over his eyes and squinted at the English squadron, trying to find what a small voice told him was not there: an escape.

"Sweet Jesus, you haven't got me yet!'' he muttered, and opened Béssac's little glass to study the Englishmen more closely.

The sixty-four was almost dead abeam now, and it was obvious *Écho* could reach across her track and weather the headland without entering the range of the big vessel's batteries. As the sixty-four was forced more and more around to windward *Écho*'s sailing ability to windward would become all the more evident. But they had more than the sixty-four to contend with.

Écho rolled heavily, and Gallant gripped the rail, watching the English ships as they began at that moment a new manoeuvre. They were fanning out into a broad line abreast. And off *Écho*'s windward bow the remaining frigate was angling over on a driving broad reach, going for the block on

Écho's track to open sea. Into the interval between that ship and the sixty-four the remaining English ship, a gunbrig, was moving, leaving only the bomb ketch, which was far astern and hove-to near the hull of the frigate Gallant's gun had dismasted. *Écho* was like a man sprinting to cross a street down which thundered a line of carriages abreast, a line of which the end carriage looked sure to smash down the man just as his foot reached for the curb. Gallant looked astern. Even if *Écho* came briskly round and tried to reach for the western shore, the bay was so strictured now that the sixty-four's batteries would reach the corvette even if Gallant ran her up on the beach.

Béssac was at his elbow, waiting. "Well, enseigne? What do we do? I don't relish an English prison hulk, but maybe..."

Gallant looked at him coldly. "I'll decide when and if we take that option, Béssac. Now pay attention to sailing this ship!"

Béssac reddened, but said nothing as he saw the fury and frustration in the marine's eyes. Finally he turned away. As he did so Gallant stepped near him.

"Sorry, Béssac. You didn't deserve that."

Béssac's smile was quick and warm. "Forget it, enseigne."

Gallant spun and squinted into the wind at the line of English ships. They were closing the trap swiftly, he thought.

"The frigate's within range of our track, enseigne. She'll likely heave-to and wait for us to come to her. She knows we can't go anywhere else." And as Béssac spoke the frigate's hull gleamed as she turned, sails rippling with dark wavelike shadows, turning until her foretopsail went hard aback and she lay waiting for the corvette. Even at this distance the frigate's gunports looked black, menacing and pitiless.

Gallant started at the big sixty-four, which was hauling round into a reach, large now off the corvette's quarter. It was obvious what would happen: the frigate would begin the pummelling of the corvette as she drove near, and might even pay off and run down against close to point-blank range for murderous broadsides or even boarding. At best the frigate would force the corvette to go about, paying away her lead over the remaining ships, until the sixty-four would move within range and her batteries could complete the destruction of *Écho*, a destruction that under a half-ton of flying metal shot would be complete and ghastly.

Gallant ran his eyes over *Écho*'s decks, at the grim and anxious faces of her men. He looked at Béssac, seeing the patience there in his eyes, the trust, the stoic calm, the willingness to fight and die if Gallant ordered it.

Again the image of his distant Louisbourg swam before his eyes, the long, final gaze of Du Chambon as he handed Gallant the vital despatch, and Philippe's face as he lay with his children in the mud.

"Mother of God, have I failed them?" he muttered.

Then he thought of Abigail, lying below in his cabin, still motionless from the blow of the stone. He thought of a storm of grape and canister smashing in through the stern gallery windows, splintering the cabin into rubbish, picking up Abigail where she lay and crushing her into nothing.

Gallant gritted his teeth and cursed at the tears of rage that welled suddenly in his eyes. He spat and moved to the forward rail, where Béssac stood braced, waiting.

"Strike, Béssac."

"Enseigne?"

"Strike the colours, man! Haul them down! In the name of Christ, do I have to chisel it in stone?"

And with savage force he kicked open the companionway door and vanished below.

"Signal from *Hector*, sir. The Frenchman has struck his colours."

"What? Has he, by God! Very good!" Commodore Fitzsimmons acknowledged the signal midshipman's report and turned to Captain Pollett, who stood with him on the broad quarterdeck of *Redoubtable*.

"Thank God, John", he said at length. "At least we can put this matter to rest."

Pollett nodded. "It was a near run thing, sir. I thought, if I may say so, that you were insane to go in there against those gunboats and the batteries. And if *Heracles* hadn't spotted her coming out and engaged her as she did, the Frenchman might have escaped."

"Quite", said Fitzsimmons, briskly. "Might have, but did not." He sniffed. "Insane or not, John, we had no choice. I have no idea what's happening in that damned Louisbourg venture. But to let that fellow get through, and perhaps put a French squadron off Louisbourg just as the siege or whatever is coming to a head..." He shook his head. "Imagine the chaos!"

Pollett studied the little corvette through a glass. The foretopsail was aback, and *Hector*'s boats bearing a boarding party were already pulling strongly toward the French vessel.

"We shall have to work off this lee shore presently", said Fitzsimmons, accepting the glass for a look. "Well, by God, there's no doubting one thing."

"Sir?"

"That Froggy's a bloody-minded man of courage, John. Be a credit to any service, including our own!"

Pollett nodded again, taking back the glass.

"Pity I had to put an end to the bastard's career", added the Commodore, almost under his breath. He rubbed his hands briskly together and began to pace the broad quarterdeck, feeling better than he had in weeks.

"Well, then", he said, matter-of-factly, "as to her disposal. Direct the *Amalie* at once to Mahon with my report of the affair to Rear-Admiral Medley. Have her take that corvette's commander and anything or anyone else of importance along with her." He adjusted his neckcloth. "Henry Medley might like to do a bit of gentlemanly interrogating as an aside. And you'll appoint a prize crew from your own ship's company. Pick a damn good officer, mind. I don't want that ship put up on some ledge after all this fuss!"

"Aye, aye, sir. May I add something else, sir?" said Pollett.

"Yes?"

"Well done, sir. You got him."

Fitzsimmons nodded solemnly. "Yes", he said. "Yes, I did, blast his garlic-sodden Papist hide!"

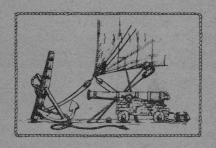

ELEVEN

To any vessel beating up against the northerlies to make the mouth of Mahon harbour, on the eastern end of Minorca, Fort Saint Philip was an impressive sight. The terraced levels and humped ramparts of its bulk dominated the southern side of the harbour mouth, its salients reaching out like the arms of a huge starfish toward the water's edge.

But there was usually little time to stare idly at the most powerful English fortification in the Mediterranean proper; it was handy and quick-thinking seamanship that was needed to thread a ship through the narrows, dodging from tack to tack all the way. The approach was almost always the same on the run easterly to the Balearics from Gibraltar. A landfall on the southern tip of Formentera; then a long, twenty-league north-easterly tack to raise Majorca out of the azure sea, and passing that shore close aboard to larboard. Then another long beat, of almost equal length if the wind did not veer to bring up first the high crown of Mount Toro, central peak of Minorca, and then, a good five leagues to the southeast, the rocks of Aire at the island's tip.

Then it was Down Helm, a northward turn into the series of tacks a league or more toward Cape Mola, to the north.

The island would be close aboard then, a high sunwashed tableland of terraces rising above cliffs, a patchwork of fields and olive groves and the whitewashed sentinel forms of windmills. Finally would come the bearing needed for the long, exhilarating reach into the three-mile harbour to Mahon: watching Mola's angle open on the bow; seeing the low hump of Marlborough Redoubt on Saint Stephen's Cove draw abeam; watching for the opening of the long view into the roads before putting the helm up, bracing the yards around as tautly fore and aft as they could draw, and standing in. It was not without danger. Once past Charles Fort and drawing Fort Saint Philip abeam, it was always grimly necessary to watch for the long shoal reaching out from Philipet Point; here the harbour was a scant two hundred and fifty yards wide. And it was always then that the tardy gunners in Fort Saint Philip would fire a last-minute salute, making it necessary to pull needed hands from sailhandling to fire salutes and dip ensigns in reply.

From where he was pacing the wind-chilled north rampart in the fort, Rear-Admiral Henry Medley, Senior Naval Officer at Mahon, was watching the entrance of a weatherbeaten gun brig with an expectant and critical eye.

He looked for the late gun salute, the sloppy clewing up of courses, the lack of crispness in work aloft. Henry Medley was a very competent naval officer, and certainly was considered by all who knew him as a brave one as well. But he was a Regulations man, to fill the great void in his appreciation of things that a stronger imagination might have filled. He believed in Method, and enforced that belief on his ships and their crews. As complete a naval officer as his age could produce, he could quote liberally and at random from the King's Regulations and Admiralty Instructions almost as soon as they appeared in 1731.

As a result he found his Commodore, Roger Fitzsimmons, to be a difficult subordinate to understand and even more difficult to control. Fitzsimmons was not a "book" man at all;

and matters had been made worse by this damned adventure Rowley at Gibraltar had set up for Fitzsimmons. Set up, in fact, entirely without Medley's knowledge. Medley was inclined to think that Vice-Admiral Lestock was right: Rowley was a choleric fool, and no more.

Medley squinted at the little brig as it thumped out an uneven but tolerable gun salute. At least Fitzsimmons had brought the matter to a head quickly, he thought, if the brig carried the news from the Commodore that Medley expected.

Well, thought Medley, it was better off done and finished. The Royal Navy's job here was to keep Spanish and French troop transports from reaching Italy, and damned hard that had proved to do at that.

He turned and stumped down off the barbette. It was time to get to his coach and jolt back along the road to Mahon. He wanted to be there to take the brig commander's report in person.

"Present Arms, damn you!" Medley barked at an inattentive sentry. The man started and almost dropped his musket before stiffening into the salute.

He snorted. Bloody disgrace to the Army. Four bloody regiments of Foot crammed into these works and not a man Jack of 'em able to give a proper mark of respect. He was still muttering as his coach clattered out the main gate westward through Saint Philip's Town.

Four hours later he was seated at his desk in the great cabin of His Britannic Majesty's Ship *Barfleur,* at anchor in the Mahon roads, staring with some amazement at the brig's commander.

"English? But who the devil is she?"

Captain Thomas shook his head. "I couldn't get enough from her for that, sir. She was below in the Frenchman's cabin being looked after by a hulking great blackamoor. He was going to go at my marines until the Frenchman's mate told him to stop."

"But the girl, man! What was she doing there?"

"All I could gather, sir, was that she was a slave of the Algerines and that the Frenchman rescued her from there when he came out and tried to slip through us. She took a stone in the head when they left. Still in a swoon when we went aboard." He smiled. "By the way the Frenchman behaved she meant a lot to him."

"How so?"

"His concern sir", said Thomas. "First thing he asked me, in good English too, was whether I had a surgeon who could look at her."

Medley snorted. "Can't abide women who get in the way of such things. What have you done with her?"

"Our surgeon looked after her in my cabin, although she'd come round by the time we put into Mahon, sir. Doctor Jennings took her up to the convent for the present."

Medley drummed his fingers on the table. "English. And you've no idea at all who she is?"

Thomas shrugged. "A few clues, sir."

"Such as?"

"She's a handsome woman. No coarseness about her, although she smelled of all that damned oil they eat. Had on Moorish robes, but spoke English. And she said her name was Abigail. Abigail Collier, was the whole name, I think."

"You think?"

"She'd swooned again by that point, sir."

Medley scratched his head. "Collier. Damn me if that name isn't somehow familiar." He sat for a moment lost in knit-browed thought, while Thomas waited patiently.

Then Medley's face lit up. "By God, Thomas, I've got it! Collier! Sir Augustus Collier!"

"Who, sir?"

"I was a new lieutenant, in the *Centurion*. Heard about old Collier. He and his family went out to Naples as His Britannic Majesty's Minister to the Kingdom of Two Sicilies. That'd be about 1737, mayhap 1738. They were taken by Moorish gun-boats just after clearing Gibraltar, the ship along with Collier and his family! By God, Thomas, it's one of his family!"

Thomas smiled. "Good fortune, sir."

Medley beamed. "Thomas, you only grasp that fact by half! The Colliers have power. And money. They're a strong name in the London market. Lot of East Indian investments. By God!''

Medley shoved back his chair and turned to look out at the harbour through *Barfleur*'s stern windows.

"Reveal this to no one for the present, Thomas. It will be important to be very sure about that girl's identity before we take any action." He turned and beamed at Thomas. "And you can be sure, Thomas, that if the Collier family express their gratitude in strongly material terms, as I'm sure they might, you can be sure I shall see to your own reward."

Thomas looked pleased. Then a frown crossed his face.

"There's the matter of the French corvette's captain, sir. What shall I do with him?"

Medley thought for a moment. "We already know what his mission was all about. That was why we set out to stop him." He glanced at Thomas. "Is he a ranking officer? Perhaps a capitaine de vaisseau?"

Thomas restrained a snicker. "Hardly that, sir. He's a colonial. Junior officer of independent companies. Not," he sniffed, "exactly an officer of the Royal Roussillon."

Medley waved a hand in dismissal. "Well, then, we hardly need bother with formalities. Put him in the keep along the quay. And when his rat-tailed crew come in you can put 'em in there with him. They can work on the repairs down there to earn their swill."

"Don't you wish to speak with him even for a moment, sir?" said Thomas, turning to go.

"Good Heavens no", said Medley, languidly. "Whatever reason should I have to speak to him?"

"To the front, march!"

The marines standing on either side of Paul Gallant stepped off along the quay, in response to the sergeant's bark. A prod in the back from a heavy cane made it clear Gallant was to do the same.

"Step along there, now", said the sergeant of marines. "There's a good Froggy." Gallant trotted to catch up.

The little party marched away from the gun brig that had boarded the corvette. Gallant had not seen Abigail since the capture, and now had no idea where she was.

Altogether Gallant felt very much at the pit bottom of his fortunes as he tramped along between his redcoated escorts. His mission was a failure, for whatever that might portend. His career seemed finished. The whole wasteful exercise had cost the freedom of *Écho*'s crew, including Béssac, who was the closest thing to a true friend Gallant had known. And now that he had brought Abigail back to her own Englishmen, likely he had seen the last of her as well.

He looked dully at the clustered fishing craft along the quayside as they passed. The marines were marching him toward the far end of the quay, where a squat stone building with barred, tiny windows was set back somewhat from the water.

Well. I shall be a felon now, as well, thought Gallant. For a brief, exquisite moment the memory of the cool, mist-shrouded forest of Cape Breton flashed through his mind.

He set his lips in a tight line. I may never see that again, he thought. Could Louisbourg still be resisting the siege?

Beside him the marines plodded dustily on, eyes blank of any expression save a flicker of boredom; stolid products of discipline and a life of unrelenting duty. To them, Gallant thought, he meant little; they were more concerned to avoid the wrath of the thickset sergeant than concern themselves over yet another prison-bound wretch.

Out of the corners of his eyes Gallant idly turned a professional look on the marines' dress and equipment. The men wore their hair unqueued, and it hung lank and greasy to their shoulders, escaping out from under the tall, grenadier-style mitres the men wore square on their heads. They had full-skirted coats with broad turned-back cuffs, and breeches in the same dull brick colour as the coats. Below these, peculiar vertically striped gaiters rose from their shoes to over their knees. A buff waistbelt supported a heavy brass-hilted hanger and a bayonet, and in front a black cartridge box. The men were cradling a weapon Gallant had seen from time to time in the hands of Bostonnais at Louisbourg: the heavy, brass-fitted musket the English charmingly called "Brown Bess".

One marine noticed Gallant eyeing him, and spat pointedly past his face.

Gallant smiled. Not lads to trifle with, these.

"Prisoner and escort, halt!" said the sergeant, stepping past them to bang his cane on the heavy studded door of the prison. A small aperture in the door slid open and a muffled voice interrogated from within.

"It's me, Cuffin me lad", said the sergeant. "Wilkins, off the old *Dancer*. Oi've got a prisoner t' swat in yer lobkin! Come on, open up!"

The voice and the sergeant bantered back and forth for some minutes, and to Gallant, who had learned a very correct English from his uncle, the conversation might as well have been in pure Arawak. He busied himself instead trying to remember what little else he knew about these English marines.

They were not, he remembered, under the control of the British admirauté, similar to his own Troupes de la Marine. In fact, if his memory was accurate, the English had only decided recently to put true marines back in their ships, and that only after their squabble with the Spanish over the *Asiento*, the African slaving trade, had brought on war. And even at that their regiments — how many were there? Nine? Or was it ten? — were almost independent companies. A rum lot meant to be soldiers and sailors, and tough enough for both.

The sergeant's profile was turned to Gallant and he could see the man bore a crude heart-shaped gunpowder tattoo on his cheek. It seemed likely that the sergeant was, in fact, quite tough enough.

The prison door creaked open, and the sergeant motioned Gallant in with his cane.

"Right then, mongsewer. In with yer 'tis!"

Gallant ducked in under the low doorway, and was momentarily baffled by the gloom until he saw the shaggy jailor a few feet away, holding open another heavy door and crooking a finger at him. With a shiver Gallant stepped through into the black space, starting as the door clanked loudly shut behind him.

"Rest easy in there, m'lord", said the retreating voice of the jailor. "Ye've much time to kill, I'll trow, ay?" The cackling laughter echoed hollowly.

Gallant ignored the clammy sweat that broke out on his brow and tried to get his bearings. Gradually he became aware that he was in a cell some fifteen feet square, into which a trickle of light came from a slit in the wall opposite. He felt his way over to it and found that by pressing his eye close against the slit he could see a portion of the main anchorage area.

He grunted. That was something, anyway.

The cell was furnished with two splintery benches, one along either side, and he sat down.

With a pang of despair Gallant felt now, for the first time, the realization of how complete his failure was. The mission was finished, and whatever harm his interception by the English would produce was no doubt beginning to unfold. His career seemingly was at an end, even were he parolled or released somehow. Louisbourg was doomed. And within him he heard a small, empty voice whispering that Abigail was gone forever from his life. Her warm laughter rang in his ears, her face floating before him in painful reality until it faded into the blackness. He half-sprawled along the bench, feeling the dark all about him, feeling the walls sealing him within it, feeling the loss and pain rising now, uncontrollable, within him. And he let it wash over him, glad of its release, hearing the tears pat on the stone floor, opening up the gate of emotion to let it wrack its way out of him until it was done, gone, finished with, and a soothing sleep settled over him.

When he woke, it felt as if centuries had passed. A squint through the slit revealed it was late afternoon. It also revealed several new vessels in the harbour, from whom curled the bright flash of the British ensign.

Gallant's eyes narrowed. Was there something oddly familiar about those ships? Realization came in the next instant. It was the big sixty-four and her consorts, the dogged pursuers and captors of his corvette.

But there was another ship just astern of them. A small trim vessel, with a blue and tan hull.

Gallant's throat caught. "*Écho!*" he cried.

He remained pressed to the slit until daylight faded, ignoring the tin tray of food that slid in below the cell door. He watched the squadron come to anchor, folding in their sails like great seabirds alighting on the water, seeing with tight lips the huge British ensign that flew from *Écho*'s ensign staff. The corvette, he noticed, was not left at anchor in the roads, but was brought alongside on a distant section of the quay, almost at too great an angle for him to see.

The light eventually faded altogether, and finally Gallant tore his eyes from the lanterns on the corvette and huddled on his bench for the night. But now the darkness and the claustrophobia of the cell were not so hard to bear. He had not lost everything, he could convince himself, as long as he could see the ship. She was still alive.

Thankful for the warmth of that thought, Gallant drifted off to sleep.

He awoke to see a thin stream of morning sunshine knifing into the cell from the slit, sweet and golden. Then he jerked upright, startled. There was shouting and oaths outside the cell door, and the sounds of scuffling. Suddenly the door burst open and two bodies were propelled through it.

"Stay in there, and be damned!" snarled the voice of the sergeant of marines as the door slammed shut.

Gallant stared at the two forms in the darkness as the thin band of sunlight illuminated for a split-second a familiar, weatherbeaten face.

"Béssac!" gasped Gallant.

"What...who...?" fumbled the mate. Then he snorted in turn. "Enseigne!"

With a bound Gallant had Béssac seized in a bear hug, pounding joyfully on the broad back.

"Béssac! Thank God! You old walrus!"

He stepped back, grinning in the darkness as Béssac sniffed and coughed to hide his own feeling.

"I'm glad to see you, too, M'sieu' Gallant", said a deep voice from the other figure.

"Akiwoya! You too?" Another hug, fierce with warmth and joy. "I can't believe it. Both of you, well and alive!" said Gallant.

"And the men? Where's our crew, Béssac?"

"Still aboard *Écho*, enseigne. They left them locked below decks when they took Akiwoya and me ashore to come here. But I overheard a sergeant say they were going to move them all ashore, and it sounded like he meant in here."

Gallant sighed. Thank the Virgin. At least they were all likely to be together again, even if behind bars.

He looked keenly at the two men. "Is anyone hurt? No one was killed by the English?"

Béssac shrugged. "A few split lips from pushing and shoving, enseigne. Nothing serious."

"Did they ask you any questions?"

"Just wanted to know who the ship's officers were. I told Guimond to keep quiet, so they'd leave him with the men."

"Good thinking. But they asked you nothing?"

"Nothing."

Béssac fumbled in his pockets and pulled out his pipe. Gallant watched the glow illuminate the mate's face as he lit the tobacco with his flint and settled back against the wall. Béssac's face looked worn and exhausted.

"Perhaps we'd better just rest for awhile", said Gallant. "That ray of sunshine means breakfast, such as it is, will no doubt be here. After that we'll talk."

He smiled at both men. "But By Christ I'm glad you're here!"

It became clear over the next several days that the English were not in any rush to interrogate the three men. Gallant's despatch still was in its belt about his body. The routine very rapidly set in: simply long periods of conversation or silence, punctuated by the arrival of food and the occasional escorted visit to the dank privy in the centre court of the prison.

Gradually Gallant came to learn a great deal of the background of his two friends, and they of his; a knowledge that subtly changed their relationship beyond that of officer to man to one of warm friendship. In more ways than he would have imagined possible Gallant came to cherish the slow, revealing conversations shared in the dark of the cell, far beyond what they did to keep their spirits alive.

After a week had passed their existence underwent a change. They were moved to a larger cell that was furnished with hard wooden bunks, and set to work outside repairing the stone and woodwork of the quay.

It was hard and dirty work, from almost first light of day until sunset. Their clothes rapidly deteriorated until the men took on the ragged and unshaven look of true convicts. Each day a massive sentry hovered nearby as they were released from the cell for work to wrestle with the crumbling stone and slime-covered pilings. The only respite came at noon, when the jailor would sullenly hand out a bowl of swill and chunks of black bread. There was rarely more than a minute to wolf the meal down before the prodding bayonet of the sentry sent them back to work.

The outside environment of clear air and sun was precious after the gloom of the cell, however, and the friends were able to talk if they kept their voices low. As the days slipped by, Gallant thought less and less of his defeat, and the worst pain of Abigail's memory had begun to fade as well. In an odd way he found a healing release in the steady routine and the constant muscular exertion. As his muscles stretched and filled, becoming strong and hardened over his frame, his mind found time to think; time to digest slowly the events of the past months and to reassess to their core his sense of life, of duty, and eventually of his own being. He came to realize that he bore the scars of having cared too much, or at least of having cared the wrong way about things. An inner toughness grew strong within him. He became more cheerful, more clear-eyed and perceptive about not only his past but even the drudgery he now found himself in. To Béssac and Akiwoya he appeared to grow. The summer of 1745 passed into the cooler days of fall, and the three men continued their work along the face of the quay as the harbour life moved about them. They watched prize after prize of French and Spanish merchantmen brought into Mahon by the prowling British cruisers, and saw their once-empty prison fill with the men from those ships.

The Acadiens of *Écho*'s crew had been put into another part of the prison and set at the repair work, and it cheered Gallant enormously to see the cocky high-spiritedness they maintained just seemingly because he was with them; late in the night the sound of their warming Acadien songs drifted into Gallant's cell to lift his own heart and those of his two friends.

The French and Spanish prisoners were set almost at once to work with the Acadiens on the quay, and they slowly came as well to follow the ragged and muscular trio who seemed to share such a warm and almost brotherly understanding. When they learned that Gallant was an officer their awe grew; it was hard to match the posing and disdainful creatures they had known on their own quarterdecks with the tanned and muscled man whose hand gripped their own with a seaman's strength in friendship. And as surely and as inexplicably as were the men of *Écho*, they became willing to follow Gallant and lay their rough-hewn loyalty at his feet.

As if to taunt the three friends with her loveliness, *Écho* reappeared from time to time in the harbour, the broad British ensign out of place as it lolled over her quarterdeck. Gallant watched the passage of the gleaming hull with newly appreciative eyes, seeing at once the meaning of what he had learned in the ship and recognizing that he loved it, as much as men can love material things. The corvette's speed had led her to be used as a Post vessel between Mahon and Gibraltar, and her presence came to be a regular event every two weeks.

Gallant did not, however, have any suspicion that the ship would figure in his life again, and sooner and more importantly than ever he might have imagined.

Shortly after the noon meal several weeks later Gallant and the men working with him looked up to see a large black coach, drawn by four snorting chestnut horses and bearing footmen in the governor's livery, rattling along the quay toward them.

"Get up 'ere! Line up, quick-like!" snarled the sentry, poking at the prisoners with his bayonet. "Not a bleedin' word out o' yew!"

Gallant and the others shuffled into a rough line and stared at the coach as it squealed to a halt in front of them. The coach window curtains were drawn almost shut.

One of the footmen clambered down from the Rumble and spoke quietly into the guard's ear. The guard swung his bayonet along the silent, watchful line until he came to Gallant.

"Yew", he said. "Step for'rard, out o' th' line."

Heart pounding, Gallant stepped forward from between Béssac and Akiwoya.

The sentry and footman did not move, and Gallant was mystified for a moment until there was the smallest of movements at the coach curtains.

He was being watched, examined, by the passenger or passengers inside. He lifted his chin and stared coolly at the window. Be damned as a Protestant, he thought.

A knock sounded on the carriage window and the footman nodded to the marine. Gallant was pushed back into line and with a snap of the coachman's whip the coach rumbled away.

"What the devil was that all about enseigne?" whispered Akiwoya through motionless lips.

"Silence, you!" barked the sentry. "Bloody well get back to work!"

For the rest of the day, even later when he could quietly talk to Béssac and the gunner alone, Gallant was at a loss to explain the event.

The evening meal had been eaten, and now moonlight was streaming in the small window over the sleeping forms of Akiwoya and Béssac. Gallant lay awake, thinking, turning over and over in his mind the meaning of the peculiar inspection. Was there a chance he was about to be questioned at last? Were the English after more information? Surely after months in prison he would not have access to anything current or relevant?

Months! Gallant's hand absently felt under his ragged shirt for the despatch belt. How long had it been since he had left Louisbourg? Three months? Four? And what was happening there? Again and again, in quiet moments, the anguish of that question twisted at his vitals, and he cursed the letter in the belt. Cursed it, as he cursed himself endlessly for failing to deliver it.

But there was always a glimmer of hope. Maybe, by some heroic circumstances or grim determination, the garrison were still holding out. Perhaps God had taken a hand and swept down a tempest that had shattered the Bostonnais' ships. Perhaps disease was rife among them in their camps, and a few precious French vessels were getting through into the harbour, and if Gallant could only get out of this prison and put Du Chambon's letter into the hands of the men next to the King in time!

With terrifying suddenness the night air was broken by a shriek of agony just outside the cell, a shriek that was almost as suddenly muffled. There was the thud of a body to the earth and the sudden patter of running feet. Many feet, all around the prison, and now sounding on the stones of the passageway outside Gallant's cell. Hoarse voices whispered to each other.

Then a heavy knock sounded on the cell door.

Gallant rolled off his bench, heart pounding, and sprang to the door, flattening close to its narrow aperture.

"Who is it!" he whispered. Almost unconsciously he balled his hands into tight fists, ready.

A voice answered, heavy, in Provençal French. "Are you French in there? Prisoners?"

"Yes!"

"Stand aside!" the voice hissed. "We're opening the door!"

Instantly two or three powerful axe blows rang against the door, and in minutes it was swinging open. Close behind it three or four dark figures stepped into the cell, figures in seamen's clothing, their faces blackened, cutlass blades gleaming in their hands.

Gallant stared at them, on the balls of his feet, ready to die fighting. "Who in God's name are you?"

The closest figure stepped nearer to Gallant, lowering his cutlass. Outside Gallant could hear noise and commotion as other men padded swiftly past the open cell door, and other cells were being opened, the axe blows ringing in the darkness.

"French, mon ami! Landing party off the *Vendée*! Twenty of us sent ashore here to raise hell before the ships come in!"

Gallant gripped the man's arm, staring. "Ships? What ships? When?"

The man chuckled mirthlessly. "They'll be in to have a little gunnery practice in exactly one hour! Six ships! Part of the Toulon squadron! We've been in the offing all night. We came in first, then they'll send in at least ten luggers to attack the ships at anchor while ours bombard Fort Saint Philip and Charles Fort!"

The noise of running feet and shouts in the building were growing, and the man was visibly edgy to move on. "We knew the rosbifs had some prisoners held here. So take your chance and get out! Now!"

Gallant's head spun. He glanced for a moment at Béssac and Akiwoya, who were struggling up out of their sleep stupor, not yet really awake.

"What can we do to help? Can you give us some arms?"

The man shook his head. "Sorry. You're on your own. But if you and these men can get out and cause a lot of upset, you'll get your hands on some soon enough! And if you can find something that floats and sails and can get you out of this cursed nest of English, out to our ships, so much the better for you!"

Before Gallant could speak the man had gone, and in the next minute the landing party were out of the prison, the sound of their running footsteps fading from the window.

Outside in the hallway the prisoners were pouring from their cells, babbling in excitement.

Gallant cursed and slapped Béssac and Akiwoya into wakefulness, stifling their sleepy grunts of surprise with a terse, rapid explanation and then propelling them out the door to still the chaos outside the cell. Gallant followed them out and then swore as his foot drove into a body on the floor. A body that shrieked in pain.

"Shut those men up, Béssac!" he barked. "Gather 'em over by the door, but don't let one of 'em out till I'm there!"

Gallant knelt by the figure. It was the gap-toothed jailor, breathing in wheezy gasps. Blood was running from the corners of his mouth.

Only one question filled Gallant's mind. A question he had nurtured over each day and night in the prison. He lifted the man's head and looked into his face.

"Tell me, man! The girl! The English girl that was with me! What have they done with her?"

The man's eyes gleamed like a rat's in the dark. His chest was heaving, and bubbles of froth were forming at the corners of his mouth.

"Oh, you...needn't worry about...her none, mongsewer. She's...safe enough in the keep o' them nuns." A racking, bloody cough convulsed the man.

Gallant shook him viciously, determined to have the full story. "Where?" he snarled. "You mean the convent? Up the hill here behind us? Speak!"

The jailor fought for breath. "Aye...her an' that damned blackamoor of her'n."

Gallant shook his head. The man was dead. Abigail, so near, so close, all this time! Suddenly he was wild to get out.

He threw aside the jailor's body and moved to the door, past the men who were staring at him, expectation and excitement burning in their eyes.

Gallant hitched up his breeches. With the men in a tense silent knot at his back, he slid over the bolt and swung back the heavy outside door.

The quay lay empty and quiet in the moonlight, with no trace at all of the wraithlike landing party. At the far end a ship could be seen, and before it, along the quay, moonlight glinted from the bayonets of slowly pacing sentries.

"Come on!" whispered Gallant horasely. "And keep low in the shadows so the sentries won't see!"

At a run the men swept down the quay, the evening air humming in their ears, the moonlight pale and cold across their faces as they moved from shadow to shadow. Not a word was said, and all that told Gallant eighty running men were behind him was the whisper of bare feet on the quay stones.

They arrived breathless at an overturned longboat and a large cluster of barrels and bales, a scant fifty yards from the ship. Gallant crouched in low behind them, eyes alert for danger, as his men moved in behind him.

Béssac arrived at Gallant's side. The mate was puffing heavily, and was pointing to one of the vessels tied to the quay. His voice was incredulous. "Sweet Jesus, enseigne! It's *Écho*!"

Gallant gaped, a pulse of joy in his veins. It was the corvette! Trim and seaworthy-looking, canvas clewed up but not stopped, singled up on her lines to the quay, lit by the soft moonlight and the orange of her stern lantern as she moved gently to the harbour swells. From her undersides came the gentle lapping sound of the water. Gallant thought he had never seen anything quite so beautiful in his life.

Akiwoya crouched, silent and catlike, at his other side. "Enseigne! I can't see anyone aboard! There's no sound coming from below decks. Are these three the only anglais around?" he hissed.

Gallant lifted his head slightly and looked over the top of the longboat's hull. Akiwoya was right. There was no sign of life aboard the corvette. Along the quayside in front of the ship three English marines paced slowly, the moonlight pale on their faces and gaiters. Their bayonets were fixed and their heads kept moving round slowly as they paced, obviously watchful and alert.

Gallant ducked back behind the boat, his mind racing.

"What'll we do, enseigne?" whispered Akiwoya.

Gallant's whisper was sharp and penetrating. "Where's that Spaniard? The one that managed to keep a knife in his boot?"

There was a pause while Akiwoya searched along the tense, huddled line of men. He was back in the next instant, a small rat-faced man at his side. "This is he, enseigne. His name's Lopez."

"All right. Now listen carefully. Béssac, get about five men and work down behind the line of bales here until you're well behind where the sentries turn about. Get as close to the ship as you can without revealing yourselves. When you see us move on the sentries, get your men aboard and barricade the hatches and companionway doors leading below. Use anything to do it. Clear?''

Béssac nodded. His teeth gleamed in the moonlight as he grinned.

Gallant grinned back. ''Move, then!''

Béssac scuttled in a crouch along the line and pulled out a few men who followed him at a run into the shadows along the quayside.

''Akiwoya, pass the word to Guimond to get the rest of the men aboard as soon as they see Béssac's people do their job. Break them up into parties: one to handle the foremast, one the main, one the mizzen. Take the turns off the lines and have 'em stand ready to put sail on her the second we need it!'' He nodded. ''Pass that along. Then come back!''

Gallant turned to the rat-faced Spaniard. ''Can you throw that knife, Lopez?''

The Spaniard bared a gap-toothed smile. His breath was foul with decay. ''Kills like a flying snake, *señor*'', he said in Spanish.

Gallant waited until Akiwoya was back crouching with them. ''Get another two men with you, Akiwoya'', he said, speaking slowly so Lopez would not miss the meaning. ''Lopez, stay close in the shadows to me when I move out. Then you...''

''Move out!'' burst out Akiwoya.

Gallant swore, ''Do as you're told, by the Christ! When I move out and distract one of the sentries over to me, you must get him, Lopez. And get him silently. Do you follow?''

Lopez's teeth showed again. ''*Si. Bueno.*''

''Akiwoya, when the other two move in to investigate what's going on, you've got to get them. With your bare hands. And they cannot be allowed to utter a sound!'' Gallant's tone was grim and deadly.

Akiwoya's eyes flashed in the darkness, and he nodded silently.

Gallant looked out toward the harbour mouth. How long was it since the landing party had freed them? Twenty minutes? Twenty-five? How many before all Hell broke loose and the quay would be alive with armed men?

"All right. Let's do it!"

Deliberately Gallant stood up from behind the barrels, weaving with the rum-sodden unsteadiness of a drunken seaman. He stepped clumsily around one of the bales and sprawled across it, staggering to his feet as he lisped and quailed out a ditty he had heard the English seamen ashore in Louisbourg sing. Between phrases he belched and spat.

> O my sweet Poll's a soft young fen,
> With a heave away, forever!
> A feather-bed jig with her I'll ken,
> With a heave and haul, forever!

Out of the corner of his eye he saw the marines spin on their heels, the musket barrels gleaming blue in the moonlight as they came level. For an instant his heart went into his mouth. Then he saw one of the marines elbow another, and the musket butts went back down to the ground. Snickers of laughter carried to Gallant's ear, and he saw one of the marines sling his musket and walk his way.

Gallant made as if to stumble, and then sat down in a sprawl, singing at the top of his lungs, putting himself fully into the act now, trying out of the corner of his eyes to look into the shadows for Lopez. He could see nothing. The marine was close now, and Gallant's heart began to race.

He staggered to his feet and roared out a particularly foul verse of the song, sniggering to himself and scratching his crotch. He let his head waggle back and forth and looked up.

"Oi, Jack Nastyface, you're into yer swill by rights, ain't you?" said the marine, good-naturedly. He put out a hand to steady the weaving drunk, who seemed ready to sprawl forward on the quay.

As his hand touched Gallant's arm the Englishman's face froze. "What the...You're not drunk! You're one o' them damned Frogs!"

The breath he drew in to bellow a warning choked and rattled in his throat. Eyes bulging and mouth working in agony, the marine fell against Gallant, hands clawing behind him at the knife that had materialized between his shoulder blades. Gallant clutched the man, ignoring the ghastly sounds coming from his throat, and held him against him until the marine suddenly went limp. Gallant cursed and struggled to hold the body upright. The marine was not a small man.

Gallant took a deep breath, praying what he said next would sound convincing.

"Oi there, Parson! Yer mate's been into his six an' tips! Come have a look!" Thank God for listening to the peculiar speech of the sentries during the quayside work, thought Gallant.

Gallant watched, his heart racing again, as the other two sentries moved cautiously toward Gallant and the man he was holding. Gallant swore under his breath, feeling the warm, sticky blood of the marine moving over his fingers. Come on!

"What's the do, Spike?" called one of the marines. They were no more than fifty feet away now.

Then a pantherish shadow sprang from the darkness off to the left, a shadow followed by others as swift. They fell on the sentries without a sound, and the struggling bodies thudded down in a twisting knot on the quay. A few minutes of terrible, soundless struggle. Then it was over, and Akiwoya was rising to his feet, huge and menacing in the moonlight.

Gallant heaved a huge breath. "Thank Christ!"

Beyond, Gallant saw Béssac's men swarming over the bow rail of the corvette, their feet drumming on the decks as they moved swiftly to bar thé escape from below. Then out of the gloom Béssac's voice echoed to Gallant.

"She's empty, enseigne! There's not a man Jack of 'em aboard her!"

Gallant vaulted over the rail and dropped to the deck, Akiwoya at his side. Béssac's men were appearing up the companionways, shaking their heads.

"Why..." began Gallant.

"A prize, enseigne!" said Béssac, snapping his fingers. "They've got her on the block for sale!"

Gallant clucked his tongue. "Béssac, the anglais are stretched to the limit! They need every ship!" He caught himself.

You fool! The entire harbour's going to explode with action and you're arguing about why a tremendous stroke of luck has happened?

"Béssac! Pick three men about the same size as those sentries. Strip the bodies and get our men in the clothing, and have them pace out there just like the English! And have the rest of the men stand by the lines as I told you!" He sprang to the rail. "I'll be back as soon as I can. But when the cannonading starts at the harbour mouth you slip and get out of here to sea, you understand? And that's whether I'm here or not!"

Béssac gaped at Gallant, opening his mouth to protest. But Gallant was already gone into the darkness.

Béssac stared at Akiwoya. "Now by Saint Peter, just what does our young rooster think he's doing, eh? What?"

Akiwoya punched the mate's belly gently. "He's like as not going to do some unfinished business, m'sieu' Béssac. And bring us a cargo to take out of here!" He winked.

"Hah? Cargo?" Béssac gaped again.

Akiwoya roared. "The girl, Béssac! the girl!"

"Oh", said Béssac, a little vacantly. Then he grinned hugely. "Oh!"

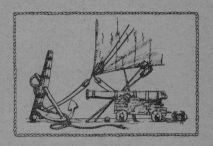

TWELVE

Gallant ran lightly through the shadows, his work-hardened feet crunching up the narrow hillside path that wound up from the harbour behind the prison. Above, on the crest of the hill, the white walls of the convent gleamed like bone battlements in the moonlight. Gallant searched each shadow as he passed, ears and eyes alert for danger, his mind alive with thought.

Holy Mother, he thought. To know that she was up there all this time! The moon-dappled path wound ever upward.

He glanced back at the harbour and its mouth, but saw nothing but the shimmering path of the moon on the sea. He bit his lip. There must be only about ten minutes left.

Abigail! A thrill of exquisite anticipation coursed through him, salted with the darkness of doubt. Would she be as he remembered? Was she at all like the form and face that tormented and enchanted his dreams? Could he find her, and get her back to *Écho* in time?

Then the white wall loomed before him, and Gallant angled off along it, running lower now, conscious of his visibility against the moonlit stone. He shortened his stride, controlling his breathing, but in spite of the night's coolness sweat began to trickle down his brow and into his eyes.

In the next moment he saw it: a small, shuttered window, no more than five feet from the ground. He crouched for a moment beneath it, took a last look around, and then was prying with his fingers at the shutters, hoping against the bar on the inside. His fingers dug into the wood...

The shutters swung open, revealing a gaping blackness. With a quick prayer Gallant hauled himself up and bellied headfirst into the opening. His outstretched hands touched a cold stone floor and he tumbled on to it, to crouch listening in the darkness.

Gradually his eyes became accustomed to the dark, and he could see a dim hallway leading away, and at its far end a door around the edge of which faint light leaked.

Gallant rose and padded noiselessly toward the door, then froze, his hair rising on his neck. From behind another door to one side the scrape of a chair sounded, and military heels rang on the floor.

Gallant flattened himself against the wall beside the door, his heart pounding in his ears. The door swung open and a beam of lantern light shone into the hall. A shadow moved in it and a tall English marine with his musket slung over his shoulder stepped through the door and, raising the lantern, began to look around the hall. In an instant the man would see Gallant where he stood.

Gritting his teeth, Gallant launched himself at the man and drove both bunched fists down on the bridge of the man's nose. With a yelp the Englishman crumpled to the floor, a dark jet spurting from his nose. Gallant swung a roundhouse punch at the man's head, but the marine ducked and lifted a foot squarely into Gallant's groin. Gallant staggered and fell to his knees as a terrible ache and nausea welled through him.

The Englishman snarled in triumph and drove a fist at Gallant's head, then a second. Gallant went down, his arms up to shield his head, the bile ghastly in his mouth. The Englishman moved in and aimed a vicious kick at Gallant's head. With desperate strength Gallant blocked the hurtling boot and grabbed the man's leg, twisting it hard. The Englishman fell hard on one knee, and as he sank Gallant drove his fist with all his strength into the man's throat. The Englishman gobbled like a turkey and clutched at his smashed voicebox, falling back against the stone wall with a scrape of his boots.

Gallant wove to his feet and scooped up the Englishman's musket. Clutching the muzzle end he smashed the butt down on the man's head with the last of his strength. The marine's mouth fell open and he sagged sideways in a heap, the blood from his nose spreading over the stones of the floor.

Gallant, his breath coming in gasps, stared at the man and then dropped the musket beside him.

Suddenly, he was seized from behind by steely arms that pinned him like a mouse in a trap. He looked down at the powerfully muscled forearms and a sudden recognition flashed through his head.

"Yussef! It's me!" he gasped.

Gallant was spun like a rag doll to look into a dark, familiar face. A face that split into a huge and delighted grin, the arms now hugging Gallant in bearish affection. Gallant's ribs creaked.

"Yussef...for the sake of the Virgin...let go! You're going to cripple me!"

But then Gallant's eye was caught by a flash of movement at the bright open doorway. A thrill coursed through his body and he scarcely noticed Yussef's arms drop away.

The figure of a girl stood in the doorway. In white convent robes, now, the folds falling softly from the same slim shoulders. And the hair was the same, lustrous, shining dark curls that framed a face on which fright was fading and where wonder and joy were taking its place.

Gallant stared. She was more beautiful by far than his memory had told him. He reached out for her.

"Agibail. It's me!" His voice broke, the emotion rendering it a whisper.

Then she was rushing into his arms, the impact of her softness against him sweet and unbelievable, the scent of her rich in his nostrils, her arms strong and silken as they clung round him. He buried his head with a low cry into her hair and felt the tears well unbidden from his eyes.

"Paul. Oh, Paul." she whispered. "Is it really you?"

For a moment Gallant could not speak, but only stared at her finally, nodding mutely as he cradled her face in his hands, kissing the tears from her cheeks.

Her hands were cool against his own cheeks. "Oh, how I prayed, Paul! Prayed for this moment! I saw you only once, from the carriage, but I knew! I knew you'd be free somehow!"

"Then it was you that day!"

"Yes, my love. They let me stop and see you. Only that once. Otherwise they've not let us out of here." She burrowed close against him.

Gallant glanced as Yussef, who was standing off to one side in the small room, the delighted grin still large on his face.

"But why, sweet? You're English! Why did they keep you imprisoned?"

Abigail shuddered. "It was terrible. A few of the younger English officers said they knew my family had money. They said they'd hold me until I could get my family to pay them for finding me." She threw back her curls in a way that brought a sweet pain of remembrance to Gallant. "Otherwise they said I'd die in here. Yussef and I."

Gallant shook his head. "And what did you say?"

Abigail tossed her head. She said something swift and liquid in Arabic that sent Yussef's shoulders heaving in silent mirth.

Gallant raised his eyebrows. "And just what does that mean?"

Abigail gave him a wicked little grin. A grin that suddenly brought back memories of the Dey's feasting hall. "I told them to copulate with monkeys, beloved", she said innocently.

Gallant hooted, in spite of himself, and hugged the little figure close.

Abigail pounded her little fists against his chest until he let her go. "Stop it, Paul! That soldier is relieved by another one in only a few minutes from now!"

Sacristi! swore Gallant silently. The attack must be only a few minutes away as well. They had to move quickly.

Gallant siezed Abigail's shoulders. "We've got to do another run for a ship. As we did before. My men have taken a ship at the quayside. They're waiting for us until the attack begins."

"What attack?"

"I'll explain later! Tell Yussef we've got to get out the window and down to the ship! And fast!"

Abigail's Arabic was short and to the point. In an instant Yussef had gathered up a few belongings and the girl's cape, and was waiting again at the door.

Gallant stared at Abigail. "There is one thing, Abigail. I'm bound for France, to deliver my despatch, at whatever cost! And after that? If you come with me it means leaving your own English."

She pressed close to his chest, her breath soft on his neck. "Don't you see, Paul? My world, my only world is you. What do you think I could feel for the English after what they've done to you, or to Yussef and me? Better the Algerines!"

"Keep silent, damn you!" You want half the night watch on our necks?" Béssac swore irritably and scowled at a few seamen who were crouched by the mizzen fiferail. The men had kept their voices low, but the mate's nerves were at a fine edge.

Béssac slapped the rail where he stood in the shadows of the quarterdeck, craning to look along the empty quay for some kind of movement other than the self-conscious pacing of the masquerading "sentries". Nothing. Damnation, he thought, where was Gallant!

Akiwoya materialized at his elbow, the whites of his eyes shining in the darkness. "Still no sign?"

"What? No. Nothing." Béssac's jaw set in a grim line. "They'd better be here soon."

One of the quay sentries had suddenly stopped pacing and was pointing, his stage whisper carrying to *Écho*'s deck.

"Fire, m'sieu'! Over there! And there!"

Béssac sprang to the outboard rail and stared. In the gloom of the far shore of the harbour a blossom of flame had burst into being, followed by another close by. The sound of shouts, screams, the rattle of muskets and the whoosh of flames carried over the water.

Écho's crewmen were gabbling and leaving their stations, moving to the rails, pointing excitedly.

"The attack's begun!" spat Akiwoya. "Where in Hell's teeth has the enseigne got to!"

Béssac slapped his fist hard against the rail in rage. "Not a man moves!" he barked. "Get back to your posts, or by God I'll have your heads! You three on the quay keep up that pacing and hold those firelocks ready!"

He swung to Akiwoya, lowering his voice. "Keep a lid on them, Akiwoya. They panic, and we're lost. I don't want this ship to budge an inch until the enseigne is back aboard. Not even if the whole damned seafront is in flames!"

More fires were burning now, and in the ships at anchor in the roads there was a flurry of activity, with lights moving and the rattle of drums echoing to the corvette. Lights were appearing all along the shore, and seaward, toward the great shadowed hump of Fort Saint Philip, a red signal rocket floated skyward.

Béssac ground his teeth and scanned quickly up and down the quay. Still no movement of any kind. There was some comfort in that; a shore party of British anywhere near the corvette might put an end to the whole exercise. And if the enseigne did not get here soon, Béssac would have no choice but to set sail.

The roar of heavy naval guns from the harbour mouth cut his thoughts short. Beside him Akiwoya swore a lurid oath, staring.

"Sacristi, Béssac! Look at that! Right into the damned jaws of the harbour!"

Between the two arms of the harbour mouth was framed a

line of tall warships, moving shadowed and ghostly through the moonlight, their sides licking tongues of flame toward Fort Saint Philip. The deep boom of the detonations rolled and eddied across the water and around the harbour, and from the fort's shadowed mass explosions flashed, explosions mixed with pink lancets that shot out toward the ships in retaliation.

Akiwoya shook his head. "How long, eh? How long can we wait while that is going on?"

"I know", said Béssac. "But we wait as long as it takes, old friend!"

The ships were close in to the fort now. The cannonading was fiercer, more furious, with flames winking out steadily now from the ships and ramparts. Dark billows of smoke began to rise over the scene, their upper curves lit with a blue glow by the moonlight.

There was a commotion on the foredeck, and one man cupped his hands to yell toward Béssac, all caution forgotten.

"Boats, m'sieu'! In among the anchored ships!"

Béssac stared, then whistled low through his teeth. Close in among the anchored English warships rowing boats could be seen now, at least six long luggers with their sails brailed up against the masts and long sweeps falling and lifting rapidly along their sides. The boats swung across the moon's path as Béssac started, and from the anchored English hulls shouts of warning and alarm rang out, and two or three muskets barked.

There was an audible grinding bump as one of the boats, then another, swept in alongside an anchored frigate. A storm of musket fire broke out from the frigate's deck, answered by a volley from the lugger. Screams and hoarse yells rang out, and the clink of cutlass blades echoed tinnily across the harbour. Muskets flashed again as the Frenchmen clawed their way up the frigate's side.

Écho was touched now by the first light from the fires springing up around the harbour, mixed with the flashes from the cannonading seaward. Béssac bunched his fists and glanced at *Écho*'s jittery crewmen. This could not go on much longer before he'd lose control. And that action was getting a little too close. If those boats managed to push in to where the corvette lay helpless at the quay, there might be serious trouble.

"Béssac! We're coming aboard!"

Béssac spun on his heel to see one of the sentries, mitre cap askew and incongruous above the grinning seaman's face, leaping over the rail aboard the ship. And right behind him, with a dark-haired girl in white robes in his arms, Gallant was sprinting for the ship's side. A pace behind him the giant Moor loped, glancing backward for pursuers.

"Gallant! Thank Christ!" Then Béssac saw *Écho*'s crewmen, staring at Gallant with a mixture of joy at seeing him and awe at the beauty of the creature in his arms.

Béssac, grinning from ear to ear, let out a mock howl of rage, and the men scattered to their posts. "By the Sweet Blood of Christ! Get back to your posts!" He gripped Gallant's hand as the latter reached the deck.

"And you can tell them to get under way, too, Béssac!" added Gallant. "That is, if you've waited long enough!"

Béssac's cheeks puffed out until Gallant thought he was going to burst, and then the mate let out an uproarious hoot of laughter. "Enough! Enough! he says! Christ save us!" He spat with relish over the rail and, all caution gone now, roared at the remaining sentries to get aboard. The men were scrambling over the rail in an instant.

Béssac turned to where Gallant stood on the quarterdeck, the girl pressed against his side, the huge Moor a pace behind. All three were staring out at the flickering scene of battle before them in the harbour, listening to the rumble from it and the popping muskets from the struggle going on alongside the ships at anchor.

Béssac planted his feet. His world was once more complete. "Ready when you are, enseigne", he said.

Gallant looked down at Abigail. "I want you to go below, cherie! Go down with Yussef to the cabin."

Abigail tossed her curls back and looked him levelly in the eye. "No. Not this time, Paul Gallant!" She wrapped her arms around him tightly, and at the mizzen fiferail the hands grinned at the look on Gallant's face. "I'm staying with you! We live together. Or we die together!"

He stared down at her for an instant. Then he smiled. "So be it", he whispered.

Gallant looked aloft, sensing the wind. It was westerly, and if *Écho* paid off by the bows there was a chance of making the harbour mouth in a single free run. He looked at the harbour, gauging the gaps between the anchored ships, and then out to where the tall French war vessels were locked in the rumbling exchange of iron death with the front. What a Hell to run through, he thought.

Gallant glanced at the helmsman, who was ready and watching him. Forward, the men had moved to their positions for making sail, and were motionless. They too, had their eyes fixed on him. It was time.

Gallant cupped his hands. "Akiwoya! Slip the bow line! Hoist the foretopm'st stay'l!" His voice was hoarse with tension. "Flat it well to windward!"

Even as the pale triangle of the staysail surged up the stay in response to hauling hands at the halliard, two other men were tugging at the bight of the sail's sheet, hauling the clew into the centre of the ship to force the corvette's head to pay off to leeward. The ripple of light from the fires and explosions in the harbour danced in orange patterns over the surface of the sail, and against Gallant's side Abigail shivered.

Gallant looked at Béssac. "Let go aft, Béssac. And set topsails!"

Béssac was almost beside himself with joy. "Oui, enseigne!" he boomed.

"Keep the helm dead amidships!"

Above their heads the canvas thumped and rustled as the broad topsails fell from the yards, curving almost immediately to the pull of the breeze. The rigging began to creak with life. The bows turned out slowly, the corvette footing ahead slightly as they did so. The long arm of the bowsprit swung into the gleaming path of the moonlight.

"Now!" barked Gallant. "Let go and haul! Set them quickly, Akiwoya! Courses, Béssac!" Gallant stepped closer to the wheel, watching the arched and filling canvas aloft with a lifting bubble of joy in his throat.

"Keep her clean full, Garcia. Dead afore the wind, mind!"

The helmsman nodded, too enthralled to reply.

With a sonorous rush *Écho* picked up speed, the dark water of the harbour hissing and gurgling as it swept along the hull and curled under the counter. The creak of the rigging was rhythmic now, working with the pressure building aloft. Under the men's feet the ship began to stir, its rebirth and sudden vitality holding them spellbound. Aloft, the sails arched in bone-white moonlit curves over the deck, and the corvette ghosted steadily out into the anchorage.

The bombardment of the fort had halted for the moment, although the topsails of the French ships were still visible behind the hump of the fortifications. It was closer inshore that Gallant's eyes were fixed, where a furious fight was raging aboard one of the anchored frigates, and musketry flashes were sprinkling the dark from the shadows beside the other hulls.

Gallant rubbed his brow. On this run they could pass along the starboard side of the big anchored sixty-four. The French luggers had taken all the anchored ships totally by surprise, obviously. But they would have little luck in boarding a sixty-four, with her masses of seamen and marines.

Béssac was at his side. "Our track, enseigne?" he said, eyes watching the flash of muskets ahead.

"Leave the sixty-four to larboard, Béssac. But pass close aboard her. Keep her between us and the luggers. The French'd think any ship in this far except themselves would be English!"

He grinned in the dark. "And we wouldn't want to disappoint them, Béssac. Hoist the English colours!"

"What!"

"You heard me, Béssac!" He indicated the big sixty-four. "Or would you like her to give us a point-blank broadside as we glide obligingly by? Her crews'll be jittery enough to sink a nightsoil barge!"

Béssac grinned in appreciation. "English colours it is, enseigne!"

As he turned to go Gallant touched his arm. "But you might have a man ransack whatever the English captain fitted out his — my — cabin with. What we need is a bedsheet or tablecloth, eh?" He pointed seaward. "When we get out there we'll need French colours hanging from every yardarm!"

A thunderous booming seaward announced that the bombarding line of French warships was once again pummelling the fort. But the batteries in the latter and in Charles Fort were replying with a vengeance. Shimmering in the moonlight, tall and slender geysers of spray were leaping up, bracketing the dark hulls of the ships.

Écho was moving rapidly now, and ahead the bulk of the anchored sixty-four loomed closer. Lights were moving on her decks, and a spatter of musket blasts sounded every few seconds. The lugger was on the far side of the big ship, Gallant noted. And by the sound of it the Frenchmen were making little headway against the numbers of the sixty-four's crew.

"A point to larboard, Garcia! Lose this wind and our chance is gone!" The helmsman grunted at Gallant's words and carefully put the helm up.

Abigail was trembling against Gallant's side, but when he looked down at her, her eyes were fixed resolutely forward on their track, and her lips had a determined set to them. Gallant silently kissed her hair.

There was a thump behind them as the heavy ensign staff was set in place, and almost immediately an enormous British ensign streamed out over their heads.

Béssac was back on the quarterdeck. "The English rag is flying, enseigne", he said, and spat forcefully over the rail. "Although I don't like the look of the damned thing!"

Gallant grunted. "Never mind, Béssac. Look ahead, there. We're almost close aboard the sixty-four, where that rag may save our necks!"

Gallant squinted forward. *Écho* was going to pass smoothly along the sixty-four's side. And if the Englishman was not too concerned with beating off the luggermen there'd be some kind of hail or challenge to answer. But what was the name the English had given to the corvette? Damn! English colours or no, the game could still be lost.

Unless...

"Béssac!" Gallant barked suddenly. "Take all the hands off sailhandling you can spare! Get 'em up on the yards or along the rail on the side toward the Englishman! And when we go by her, you're going to cheer!"

Béssac stared. "Cheer, enseigne? Them?"

Gallant gripped his shoulder. "English fashion, Béssac! Hip, hip, and huzzah! Don't you see? I don't want to have to answer a challenge!"

The mate saw the light, and without a word was moving forward rapidly, pulling men from their posts.

Gallant looked forward. A few seconds more and they would be almost under the sixty-four's counter. But Béssac had been swift: already there were men out along the footropes of the yards and standing along the larboard rail.

Écho swept on, the sixty-four looming higher and higher above the bows. The musket blasts and the voices and shouts of the struggle on the big ship's far side were muted now. The English must have finished with them, thought Gallant.

Béssac bounded back to beside the wheel. "In place, enseigne." He stared at the sixty-four. "By Christ, what a monster! We'll pass no more than fifty feet off her!"

The rush of water along *Écho*'s side sounded louder now, reflected from the sixty-four's side. *Écho*'s speed under her taut canvas suddenly seemed magnified, and she rushed in under the loom of the bigger vessel with breathless speed.

Gallant bit his lip, stealing a quick glance up at the ensign overhead. Would they roar past her without even a word? No. The Royal Navy would never be that loose.

And there it was, a voice echoing out of the night, from high above on the sixty-four's deck.

"...ahoy! What ship are you!"

Gallant nodded at Béssac. "Now, Béssac!" he hissed. "After my call."

He cupped his hands, working his lips to sound the English words. "Well done, sir! And huzzah for old England!"

"Huz-zah! Huz-zah! Huz-zah!" *Écho*'s men put their lungs into the cheers, and the brave sound echoed and re-echoed off the oaken walls of the sixty-four as the corvette drove past, the British ensign winging majestically out from its staff.

Christ in Heaven, thought Gallant, we must look tremendous. But did it work?

For an instant there was no sound other than the surge and rush of the sea along *Écho*'s side. All aboard *Écho* were frozen in place, tensely waiting. In an instant the corvette would be clear of the shadow of the huge hull, and away from the menace of its guns.

Then it came. A ringing cheer, three short barks of British seamen, echoing out of the dark of the sixty-four's hull toward the corvette.

"Oh, Paul! It worked!" breathed Abigail at his side. And in the next instant *Écho* plunged out of the shadow of the sixty-four's hull full into the broad flood of moonlight.

Gallant was scanning off the bows. "Béssac! The luggers! Where are they?"

"One, two to larboard, nearing that frigate that's aflame, enseigne!"

The lookout in the foretop called down, his voice thin with excitement. "Deck, there! The rest are closer inshore, M'sieu'! Except for two that are tangled alongside the big sixty-four!"

Gallant cupped his hands. "On our track ahead! What is there on our track ahead!"

Béssac and the lookout replied together. "Nothing, enseigne! Clear water to the harbour mouth!"

Gallant and Abigail looked aft, back toward the anchorage. The light from the burning frigate was lighting the whole scene now in a lurid glow. And now the luggers could be seen clearly, so brave and incredibly small against the mass of the ships they had attacked.

Gallant kissed Abigail's hair. "Only one more obstacle. That storm of fire those ships are exchanging with the fort. If we can get through that — we're free!"

Béssac was back on the quarterdeck, puffing with exertion and excitement. "The hands are at the braces, if we need to wear or tack our way through that mouth, enseigne." He scratched his head. "They're giving the fort the Devil of a pounding!"

Gallant looked up at the moonlight on the sails. It was clear and brilliant, and the canvas glowed in ghostly blue splendour. And ahead of them the track of the moon on the water shimmered like beaten silver.

"Béssac, unless they're blinded by smoke those ships will have good visibility. If we hang ourselves with French colours, anything white, they'll be able to see it." He pursed his lips. "I'm willing to bet they'll not fire on us!"

Béssac pointed at the mass of Fort Saint Philip. "But the batteries ashore, there, enseigne!" he said. "If the French can see us, the English gunners'll have an even better view! And we'll be sailing right past their line of fire! And do you see the volume of fire they're putting out against those ships?"

Gallant glanced ahead. The line of French warships had worn and were standing out to sea once more. From the ramparts of the fort an almost constant ripple of pink flame showed, filling the air with the rumbling of the detonations and bracketing the French hulls with a forest of leaping geysers.

Gallant licked his lips. "How long, Béssac? How long will we be in the arc of fire from those batteries?"

Béssac was silent for a few moments, calculating *Écho*'s speed through the water, looking long at the harbour mouth.

"Fifteen minutes, enseigne. Maybe twenty. And thats only if we hold this speed." He clucked his tongue. "Who knows what the winds are doing in the narrows there."

Gallant set his jaw. There was no way around it. They were committed now, to freedom, to getting out that mouth to sea. And it was the last obstacle, the last of so many since Gallant had first been charged with his mission back so long ago in the governor's cabinet at Louisbourg. He would not stop now!

"Tell the men to prepare themselves as best they can, Béssac. And be ready for some rapid sail handling and course changes if I call for them!"

Béssac looked at him. "We're going through, then."

Gallant nodded, looking into Abigail's eyes. She closed them and pressed her head to his chest.

"We're going through."

Écho moved steadily and swiftly toward the narrows. Aloft, the men were hoisting the makeshift French colours that had been put together from the linen in the ship's great cabin. The British ensign came down from the stern staff and was replaced by a linen bedsheet, set in place with much satisfaction by Béssac.

"There, by Christ," he said. "It may be a bedsheet, but it's a Bourbon bedsheet!"

Gallant looked at the dark mass of Philipet Point, to the left of the harbour mouth. There was a battery there, he knew, at Philipet Fort. But why had there been no fire from it?

It was worth a chance. "Béssac, wear her over a point or two to larboard. Put her as close alongshore of Philipet Point as you dare! But be ready for my call to swing to starboard in a hurry, eh? Hands at the braces and sheets, ready!"

Béssac nodded, and Garcia was already turning the wheel. Aloft, the yards creaked in their lifts as *Écho* swung toward the shadow of the shore.

Gallant eyed the mass of Fort Saint Philip. The French battle line had moved out of range, and the batteries were silent. The corvette was almost abeam of Philipet Fort, which still lay silent as the corvette glided past. When would Saint Philip open fire! In a minute, they would be almost atop the long shoal that reached out from Philipet Point.

A pink flash on the ramparts of Saint Philip startled him. The another lit the night. And another, the hollow boom of the guns echoing round the corvette.

With a punching sound and a hiss, an enormous geyser of water leaped up directly in front of *Écho*, followed by two more almost in the same spot.

"Sacristi, they've got the range already!" Gallant swore. "Now, Béssac! Haul round ten points to starboard! Braces and sheets!"

Sails whiplashing aloft, *Écho* swung nimbly round to starboard until the bowsprit pointed almost dead on the ramparts of Saint Philip. The yards squealed round and *Écho* knifed into the middle of the channel, reaching for the far shore. A second salvo rang out from Saint Philip, the shot falling almost exactly where *Écho* would have been had Gallant not swung her about.

Béssac's white face appeared at the foot of the ladder to the waist. "God, enseigne, did you see that?"

Gallant spat to clear his dry throat. "I know, Béssac! We're into a bad business here. Keep her steady on this heading till we put Philipet on our quarter! Then we'll swing back!"

A rippling line of flame swept along the near rampart of Saint Philip, and in the next instant two huge geysers hissed up inches from *Écho*'s side, Gallant hugging Abigail close as the heavy spray splashed over the quarterdeck. In almost the same instant, several thumps sounded overhead as balls tore gaping holes in *Écho*'s canvas. And ahead, in the forecastle of the ship, there was a smashing impact as another ball drove into the corvette's side.

"Take her round, Garcia!" Gallant barked. "Wear her to larboard, fifteen points! Béssac, the braces and sheets! Quickly!"

Even as he finished the order two more shot crashed into the corvette, the deck trembling beneath Gallant's and Abigail's feet with the impact. There was the smash and clang of ironwork this time.

And the screams of mangled men.

"Damn their eyes!" swore Gallant. Abigail was crying now, her hands locked in the material of his shirt.

Écho swung on her new course, and Gallant said a small prayer as three more geysers towered up from the water, again where the corvette would have been but for her turn. Sweet Mother of God, were the English gunners magicians?

He glanced ahead. *Écho* was into the wider mouth of the harbour now, between Saint Ann's Point and Charles Fort. Tantalizingly, open sea lay over *Écho*'s bowsprit. But Gallant knew that another treacherous shoal, the Saint Ann, reached out from that point, and *Écho* would rip her belly out trying to cross it.

He swore. *Écho* would have to angle back in toward

Charles Fort and Saint Philip once more. Once more into the foreground of those gunners' ranges.

Seconds after another wave of flashes swept the ramparts astern, the corvette was bracketed by splashes. The water rattled onto the quarterdeck, and Gallant drove his hand across his eyes to see. Not a hit this time. But in another instant?

"Round again, Garcia! Wear to fifteen points to starboard! Béssac!" he shouted through cupped hands. "Set them again!"

Écho dipped round, the moonlight washing over her and moving the lacework shadows made by her rigging across her deck planking as she turned.

Gallant looked ahead, heart pounding. Could they make it this time? And how long had they been under those guns? Was it the twenty minutes?

Another salvo sounded shoreward, and this time the shot was laid with deadly accuracy. Round after round slammed into the corvette, and the canvas aloft shook with the impact. Wood and iron fragments were flying everywhere, and the shouts and screams of injured men rose again on the air. Before Gallant's eyes a seaman clutching a topsail sheet was smashed into a dark pulpy mass against the larboard rail by a ball that left a gaping hole in *Écho*'s starboard bulwark.

Behind them Gallant heard Garcia gibbering, and turned to see him staggering, the wheel spinning unchecked, jets of blood pulsing from both wrists. The man's hands had been cut off.

"Dear God!" cried Abigail. In the next instant she had ripped strips from the hem of her robe and was kneeling beside Garcia, who had fallen whimpering to the deck. Her tears streamed down her cheeks, and she moved her lips in prayer as she twisted tourniquets round the pulsing stumps. In the black moonlight the blood spilled over her robes like black ink.

Gallant seized the wheel and spun it savagely back until *Écho*'s canvas ceased its maniacal luffing. Geysers were leaping up all around the ship, smashing down sheets of spray over Gallant and Abigail, who now had Yussef kneeling with her, over the men struggling to free themselves from the wreckage in the waist, over Béssac as he raged on the foredeck with the men clearing away splintered rails and snarled lines to dig for the screaming shipmates buried beneath the mass. *Écho* staggered again as shot punched into her, and part of a yardarm, its gear trailing, swung down in a vicious arc scant inches from Gallant's head to crash on the deck in front of the wheel.

The deck was a chaos of wreckage and staggering bodies, unreal and nightmarish in the alternating blue moonlight and the pink flash of the shore batteries. Gallant stared as the sails aloft twitched, the flying shot ripping hole after hole in the canvas. Already the maintopsail was more a rag than a sail, streaming in tatters in the wind.

Then Abigail was beside him, her hands clinging round his arm, her tear-streaked cheek pressed to his shoulder. She was pointing ahead over the bows.

"Paul, look! The French ships!"

There was another smashing impact into the corvette below their feet, but Gallant ignored it. He gazed forward over the corvette's bows, unable to say anything.

In a stately and majestic line, the tall pyramids of their sails taut and blue-white in the moonlight, the line of French warships was tacking beautifully in toward them. Already broadsides were booming out from the lead ship toward Saint Philip, the pink flames lancing out in regular succession. The tall line swept in, their speed magnified by the corvette's own, their massive walls moving in to shield the corvette as she moved now into their lee.

And there was something else. Something that brought a lump to his throat and sudden tears, uncontrollable, to his eyes.

They were cheering them.

Abigail laughed and cried at his side, the relief and exhaustion in her voice.

"Listen, Paul. Oh, dear God, listen to that!"

The cheers echoed from each tall ship as it swept past, their far side guns lashing out at the fort, the voices of the men carrying strong and vibrant across the water, the white Bourbon ensigns proud and defiantly streaming as the ships in turn paid their salute to the battered little vessel that lay lifting now in the ocean swell it had fought so valiantly to reach.

THIRTEEN

Cornet Mercier Auphan de la Gravière pulled his grey gelding to a halt on the rise of the last hill on the dusty high road between Marseille and Toulon. He took off his tricorne and slapped at the dust on his russet breeches, the taste of grit in his mouth.

He let the horse rest a few moments as he swivelled round in the saddle to look at the view. Here the headlands were so visible that Gravière could see almost along to the rocky tip of Cap Cepet, at the mouth of the Great Road of Toulon.

He smiled, a feeling of satisfaction filling him. It had been a long ride overnight, and he was glad the end was near. For the twentieth time he checked the fastening on the despatch case which hung on his saddle above his pistol case.

"Can't be too careful, mon ami", he said to the horse. Not that he cared too much about a routine despatch to the commander of a run-of-the-mill colonial corvette.

He clamped the hat back on his head. Routine or not, he could deliver the despatch by noon, if he made good time. Then there could come a good meal at Ozerac's in La Seine, and maybe the warm bed of one of Ozerac's wenches...

The cornet whistled to himself. It might be a good day yet. He kicked the grey into a trot.

It took Gravière another hour before he reached the fork in the high road just before Brugaillon and turned off, and another half-hour before he was cantering past the red tiled roofs of La Seine and on, the Balaquier Tower looming at water's edge on his left as he passed along the Cap Cepet road. He led the horse down the road to the hospital there, and finally turned on to a narrow track that wound steeply down to a small cluster of boatmen's shacks on the beach.

He waited a moment before dismounting, pleased with the view. From where he sat he looked out into the broad bay of the Great Road, the opening of the Little Road and the mouth of the Toulon basin itself lying to the left. It was marked on the far shore by the plinth of the Great Tower, and a little to its right Gravière made out the familiar low form of Fort Saint Louis.

He smiled. God, this sea air was magic to see with! Toulon itself lay hidden at the far end of the Little Road, directly behind the Great Tower. By standing in his stirrups the cornet could see the ramparts and rooftops of the city proper. And in the Little Road the massed shapes of the Toulon squadron rode at anchor, an impressive and beautiful sight half-hidden in the dispersing late morning haze.

A ragged child appeared out from the nearest shed and reached as if by long habit for the grey's reins.

"Holà, boy!" said Gravière, good-naturedly, as he swung down from the grey and tossed the boy a coin. "Where's the corvette? The *Écho*, is it?"

The boy's face lit up. "Anchored close aboard the Aiguilette Tower, m'sieu'! An' a pretty ship it is too! D'you not see it there?"

Gravière scanned the harbour again.

"Ah yes, there it is." He sniffed. "Small, isn't it?"

"But a proper little ship, m'sieu'!" said the boy.

"Proper or not, I need a boat to get to her." He tossed the boy another coin. "Fetch out one of your cutthroat brothers, will you?"

The boy slunk away, crestfallen, into the shed.

Aboard *Écho* Paul Gallant squinted into the morning haze toward the shore, making sure of what he thought he saw. Then he nodded, his lips a tight line.

"It's come at last, Béssac. A courier. A reply at last."

Béssac shrugged. "Four days since we put in here and sent your damned letter off, enseigne. Not bad time."

Gallant glanced at him his eyes alive with feeling.

"Time!" He shook his head. "God knows what time I needed to get that message through for aid to get to Louisbourg! God knows what's already happened there. What could have been avoided if only...!"

Béssac grunted. "Well, enseigne, a miracle is always possible. The siege might have failed. Or they might still be holding out, in which case the message may not be too late at all."

Gallant was silent for a moment. "Yes, I suppose. But I have a feeling, Béssac. I just have a feeling."

He turned and watched the tiny shape of the boat which was moving out from shore toward the corvette.

Half an hour later Gravière was standing on *Écho*'s deck, and there was very little disrespect in his eyes as he looked about. The ship was clean and showed the efforts of either good spirit or discipline, or perhaps both: the lines were coiled or cheesed with naval regularity and order; the brightwork was gleaming; and the bronzed young enseigne in a new-looking Compagnies and threadbare, the large turned-back blue cuffs frayed and don't break patched along the edges. The brass buttons had none of the parade-ground sheen of the Toulon garrison. The veston and breeches of blue serge were worn and showed signs of frequent repair.

Franches uniform who stepped forward to meet him looked anything but unprofessional.

Gravière took one last look around the ship and noticed that the hardy-looking crewmen, Acadiens almost to a man if he had heard right, were clustering close to hear what was about to happen.

Gravière raised one eyebrow ever so slightly. That clinched

it. The men had to be from the Americas. A French crew would have stayed as far away as possible from the doings of officers. It usually portended too much trouble.

The cornet shrugged inwardly and raised his hat. Appearances, appearances, he said to himself.

"Enseigne Paul François Adhémar Gallant, I presume?"

Gravière was pleased and startled at the court-perfect salute that came in reply. "Your servant", said the enseigne.

"And yours", said Gravière agreeably. He stepped closer to Gallant and took his hand, feeling the powerful grip with surprise.

"Mother of God, you don't know what a pleasure it is to meet a gentleman, Gallant. I had expected..."

Gallant smiled. "A peasant?"

Gravière's answering smile was genuine. "To be frank, yes!" He looked round the ship. "The Minister is a fool. Seeing you and this ship and..."

Gravière froze, momentarily at a loss for words. An exquisitely beautiful young woman in a simple gown had appeared up the aft companionway. She moved to Gallant's side with an easy grace, her dark and lustrous eyes examining Gravière with friendly interest.

Gallant's expression was humorous. "Recover yourself, my dear Gravière." He raised his hat. "May I present my betrothed, Mademoiselle Collier? She speaks but little French, I may add."

Gravière beamed. The girl's dark beauty was a revelation after the powdered dolls of Versailles. "Her beauty is eloquent enough", he offered gallantly.

Gallant translated, and the girl's laugh was liquid and delicious. Gravière was won at once.

Gallant's expression sobered. "But I presume you have come for a reason, cornet. Perhaps a reply to my report to His Majesty? We have been waiting anxiously for some time."

Gravière ripped his eyes away from Abigail and nodded.

"Yes, of course. I do indeed carry a despatch for you." He opened the pouch. "I'm afraid I know the clerk who wrote it out. His writing is as indecipherable as Chinese. I've read them before, of course, so if you would permit me?''

Gallant paused only a moment before nodding.

"There is nothing confidential, I assure you", went on Gravière, and then stared over Gallant's shoulder.

Behind the enseigne three other men had moved in to stand as if supporting the couple: a huge turbaned Moor, an equally huge African, and a grizzled seaman who had the look of deepsea command written large upon him.

Gravière raised his other eyebrow. "You...do have an extraordinary crew, M'sieu' Gallant."

Gallant's laugh was warm and reassuring. "Our friends, cornet. Friends and shipmates. But please, the despatch?''

"Forgive me. If you'll permit me..."

Gravière broke the heavy red seal and unfolded the document.

He looked up. "Do you want the endless introductory phrases?''

"God, no!" said Gallant. "The details, cornet."

Gravière read for a few moments.

"I regret to inform you that His Majesty's forces in Isle Royale, specifically the Fortress of Louisbourg, have been taken by English forces from their American colonies."

Gallant swore a startling oath. "When?" he rasped.

"After a siege of forty-nine days, it says, my dear Gallant. A goodly resistance."

Gallant had turned to the rail and was staring out over the water. "For nothing", Gravière heard him say. "All for nothing!"

"I beg your pardon?" said Gravière.

Gallant had turned back, a noticeable redness in his eyes. The girl saw it and moved to him, her arm linking in his own.

"I...apologize, Gravière", said Gallant, hoarsely. "My manners are inexcusable. I...it was merely a matter of some personal concern." He cleared his throat. "Please go on."

Gravière read further. Then he raised his eyes and looked at Gallant with new appreciation in them.

"You will receive the Cross of Saint-Louis, enseigne. For meritorious conduct as a Christian gentleman."

Gallant stared. "You're joking."

"Not a bit. Something about persevering to complete your assigned mission at all costs, even though faced with apparent failure, delay, and so forth. It goes on at some length." He smiled. "Congratulations!"

The girl said something. Gallant, a dazed look on his face, said, "Please. What else?"

"His Majesty has decided that it is the will of God for the present that France should accept the loss of Isle Royale and the Fortress of Louisbourg."

Gallant's face was grim. "Yes."

"His Majesty has for the moment given instruction through the Minister of Marine that his subjects from that colony are to be resettled in France as per the terms of the surrender agreement, but only until such time as they may return through the fortunes of war or diplomacy. If ever, of course." He looked at Gallant. "You are offered the option of resigning your commission and joining your family at..." Gravière cursed and squinted at the crabbed handwriting. "At La Rochelle", he added finally.

Gallant's eyes were empty. "I see", he said quietly.

Gravière read further and spoke again after a moment.

"Or", he said slowly, "you may remain in the service of France. In command of this ship. As a lieutenant."

Gallant's head snapped up, his eyes flashing. "What?"

Gravière went on. "The *Écho*, corvette, and its crew will be entered in the Navy and may remain under your command, inasmuch as you are by and large countrymen. If you choose to accept you will immediately inform the secretary of His Excellency the Duc d'Anville, Governor of Galleys, who will see that orders, dispositions and settlement of accounts are passed to you."

Gallant nodded, his eyes aflame.

Gravière folded the document and handed it to Gallant. "Frankly, my dear Gallant, the King has a mad scheme afoot. He intends to send d'Anville off to retake your Isle Royale in June. Eleven line-of-battle ships, a clutch of others, transports, and so on. Three thousand troops as well." He touched his brow with a delicate handkerchief. "I'd suppose you'd be going along."

Gravière noticed the faces of the eavesdropping seamen with some irritation. Everywhere they were suddenly grinning like fiends.

He turned back to Gallant. "So there's your choice, enseigne. Pardon. I should say lieutenant."

Gravière squinted at the sun. "Dear me, I must be going." He turned to go over the side to his waiting boat, and Gallant stepped forward to help him down to the first of the battens.

The cornet looked up at the little group on the corvette's deck before he went down. "Good luck in making your choice, Gallant!" he said.

As the boatman pulled away Gravière settled comfortably into the cushions in the stern sheets. Good job well done, he thought.

Then he sat up with a start and spun around.

"Sweet Virgin", he said to the boatman, but as much to himself. "Why are those men cheering like idiots? And look at that fellow Gallant, kissing that creature in front of them all!"

He pulled his hat down over his eyes and for a few moments watched the embracing couple and the cheering men who clustered round them. Then he settled back into his seat with a half-smile on his face.

"But cursed if I wouldn't like to be in his shoes, somehow!" he said to himself.